Death at
a Scottish
Christmas

Also available by Lucy Connelly

The Scottish Isle Mysteries

Death at a Scottish Wedding
An American in Scotland

Death at a Scottish Christmas

A SCOTTISH ISLE MYSTERY

Lucy Connelly

CROOKED
LANE

NEW YORK

Copyright © 2024 by Candace Havens

Published in the United States by Crooked Lane Books, an imprint of The Quick Brown Fox & Company LLC.

Crooked Lane Books and its logo are trademarks of The Quick Brown Fox & Company LLC.

Library of Congress Catalog-in-Publication data available upon request.

ISBN (hardcover): 978-1-63910-930-2
ISBN (ebook): 978-1-63910-931-9

Cover design by Jim Griffin

Printed in the United States.

www.crookedlanebooks.com

Crooked Lane Books
34 West 27th St., 10th Floor
New York, NY 10001

First Edition: October 2024

10 9 8 7 6 5 4 3 2 1

To Dad and Gigi.
Thank you for being my
favorite cheerleaders.

Chapter One

I'd never taken a month off work in my life. While living in Seattle, I worked in the ER through the holidays for several years. I preferred being busy to sitting at home alone, and I'd never been one to celebrate. This was why I'd been unprepared for the month off I'd been given for the December holidays for my new position as the doctor for the Sea Isle, Scotland, residents.

The people here took their holidays seriously. While I would take the occasional emergency, the town had been informed that I was on vacation until January 3.

It was only December 10, and I'd already bought and wrapped most of the gifts for my friends, reorganized my bedroom closet, and planned a spring getaway to Spain. I'd cleaned off my desk and read all the medical journals I'd been behind on the last few months.

Now what?

As if the universe had an answer, my cell phone rang.

"Em, I need you to do a big favor for me," said Mara, my best friend and manager of the Pig & Whistle Pub around the corner.

"Did I forget something?" I'd signed up for various volunteer duties for holiday events in Sea Isle. Most of the organizing had already taken place, but I was in charge of following up on a few of the details. I liked that the town had been so kind to me when I arrived, and I looked for ways to give back when I could.

"Not at all. The band's bus broke down about thirty minutes out of Edinburgh. The band is supposed to play for our big kickoff of the season tonight. Is there any chance you could follow me there to pick them up? I can fit their instruments in the back of Grandad's truck and carry a couple of them in the front, but I don't have room for the rest of the passengers.

"And the catering van is at the shop for repairs. It won't be ready until later this afternoon. We need your SUV."

I wasn't crazy about driving in the Scottish weather, but the roads were clear. It hadn't snowed in a few days. "Of course I'll help. When do you want to leave?" I asked. Mara was always there for me when I needed her, and I wouldn't let her down.

* * *

By the time we found the bus, the sky had grown dark, and snow threatened. The temperature had also dropped a few degrees, and I was freezing on the side of the road while I helped load their bags into the back of my SUV. I prayed we made it back before the skies opened up.

"Sorry about this," said Bram, the band's lead singer. Mara had introduced us all, and they'd been very polite, unlike what I'd expected from one of the most popular bands in Scotland (well, the UK, according to Mara). I'd always thought rock stars were rude and unkempt, and that they broke things in hotel rooms.

Stereotypes, Em? I smiled. I should have known better. People in Scotland, in general, were quite kind and friendly.

If Gerard Butler had a doppelgänger, it was this guy. He was beyond handsome in his cable-knit sweater, navy wool jacket, and cap that matched. He didn't seem to mind the cold at all.

"No worries," I said as they loaded into my car. "I don't mind."

He sat in the front passenger seat and smelled of bergamot and sandalwood. I almost asked what kind of cologne he wore. It was that intoxicating.

Three of his bandmates sat in the back.

"You're American," he said. "That is unexpected."

I smiled. "I moved to Sea Isle only a few months ago. I'm the town doctor." My job also included being a coroner, but it wasn't a fact I liked to share. Rightfully so, dealing with dead bodies tended to freak most people out.

"A doctor," the manager, Davy, said from the back seat. "We're sorry for taking your time. I'm not sure what was going on with the bus. It's the first time we've had anything other than a puncture."

"Impressive," said Destinee, the only woman in the band. "And they have you traipsing about pickin' up strangers on the road. We're sorry for that." Her Scottish brogue was heavier than the others. She had a husky sound to her voice.

I laughed. "Mara's my friend, and she needed help. I'm off for the holidays, so it's no big deal. I'm happy to help."

"Aye, and we're grateful," Bram said. "Right, Destinee?"

"Aye," she agreed.

"Bram's right," Davy said. "We are grateful. Like I said, never had any trouble with old Nessie before."

"Nessie?"

"Name of the bus," Bram said. "Davy said it. Not a peep of trouble before today."

"Probably that fan of yours sabotaged her," Destinee said. "She did leave you another note last night, right? Probably wanted to lock you in her basement and make you play love songs for her."

"Destinee." He sighed.

"Do you have a stalker?" I asked.

Bram sighed. "Comes with the territory," he said. "Just an overzealous fan who has some trouble with reality. I don't think anyone sabotaged the bus. It's on the older side. We're just lucky we haven't had trouble till now. Nessie's taken us all over Europe. She had done her time."

"Hmpf," Destinee grunted from the back.

I knew the band was very popular, but so famous to have a stalker? Mara was great about getting some of the best local talent into the pub. She used to live in Edinburgh and was hugely into the music scene before she chucked her high-paying but unfulfilling job and became the manager of her grandparents' pub.

But from what I understood, this group of musicians was different. They were the top sellers on this side of the pond, as in the number one band in all the UK and Europe. I'd meant to download some of their music today but hadn't had the time.

"How did you all become a band?" I pulled forward on the coastal highway, praying the snow would hold off until we reached Sea Isle.

Bram told the story of meeting Destinee at university, and after he and the others graduated, they gave themselves five years to make a living.

"That was fifteen years ago. This is our first gig back in Scotland in a year," he said. "We've been touring eastern Europe and Davy, our manager, has created a huge online following for us all over the world. We're doing much better than we ever imagined."

"I'm surprised you agreed to do such a small party."

He laughed. "We didn't have much choice, as Destinee grew up down the street from Mara in Edinburgh."

"Oh?"

"You are friends with our Mara. So, ya know you can't say no to her." Destinee laughed.

"True."

"Besides, we wrote some new songs while we were on the road," Bram said. "We've been rehearsing them the last few weeks. Best to try them out on a smaller audience. It was the perfect opportunity for us."

His hand had a slight tremor, and he crossed his arms.

I wonder what that is about?

"I can't imagine what it takes to write a song. How does that even work?"

I enjoyed learning about their songwriting process and the anecdotes from their travels. I was sad to see them go when I dropped them off.

"One thing, Doc," Bram said as he shut the hatch on the back of the SUV.

He approached the driver's side, and I rolled down the window.

"What is it?"

"Save me a couple of dances later. I do love a brilliant woman." He smiled and then walked away. The man oozed charm. And darn, he smelled amazing. I had to find out what kind of cologne that was. I'd use it as an air freshener if I could.

When I glanced in the rearview mirror, my cheeks were pink.

Well, that was unexpected.

* * *

A few hours later, I'd dressed in my favorite jeans and boots. I topped my outfit with an emerald-colored sweater and even donned a bit of makeup. It had nothing to do with the lead singer asking me to dance with him.

Okay, maybe a little bit.

When I reached the pub, the party was in full swing. The crowd inside typically would have deterred me, but the tent over the back garden was huge and held several hundred people. That was my destination, as my friends were already holding a table for me.

As I maneuvered my way through the pub, I found Mara arguing with Ewan, the laird of Sea Isle, and the mayor, as well as the constable. He, too, was as handsome as they came, and we butted heads constantly. Rarely were we in the same room and didn't argue.

They blocked the opening to the tent out back.

"How was I to know, Ewan? You never talked about it," Mara said.

"I asked you not to invite them." The edge in his voice was unmistakable.

"Destinee and I are friends," she said. "Look at this turnout—in December. We need the business. We've never seen anything like this during the holidays. I understand why you're upset, but it's too late now.

"They are about to go on, and I have to introduce them."

"They shouldn't be here," Ewan bit out.

Mara crossed her eyes. "Look, I have to bring in business during the winter months. You understand that better than most. And like I said, Destinee is a friend. They're doing this for nearly nothing and as a favor to me. I actually never expected them to say yes. This is a huge bonus. Please, don't cause a scene."

"Is everything okay?" I asked. I smiled so they wouldn't know I'd been listening.

"I, uh . . . Ewan isn't a huge fan of the band." Mara grimaced.

"Doc," Ewan said as he turned. "You . . . you look nice. I need a pint." He pushed past me.

"What was that all about?"

My friend shrugged. "Long story. I'll explain later. I really do need to introduce the band."

I followed her into the tent, and my friends Angie and Jasper motioned me over to a table on the far side. Jasper owned a bakery in town, and Angie had several shops throughout Scotland that sold everything from kilts to the oversized puffy coat I'd worn over my outfit to the pub.

I hugged them and then sat in the chair they'd saved for me. The crowd in the tent wasn't much better than the pub, and so many bodies made it warm. I slipped out of my jacket and put it on the back of the chair.

"There are so many people," I said.

"Most of them are townies," Angie said. "Mara wanted to keep it local. We might not have gotten into the pub if she'd advertised it. This is the first time the band has played in Scotland in a while."

"It always amazes me how Mara can get such big names here to Sea Isle," Jasper said.

Angie laughed. "When she was in advertising, she ran with a pretty wild crowd and made a lot of friends when they went clubbin'."

"Hard to imagine her that way." Jasper shook his head. "She's so—"

"Down to earth," I said.

"Aye."

"Where's your husband?" I asked Angie.

Her eyes lit up. "He's in London on business. Lots to clean up after all that mess with his dad," she said. "But things have turned in Damian's favor. He said to say hello."

Thanks to her father-in-law and his co-conspirator, Angie's stepmom, our lives had been in danger at her and Damian's wedding. But we survived, and the culprits were in jail for a long time.

"Oh, here they come. Our Mara looks like a boho princess tonight." Angie clapped.

Our friend did look like a princess, dressed in wide-legged jeans and a lacy, long-sleeved top, with curls piled on her head.

"Hello, friends. We're here to kick off the holiday season, and who better to help us than Bram and the Stokers."

I coughed back a laugh.

"What's so funny?" Angie asked over the roar of the crowd.

"I didn't know the name of the band."

"Don't judge 'em by it," Angie warned. "You're going to love them."

I wasn't so sure about that. But I was proven wrong a few lines into the first song. Bram's voice was beautiful, and it was magic when he and Destinee sang together. After the first song, the crowd surged forward.

"Told ya," Angie said.

I nodded.

"I'd like to dedicate this next one to Mara and the good Doc, who saved our souls on the side of the road today." He glanced back at the band. "There might be a song in that line."

They laughed and then launched into a tune about a beautiful woman who had to choose between two men, and Bram was begging her to choose him.

I might have blushed a bit when he focused on me.

"Bloody hell," Ewan grumbled from behind me.

As if he'd heard Ewan, Bram looked behind me. He grimaced and then went on with the song.

Why was Ewan so against the band being here, and what kind of history did he have with Bram?

The crowd had grown even larger by the time the musicians had finished their first set.

"I'm callin' the fire marshal," Ewan grumbled again. While we didn't always get along, it was strange for him to be so grumpy in public. He was usually in his element, surrounded by the village folks who adored him.

"What's in his craw?" Angie asked.

"No idea," Jasper said. "Anyone need a drink?"

I'd downed the last dregs of my pint. "Thanks," I said.

Being a friend of Mara's, he scooped up the glasses. We all took our dishes to the kitchen when we ate or drank at the pub. It's what friends did.

Angie's eyes widened, and I turned to see what she was staring at.

Bram held out his hand to me. "Lass, I believe it's time to dance." The jukebox played an old Ed Sheeran song—a slow one.

I didn't bother refusing. It would have been rude. Besides, he smelled so good it was as if his scent drew me nearer.

I tried to ignore the fact that my cheeks had warmed. Hopefully, he'd think the pink was from the heat in the tent.

"I like your music," I said.

"Thank you." He pulled me into him, with only a few inches of space between us. "We tour America in two months, so good to know we have some appeal with the Yanks. What part of the States are ya from?"

"I grew up around San Francisco but spent most of my adult years in Seattle working in emergency medicine."

He shook his head. "I barely made it through university. I can't imagine how much studying that must have taken. Why'd ya move here? America has everything."

I laughed. "A slower pace of life and a place where I could truly start over."

He held his head back. "Why would you need to do that? You're beautiful and smart."

My cheeks heated. "Thanks. Maybe I'll tell you the story some-day. But the gist is, I had a chance to run away and took it."

"Any chance you came over for Ewan?" He nodded toward the constable, who scowled at us.

I snorted. "Not likely. He can barely stand to be in the same room with me, but he is the one who hired me."

"I'd say he'd like to do more than be in a room with ya." Bram grinned. "His eyes are burnin' a hole into my soul."

"About that—how does he know you?"

Bram twirled me around so I could no longer see Ewan.

"It was long ago, but we have a bit of bad blood between us."

"Oh? Can you tell me about it?"

"Friends with his brother for a time."

I didn't know he had a brother. He had a huge family, but I'd only ever met him and his housekeeper. "And you had a falling out?"

"You could say that. Ewan caught me in bed with his fiancée at the time."

"With his brother's fiancée?"

"No, lass. Ewan's. I'm not proud of it."

What?

I stumbled a bit. The way the people in Sea Isle gossiped, especially to their doctor, I was surprised I'd never heard anything about this. As a public figure, the constable was fair game. But this town loved him.

"Like I said, it wasn't my best moment, but I dinnae know who she was at the time. She came to one of our shows and invited me home with her. How was I to know she was the fiancée of my best mate's brother?"

I didn't know who she was, but I disliked her. Any woman who would do that wasn't worth Ewan's time.

Look at me being protective of him.

"What happened?"

The other man shrugged. "He punched me in the nose and then walked out. That's the last I saw any of the Campbells."

No wonder Ewan was so angry about the band being here. They probably brought back terrible memories from the past.

I understood that sort of betrayal more than most. My husband had cheated on me most unexpectedly. It was part of the reason I'd run away from Seattle. Even though the hospital had kept things quiet after my husband's death, everyone still knew what had happened. I couldn't stand the looks or whispers. If I hadn't ended up here in Scotland, it would have been somewhere else.

For some weird reason, guilt assuaged me, and I wanted to leave the dance floor. While Ewan and I didn't always get along regarding cases, I had mad respect for him. He took his responsibilities for the town and its people seriously. He was a good man. Even I could see that.

"I've lost ya," Bram whispered the words.

I smiled. "No. It's all in the past, right?"

"Aye. Some people hold on to the past, though."

"True."

He twirled me around again, and Ewan was no longer staring us down.

The song ended.

"Thank you for the dance," I said. "I should get back to my friends."

"Lass, meet me after the last set. I want to get to know you." Full of charm, he gave me a grin.

Part of me yelled "Yes!" It had been a long time since a man had shown an interest in me. The more sensible side of me forced a smile. "Thanks again," I said. Then I walked away.

There was no way I could even think about flirting with Bram after what had happened to Ewan.

I guess I'm more loyal than I thought.

"That was cozy," Angie said. "I had no idea you knew him. If I weren't married to the most handsome man on the planet, I might be jealous." She laughed. "I took a picture so you had proof." She showed me her phone. He was staring down at me with interest, and man, he was handsome.

No.

I waved a hand. "He was just thanking me for picking them up when their bus broke down."

"He couldn't take his eyes off you," Angie said. "I'd say it was more than that."

"No," I said. "At least, not for me." One thing I'd always been was loyal. Even though the incident with Ewan's fiancée happened years ago, it bothered me. Though, according to Bram, it hadn't actually been his fault. He hadn't known who she was.

A bit of the sparkle had gone out of the night, and I saw Bram in a different light. He was used to going home with women all the time. I had no judgment but didn't want to be another notch on the bedpost.

Silly? Maybe, but I'd be steering clear of the band leader.

* * *

The following day, I headed to the pub for a full Scottish breakfast and Mara's coffee, which was tasty and known to wake the dead.

I had a bit too much Guinness the night before, and clearing the cobwebs from my brain was first on my agenda.

I was about to go into the Pig & Whistle when I caught a reflection of something shiny on the glass door. I turned toward the beach and lifted my hand to shade my eyes from the sun. Something stuck out of the sand, but I couldn't tell what it was.

I crossed the coastal road. On the other side, I stopped.

"Bram? Is everything okay?" He sat in the sand with his hand holding his guitar upright. He was so still it was eerie.

"Bram, it's cold. Why don't you come inside?"

He didn't seem to hear me, or he was ignoring me. I shivered in the cold.

Maybe he's meditating. I should leave him alone.

But something wasn't right about the way he sat hunched over, and he didn't have a heavy coat on. The temperature was in the twenties.

I made my way down the sand and stood a few feet away.

"Bram, are you okay?"

I moved closer and then took his pulse. His tan skin had turned a scary shade of white.

This isn't good.

"Doc, what's going on?" Ewan asked. I hadn't heard him walk up. And I might have jumped and, um, yelped a bit.

"He's dead," I said. "Very, very dead."

Chapter Two

Knowing that time was everything when one found a dead body, I pulled out my phone and started taking pictures. There was no outward sign of trauma. It was as if he'd sat down to watch the water and fallen asleep—permanently.

"Tell me what you need." Ewan asked.

"Abigail, the evidence kit, and someone to cordon off the area." My head throbbed. "And a cup of coffee." Breakfast would have to wait, but I needed to clear the cobwebs with some caffeine.

I didn't feel bad calling my able assistant, Abigail, so early. She'd be furious with me if I didn't.

After taking some preliminary photos, I walked the area around him to look for anything suspicious.

Nothing. When I'd met him the day before, he didn't show any outward signs of drug use. But that didn't mean he wasn't a user. We'd be checking for that later. He wore a long shirt and jeans, the same thing he'd had on the night before. He wore a wool coat, but it didn't seem warm enough for the weather. The Scots were tough, but in this cold, even the heartiest of them needed to bundle up, and it had been below freezing the night before.

As a doctor, I'd taught myself long ago to keep my emotions out of the job. Still, it was sad that the world had lost such a beautiful singer. No matter what else he'd done, his music was exceptional.

By the time Abigail showed up with my kit and some coffee, I'd done as much as possible without my tools.

We worked together in tandem like the well-oiled machine we were. The flash of sun from the morning had gone, and a light snow had started to fall. I worried about it washing away any helpful DNA or fibers.

"Let Ewan know we're ready to take him back to the lab. Have you had breakfast?"

"Nay," she said.

"I'll grab us some to go from the pub. You stay with the body. Where is Tommy?" Her brother was my gardener and all-around fixer-upper around the four-hundred-year-old church I lived in up the hill. Tommy was on the spectrum, but he was every bit as brilliant as his sister.

"Up at Ewan's being well looked after. I'll call up for him once we get the rock star settled."

"So, you know the band?"

"Aye," she said. Then she was on the phone giving orders. She was a bit meek and unsure of herself when I first met her. But she wasn't anymore. All she needed was a bit of self-confidence, and the strong woman underneath shone through.

"Don't let the body out of your sight," I said. "Please."

She laughed. "We won't be letting that happen again."

We'd once had a body stolen from my lab, and not long ago, someone had broken into our makeshift lab at a castle to tamper with evidence. One couldn't be too careful.

I headed up to the pub. When I walked in, the place went silent. All eyes were on me as I approached Mara at the bar.

"So, is it true? Bram is dead?" she asked in her straightforward manner.

I opened my mouth, but she held up a hand.

"Before you say it's part of an ongoing investigation, two of Ewan's men have already said it was."

"Right." I turned to face the rest of the pub. "But before any rumors begin, I have no idea what happened. We'll have to run some tests and do a full workup. It's an—"

"Ongoing investigation," the crowd said in unison. I laughed. Ewan's famous words were well-known by all.

"Right, but it would be great if you could keep the news to yourselves. We don't need the media making assumptions." I said the words even though I understood they were useless. My guess was word had already gone out on social media.

I turned back to Mara. "I need takeaway breakfasts," I said. "Two, make that three, full Scottish." I had a feeling Ewan would be joining us for the autopsy. And yes, food and autopsies don't usually go together, but keeping up one's strength for work was best.

None of us would feel like eating afterward.

"I'll tell Gran. She's in the kitchen this morning." She went away. When she came back, I'd pulled out my notebook.

"When was the last time you remember seeing him?" I asked her.

She leaned on the bar. "Like I told Ewan's guys, they closed down the pub last night," she said. "I had to shove them out the door. That was a bit after midnight. They were staying up the mountain at Mrs. Beatty's B and B. Since their bus was broken, I had one of my bartenders help take them up in the catering van. The manager, Davy, rented a car yesterday, but they didn't fit with all the equipment."

Mrs. Beatty's was a Victorian bed-and-breakfast in the other part of Sea Isle up the mountain. A strip of pastel-colored shops and restaurants was on the coast, but the other half of town was up the hill. It was filled with old stone buildings, shops, restaurants, and the courthouse and library.

Our village may have been small, but it was self-sufficient. We had everything a person might need, from clothing stores to bakeries and books.

"Do you remember anything after that? Did you see him wander down to the beach?"

She shook her head. "Nay. I was knackered by the time we got them out the door. I locked up and then headed upstairs. I took a shower and don't even remember going to bed. But the alarm went off way too early this morning."

"Did you see anyone giving him trouble? Maybe a fan? Or one of the other band members?"

"Nay. When they left, they were all singing Christmas carols together. I would have let them stay if I hadn't been so tired. It was beautiful. They seemed happy after their set. The mix of new and old songs had gone over well with the crowd. It was a great night."

"I agree." It was a great night, but then the talented singer ended up dead on the beach.

I'd been a witness to most of what happened the night before. The fans had been eager to hear the new songs. They often sang along with the older ones. There were murmurs when the band announced new tunes, but the applause at the end proved the music was a hit.

And I'd been right there along with them. The band was one of the best I'd ever heard. Not that I had much experience with music. I enjoyed it, but that was about the extent of my interests.

"So, you don't remember anyone acting strangely?"

"I'm sorry, Em. I feel like I'm letting you down. But we were so busy last night. After I announced the band, we were smashed at the bar and in the kitchen. We ran out of food and had to close the kitchen down."

"Well, that was good for business, at least."

She pursed her lips. "I can't believe he's gone. We were just . . . it's so weird."

"It is, and I'm sorry."

"I'll make sure my team is available to chat with you and Ewan, but I feel like if they'd seen something, they would have let me know."

I nodded.

"You don't think he was killed in here, do you?" Her eyes went wide. "I can tell you we found no blood or crime scene last night. He walked out of here. That much I remember."

I smiled. "Thanks."

Her grandmother came out with a large paper bag filled with food boxes. "How are you, luv?"

"I'm good, thank you. How about you?"

She shook her head. "Sad business."

I nodded. "Did you notice anything last night? Maybe someone arguing with him?"

The noise behind me died down as the customers listened to the conversation. I'd grown used to the village being involved in investigations.

"Nay. Sorry, luv. I was in the kitchen all night. By the time we were done, I stumbled to the car and went home."

"You'll both let me know if you hear anything?"

"Aye," Mara said.

"I added a few extras," Mrs. Wilson said as she handed me the bag. "We have to keep your strength up."

"I appreciate your kindness," I said. "And you're sure you don't remember anything weird from last night?"

"Oh, lass, we were heavin' it was so crazy behind the bar and in the kitchen," Mara's gran said. "The whole time is a blur of faces. Sorry."

I smiled. "Don't be. You did a great job." I took the bag but then stopped. "Has anyone sat where the band was last night?"

"Aye, we were full up this morning," Mara said. "Why?"

I shrugged. "I just wondered if maybe one of them left something behind."

"Or if there might be bloodstains." Mara frowned. "I promise, it was the normal cleanup last night. No blood. And we didn't find anything unusual."

"Maybe reserve that area for a bit. I'll send one of Ewan's men to look around before the lunch crowd arrives. I know you're right, but it's best to make certain."

"Done," Mara said. "But fair warning, we scrubbed to the corners before we left last night. Does this mean you think it was foul play?"

The conversation in the pub ceased again. The townies listened with bated breath.

I shrugged. "I've no idea, to be honest. Oh, when they were partying after the set, was there anyone outside of their group hanging around?"

Mara nodded. "Several fans wanting autographs. Some young girls were trying to get their attention. I think Davy said something to them, though. They went off in a huff."

"Okay, good to know."

"So, you think someone killed him?" She whispered the words.

He had seemed perfectly healthy the day before, but one never knew. "That's why I have to get back to the lab."

"Let us know if you need anything." Mara handed me another container with four cups of coffee.

"This is a great start." I held up the coffee.

*   *   *

Back at my practice, I found Abigail and Ewan in the kitchen. I put the food on the long quartz counter, or bench, as they called them here. The kitchen was too big for me. I'm not much of a cook. It had a fancy hob that kept the area warm throughout the year. So, I spent more time here than I had in the one I had in Seattle, but more because it was a cozy place to read a book and drink coffee and tea.

"What's up?" I asked.

"I've drawn for toxicology," she said. She wore a lab coat, and her hair was piled on her head. "But we were waiting for you. I've lined up some bins. We have the evidence bags ready. I didn't want to do anything more until you arrived."

"Well, I thought it best we have breakfast before we begin," I said as I held up the bag of food.

Ewan opened his mouth, but I held up a hand.

"I know you're in a rush. I'm asking for half an hour to clear the cobwebs and eat. We have no idea how long this will take."

"I was just going to say that sounds like a good idea," he said grumpily.

Abigail may have hidden a laugh behind her hand. There was no way he was about to say that, but I let it go.

We ate quickly while discussing what we'd found so far. Ewan's team was at the B and B gathering evidence from Bram's room and the public areas in case foul play had been involved.

"What about the others?"

"Still asleep," he said. "We are leaving them alone for now. That is, until I get more information from you."

We ate quickly, and then it was time to get to work.

We bagged and tagged, and Abigail pulled fibers. Some she would test, others we would send to the labs in Edinburgh or Glasgow. Thanks to Ewan, we have a state-of-the-art facility here in Sea Isle, especially for a practice in such a small town. There were times when we were blocked off from the rest of the world because of winds or snow, and having so much on hand meant we could treat the majority of emergencies.

As the coroner, I didn't need to do an autopsy. I could have sent the bodies off to a larger town. But I'm a bit of a control freak and perfectly capable. I've also discovered an innate curiosity in trying to find out how people have died.

After a quick overall examination, the cause of death was not readily available.

"I wonder what the rip on his jeans is about," I said aloud. "I don't remember that being a part of his outfit last night."

We cut off his clothes and carefully placed everything in evidence bags that Ewan helped us log.

Oh. Ewan. He might be considered a suspect if there had been foul play.

Hmm.

"Is it okay for you to be in here?" I asked.

"I'm the constable, so yes."

"No, I mean, if there was foul play—you and the deceased weren't exactly on speaking terms. You like investigations to go by the book and . . . well, I know you didn't kill him. But you weren't happy about him being in Sea Isle. I may not have been the only one who witnessed your argument with Mara or noticed you shooting daggers with your eyes at Bram all night."

Abigail's eyes went wide.

"Doesn't mean I had reason to kill him. What happened was years ago, I have just never been a big fan and was voicing my opinion. People have a right to do so. Are you calling my professionalism into question?" He gave me a look that might make a lesser human wither, but I was used to his grumpiness. Mara joked it was part of his charm.

"Of course not. You are the most professional person I know. I just don't want you to get into trouble later."

"Any chance we can get a time of death?" he asked.

"Are you trying to plan your alibi?" I was joking, but Ewan's face was not.

"I dinnae kill him," he said. His brogue was coming out a bit more pronounced. That happened when his temper flared, or he was tired.

"From his liver temp, and the state of the body, I'd say we're looking at about six to eight hours ago. The body was half frozen when I found it, so it's going to be difficult to give you an exact time."

He glanced at his watch and then made a note on the clipboard he held. There was no way he'd hurt anyone, but I didn't want him to get in trouble later if his dislike of the deceased ever came up. And this was a small town. People knew about his past. It would definitely come up at some point.

"We know he left the pub just after midnight," I said. "I spoke with Mara, and she said she had to shove them out the door about then. But everyone in their group seemed in a good mood, and they were caroling as they left. If there was foul play, it had to have happened when they were at the B and B."

"I've got my men waiting for the rest of them there. We need to know if he went back with them or stayed behind. That will give us a start."

"You're acting like there was foul play," I said.

"May have been," he said. He held up the sweater Bram had been wearing. The inside of the collar was covered with dried, and frozen, blood.

I hadn't noticed that when I found him sitting on the beach, but then his clothes had been frozen to him.

"We need to flip him, carefully," I said.

They helped me turn the body. I lifted his long hair off his neck. The strands were matted together with blood as well. And there it was.

A perfectly round puncture right into the stem of the brain.

"What made that?" Abigail asked.

"I have no idea." But Ewan's instincts were correct.

Something was definitely not right.

"I'm fairly certain we're looking at murder."

Chapter Three

After checking the body for other injuries and not finding anything, I went back to the puncture wound. It was tiny and perfectly round. But there were some jagged edges just inside. We measured the wound. It was larger than a hypodermic needle, but not by much.

"I need a scan before I take out the brain and disturb anything," I said.

We loaded him onto a gurney and rolled him through my house to the lab at the back of the clinic where we kept the larger machines. Thanks to Ewan, and Sea Isle, we could do everything from MRIs and CAT scans to X-rays, and we had surgical suites. Abigail worked on the scans while Ewan and I headed back to the autopsy room.

"What are you thinking?" he asked impatiently.

"I'm not thinking anything quite yet," I said. I understood why he needed to know. We were talking about murder, and every second counted. "I need to see those scans first."

"What about the puncture? What made that size of a wound?"

"Ewan, I promise you I have no idea. I thought at first it might be he was injected with—Wait a minute."

I hurried back to where Abigail was. The scans were just coming up on her machine.

We pointed to it at the same time.

"What is it?" Ewan asked.

"Embolism, a large clot in his brain, which blocked the main artery. He probably presented with stroke symptoms before he died."

"Could it have been caused by some kind of natural clotting of the blood or something?" he asked.

"They can be, but this one . . . My guess is someone pumped the air into his brain stem. And a few minutes later he was dead. I don't know exactly what they used, but I don't think it was a hypodermic needle."

"So, definitely murder?"

I shrugged. "He maybe could have jabbed whatever it was into his own neck, but I doubt it. There are much easier ways to kill oneself. But we would have found the weapon in his hand. The odd thing is, there are no defensive wounds. Like, none. He didn't put up a fuss."

"Maybe, he passed out before they killed him," Abigail added. "Was he drinking a lot?"

"I have no idea," I said. I'd have to ask Mara. "So," I continued. "Someone pumps air into his brain, creates an embolism, and it causes his body to shut down. That's my best guess at the moment. And it is a guess. Clots can happen at any time. He could have been injured weeks ago and one formed, then let loose at an inopportune moment.

"If we hadn't found the puncture wound . . ."

"That's how you think he died," Ewan said.

"I'll know more once we have some of the tests back. But there is definitely an embolism. And it's large enough to block the artery. But until we can find what caused that puncture . . . like I said, it could have happened somewhere else in the body and traveled to the brain, but it would have hit the heart first.

"The puncture is close to the brain, so that would be my best guess. And again, I have to stress it is a guess, Ewan."

One of the machines dinged, and Abigail went to check on it. She printed something out and brought it to me.

"Wow. That's an interesting cocktail of substances, most of which our tests can't identify," I said.

"And only a partial list," she said. "The rest won't be finished for a couple of days. And then there's what we had to send off."

"What do you mean?" Ewan asked as he stared over our shoulders.

"His blood alcohol level was high enough to be toxic to his system, but there's also some others we can't identify and Chlormethiazole."

"What's that last one?"

"Sleeping tranqs," Abigail said. "But a much larger dose than normal."

"He was also drugged?"

I shrugged. "Or he took them himself. It wouldn't be the first time a rock star overdosed." It was sad but often a side symptom of the business. "There's a good chance after all that, at these levels, he may not have woken up even without the embolism."

"Could that mean he'd planned to self-harm? I mean, did he ingest the drugs on his own, or were they mixed into something?"

Abigail and I glanced at each other.

"What?"

"I can tell you the drugs weren't forced down," I said. "His mouth and esophagus were clear. We would have seen signs of trauma if they had been forced. That said, it doesn't mean they weren't hidden in something else."

"What do you mean?" he asked.

"She's thinking about what happened before Angie's wedding. The poison in the water."

"Right. What you're saying is, it's possible any or all of the drugs might have been put in something he drank or ate, and someone stabbed him in the back of the neck and gave him an embolism."

"Overkill," I said. I hadn't meant to say it out loud, but Abigail and Ewan nodded in agreement. "I mean, he could have taken some of the drugs, and then the others, or . . . Like I said, drugs are rampant in that business. I saw it a lot when I was in Seattle. Toxicology should have identified them quickly if it were cannabis, cocaine, oxy, or any of the regular street drugs. But the tests didn't.

"Then there is the stabbing. That adds a different element to the situation. I think someone was trying to make sure Bram never woke up. Whether that was himself or someone else, that's something yet to be determined."

*　　*　　*

By the time we'd finished with everything, it was well past lunch. I washed up, and Ewan received a call.

"The band members are waiting to be questioned," he said. "Would you like to come with me?"

He wasn't always so open to me helping out in that regard. I usually had to figure out a way to go alone if I wanted answers.

"Yes, thanks." I ran upstairs to do a quick change. Less than a half hour later, we were shown into the front parlor of the B and B. The inside rooms were every bit as charming as the gingerbread exterior. I was surprised by the modern Victorian appeal of the rooms. They weren't decorated with the stuffy grandma decor I'd been expecting.

Destinee and Davy sat on one side of the well-appointed front room. And the rest of the band was on a sofa near a fire. There was a massive Christmas tree in front of the window, as well as decorations along the walls and bookshelves. It had a very homey feel and was perfectly designed too.

"What's going on?" Davy, the band's manager, stood and came toward us. "Where is Bram?"

"I'm Constable Ewan McGregor, and you are?"

"Davy Albright," he said. "I'm the band's manager." He seemed to notice me behind Ewan, and he frowned. "Doc, is everything okay? Do you know what's happened to Bram?"

"Mr. Albright, if you'll have a seat." Ewan motioned toward some chairs. "We need to speak to your group."

Davy frowned but did as Ewan asked. The constable had a commanding way about him that had most people doing exactly what he wanted.

Destinee turned toward us, but she didn't look so great. Her hair was mussed, and it appeared not all of yesterday's makeup was off. Her eyes were bloodshot, and she was extremely pale.

"I need to know your movements after you left the pub last night," he said to the group.

Everyone just stared at him with quizzical expressions on their faces. As I glanced around, I made a note to see if any of them looked suspicious, but they just looked exhausted and confused.

"I dinnae understand what is happening," Davy said. "I'll ask you again, where is Bram? Did something happen to him? Why won't you tell us where he is?" His voice was a mix of desperation and anger. I couldn't blame him. This had to be confusing.

"I would appreciate you answering my questions." Ewan didn't give in to his demands. He could be stubborn that way.

I took a notebook and pen out of my bag. Destinee watched me carefully.

"I think we'd be more open to answering your questions if you tell us what's going on," Davy said. "And where the bloody hell is Bram?"

"Yeah, what did he do this time?" Destinee asked. She rubbed her forehead.

"I'd like you to answer the question," Ewan said. He moved to stand in front of Destinee. "Where did you go when you left the pub?"

"Here," she said softly. "Davy rented a car for us, and the bartender brought our equipment up in the van."

"And Bram was with you?" Ewan asked.

She nodded and then grabbed her head as if the motion made it hurt worse. "Why? Is he missing?" She glanced around the room frantically, and then grabbed her head again.

"Constable," Davy interrupted, "please tell us what is going on." He appeared genuinely worried. They all did, which meant they probably didn't know anything about what happened to Bram.

I peered over at Ewan and realized that he'd been looking for their reactions.

"We found your friend on the beach," Ewan said. "He was pronounced dead at the scene."

There were gasps all around.

"No," Destinee cried out. "It—He was just—No. He can't be gone. He's upstairs sleeping or at some chippy's house. It isn't him." She sobbed and put her head into her arms. Davy put a hand on her shoulder.

"Are you sure?" the drummer, Liam, asked. He'd ridden with Mara, so I didn't know him that well. Not that I knew any of them, really. But I'd spent time with Bram, Destinee, Davy, and Boscoe, one of the guitar players, while we'd driven to Sea Isle. I couldn't imagine any of the band members killing their lead singer. They all seemed to be great friends.

But then victims were usually murdered by people they knew. I couldn't allow myself to forget that.

"Yes," Ewan said. "One of you, or a family member, will need to formally identify the body, but it is him."

Davy cleared his throat. "I can do that. I cannae believe this though. We . . ."

"You what?" Ewan asked.

"We were all just together. As Destinee said, we came up together in the car. We had a few more drinks in here, and then we went off to bed."

"Did any of you see Bram go into his room?"

Henry, who worked with Ewan, had just come in, but he stood at the side.

"He said he was too wired." The drummer took a sip of his tea. "He had some new songs rolling around in his head. Told us that your wee town was inspiring him. He does that. Goes off on these manic phases, and he can't be bothered with anything else. We left him down here by the fire with his guitar and his notebook."

We'd found the guitar, but there'd been no notebook at the crime scene. And how did he get down to the beach? It was nearly a mile, in the cold, down the mountain. Why would he walk down in the middle of the night?

And someone had stabbed him.

But who?

I surveyed the room. Destinee was still crying, albeit a bit softer than before. The drummer sniffed. Davy was pacing back and forth. Boscoe and Render both had their heads in their hands. I couldn't see their faces.

"What are we going to do?" Davy said. His eyes went wide, and he looked like he'd just had a terrible fright.

Well, he'd lost a friend. That made sense.

"About?" Ewan asked.

"The bloody tour. The band finally makes it back to America, and Bram . . ." He stopped and glanced up. "Sorry. Sorry. I sound like a heartless arse. I get it. But . . . Did he—did he do himself in?"

"No." Destinee shouted. "He was a selfish bastard sometimes, but he wouldn't do that to us, Davy. Why did you even say that?"

I opened my mouth, but Ewan gave me a look. I shut it again. I was more a cards-on-the-table kind of person, but that wasn't always helpful in an investigation. The less one spoke, the more others tended to fill the silence. But the constable was much better with those silences than I was.

"We will know soon," Ewan said. "Do any of you know if he had a substance problem?"

Boscoe snorted. "Not likely. He hated everything to do with drugs. Would kick us out on our arses if he caught us at it. It was one of his only rules. That, and showing up on time for rehearsals."

But he had drugs in his system. Interesting.

"And not drinking during shows," Render added. He sat back in his chair.

"What they're saying is true," Davy said. "We have a strict clause in their contract for no drugs."

Destinee raised her head. I handed her a package of tissues I carried in my bag.

"Thanks," she said softly. "He had a problem in uni back in the day," she said. "After he got clean, he wouldn't touch the stuff. But I'll be honest, I've been wondering—"

"Destinee," Davy said sharply.

She shrugged. "You all know. He's been strange lately. Forgetting lyrics and spacing out. It happened twice onstage in the last six months. Could be he was using again."

"Nah," Davy said. "We'd have known. And the doctor said it was exhaustion."

"What are you even saying, Destinee?" Render asked. "We were there from the beginning. After everything he went through, he swore off the stuff for good. He wouldnae fallen off the wagon."

She sniffed again. "I know what we all think, and it's been twenty years," she said. "You all have to admit he has been off the last part of the year. How can we know what he was up to? And last night, he drank more—" She started crying again.

"Drank more than what?" I asked softly.

"More than he has in a long time," the drummer said. "She's right. He's been a bit off for months. I thought he was just excited about getting ready for the new tour."

"No different than every time before when we were preparing for a tour," the bass player said. "What no one will say out loud is Bram had a manic personality. Extreme highs and lows, and everything between. That brain of his was brilliant, but . . ."

"He was a bloody brilliant artist, you twat," Destinee said. "Don't you go off on him now. He's the only reason you're still around after what you did."

She sobbed harder and then took off up the stairs.

What a mess this was. It might have been better if we'd tried to chat with them one at a time rather than as a group. But I understood Ewan's reasoning. Hit them all at once and gauge their reactions. Then watch the group dynamics, which had been fascinating.

That said, it was obvious everything wasn't as happy within the band as one might have been led to believe. I would have never guessed any of this drama as I watched them interact in the car and onstage the day before.

But there was a possibility that one of them killed him.

But I hadn't a clue who that might be.

What I couldn't say, without risk of Ewan murdering me where I stood, was that he didn't have the organs of a long-time drug user, and we'd found nothing that would have made me think differently.

I had a weird feeling, but I couldn't quite place it. My gut told me this story was much more complicated than any of us might imagine. And I needed to go over everything again.

The drummer's hands shook. The bass player didn't seem to meet anyone's eyes. Davy seemed like he might come unglued at any moment. Everyone looked suspicious to me.

But had one, or more, of the band members tried to kill Bram?

Ewan continued to watch them all, as did I.

Someone confess. I wanted to scream the words, but that wasn't how this worked.

If someone in the room had killed Bram, I hoped we'd figure it out quickly.

At least before they tried it again.

Chapter Four

The room at the B and B where Bram had stayed before his death was enormous. It took up most of the third floor and had a private living room, huge bath, study, and bedroom with a fireplace. I hadn't realized Mrs. Beatty had such fancy accommodations. Now I understood why the band chose to stay here.

There were a few other inns and B and Bs in Sea Isle, but I didn't think they would be as nice as this one.

While Ewan's men had searched the area around the B and B already, I asked if I could have a look around his room. I'm not sure what I thought I might find, but I wanted a better idea of who the singer really was. Since they'd finished the forensics in the room, Ewan, for once, hadn't seen the harm in me looking around.

The bed was made, and his bags were neatly packed as if they hadn't been touched. "They didn't take these in for evidence?" I asked after Ewan let me in the room.

"They went through them but didn't find anything. Feel free though. Will you be okay for a bit? I need to speak with Mrs. Beatty, the owner of the B and B."

"Yes, I'll be fine. I'll meet you down there when I'm done."

After putting on my gloves, I went through the small leather bag that sat on a chair near the bed. There was a change of clothes, and

I discovered the singer wore boxer briefs, but other than that, there wasn't much on the personal side.

There was a carry-on suitcase in the wardrobe, but it was more of the same, just clothes. In the bathroom, I found his toiletries. There wasn't even an aspirin, and certainly no signs of any sort of drugs. Nothing we'd found in his system was in this room or his things.

If he were an addict, and I knew he wasn't, he'd have a stash. After going through the room, I searched the bookshelves that surrounded the fireplace, and looked under the pillows for anything he might have been trying to hide.

Nothing. No drugs, or the notebook everyone had been talking about, could be found. They'd said he'd been writing, but we didn't find it on his person, and it wasn't in here. Wind rattled the windows. Even though the radiators sputtered warmth around the room, I shivered. I had a sense someone was watching me, but there wasn't anyone else in there with me.

After checking the bathroom again, I went downstairs in search of Ewan. My phone buzzed as I hit the foyer. It was Abigail.

"The lab in Edinburgh is backed up, but there are some strange anomalies in the test results," she said.

"Let me guess. He isn't a drug user."

"Not that I can find," she said. "How did you know?"

"I've just been through his room. I couldn't even find anything over the counter. There's no stash, at least not in there."

"The drugs didn't make it to his liver—well, not much," she said. "I ran some of the tests you asked for on his heart. All of them came out clean. I've been over every inch of him again and cannae find any other needle marks. I even checked between his toes, and, um, other places."

I pursed my lips. "Thank you, Abigail, for being so thorough."

"'Tis my job," she said in that matter-of-fact way of hers.

"Is there anything else?" I asked.

"Nay, though Mr. Guilford's son, Danny, called. He says his granddad won't come in, but he definitely needs looking after. I told him you were on holiday, and said they should go into Edinburgh, but his granddad is not having it."

"Let me see if I can have Ewan run me by," I said.

After I hung up, I went in search of Ewan. He was talking to Davy, but the rest of the band wasn't around.

When I walked in, they stopped talking and looked over at me.

"Everything okay, Doc?"

I nodded. "When you're finished, I wondered if you could give me a ride to the Guilfords?"

"Aye. We're done for now," he said. "I'll be back tomorrow for the individual interviews. Give you all a chance to mourn your loss. I'll also be contacting the family."

Davy shook his head. "We were his family," he said. "His parents died years ago, and he didn't have any siblings. He might have the odd aunt or uncle, but he wasn't close to any of them. Render and his family took him in years ago. I'm sure he'll be the one to tell them."

"Noted," Ewan said.

"I'll need to make, uh, arrangements," Davy said. "Is it okay to do that? Do you know when we'll have the body back?"

Ewan glanced at me.

"The labs are backed up," I said. "Until we can get see some of the results, we'll have to hold on to the body, I'm afraid."

"Can you at least tell us how he died? Did he kill himself?" the band manager asked.

"That's the second time you asked that," I said. "You all mentioned his moods, but was there more to it? Is there something you can tell us that might further our medical investigation? The tests take time, and it would help to have some sort of direction."

Davy shrugged. "Destinee was right about him being off the last few months. He's been a bit distracted, but I wouldn't say he was down. Not until the last few weeks. He seemed—I don't know how to explain it—edgy at times, though he was more thoughtful around us. More so than he ever has been before. But also sad. I asked him a couple of times if he was okay."

"What did he say?" Ewan asked.

"That he was working through something but that he'd be fine."

"And you had no idea what he meant by that?"

Davy sighed. "Nay. Like I said, he was a moody bugger. When he was writing, and he had been the last several months, it was like he dredged up the past to put it into words. I guess I thought maybe that was what happened."

"What about his fans?" I asked.

"What do you mean?"

"When we were in the car yesterday, it was mentioned he had a stalker, right?" That drive seemed like it had taken place months ago. So much had happened since then. It was strange to be investigating his death when he'd been so vibrant and alive the day before.

I wasn't sure I'd ever get used to this part of the job. In the ER, I assessed and dealt with my patients quickly and efficiently. Even as a GP, I was pretty fast most days. But these investigations took a great deal of time and thought, and a skill set I was still developing.

I tried to think of the cases as a diagnostician. It was a very different sort of thing trying to find out how someone died.

"He's had more than one stalker," he said. "But they are usually harmless. I don't think any of them would try to hurt him. Worship him, yes. But nay, they would not have killed him."

"Still, we'll need names," Ewan said. "And access to his computer and emails."

"Don't you need a search warrant for all that?"

"He's dead. Is it necessary?" Ewan said. "Is there something you're hiding?" The constable was nothing if not direct.

"I'll see what I can do," Davy said.

* * *

34

A short time later, we were greeted by a flock of sheep at the Guilford farm. There were some with sweet, black faces. There were others that looked like giant, white cotton balls.

Ewan beeped his horn lightly, and the sheep gradually moved out of the way.

"Looks like someone left the gate open," he said. Then he was out of the car herding the sheep into a nearby paddock. I got out of the car to try to help, though I wasn't sure exactly what I was supposed to do.

I waved my arms around a bit. "Go, sheep, go." I yelled. The wind whipped around me, wrapping me with its icy fingers. It was several degrees colder this high up the mountain, and my nose and hands were frozen.

Danny ran out of the house to help. In a matter of minutes, they had them all in the paddock.

"Sorry about that," he said. "I was feedin' 'em when Pauline called out and said Granddad had fallen again. I raced in and must have forgotten the gate."

"No trouble," Ewan said.

"Tell me what's happened with your grandfather," I said. "I'm afraid I don't have my kit with me, but I thought I could stop by and see what was going on," I said.

"We're grateful," Danny said. "After tea, he was headin' to sit in his chair, and Pauline says his legs just gave out on him. I tried to pack him in the lorry, but he wasn't having it. Says there's a bad storm on the way, and he won't be missing out on his bed. I'm truly sorry we interrupted your holiday."

I smiled. Mr. Guilford was stubborn and quite set in his ways. I adored him, though.

"No worries," I said. "We weren't far away. I thought I'd stop by. If I need my kit, I can come back, or Abigail can run it up."

"Thank ya," Danny said.

The house was a roughly built stone cabin, but thanks to the log burner in the central room, it was toasty warm. There was a

Christmas tree in the corner with loads of lights and tinsel. The tinsel made me smile. And there were brightly wrapped presents under the tree.

Not since I was a kid when my grandma let me help her decorate for the holidays had I seen tinsel. I didn't even know they still made it.

Which reminded me, I needed to get a tree for my house. When I lived in Seattle, I never decorated for the holidays. It seemed a waste of time and effort since me and my husband usually worked through the holidays so our staff could have time off. We had Chinese food on Christmas Day, and sometimes we gave each other gifts. It depended on the year and what we had going on at the time.

That life no longer felt like mine.

"Oh, thank you, Doctor McRoy, for coming," Pauline said as we entered the house. "Fair warning, Granddad is in a right mood."

I smiled. In my many years as a doctor, I'd dealt with my fair share of grumpy old dudes.

The elder Mr. Guilford was in a recliner in front of the television, watching what I could only assume was an old football match. I knew enough about sports to understand the season was well over for this year.

"I hear you've been practicing your flips to join the Scottish gymnastics team," I said as I moved beside him.

He snorted but looked up at me. "Doc?"

"It's me. Ewan and I were in town, and I thought I might stop by to see how you're doing."

He pointed to the television. "Well, we're about to lose again, but we'll be better next year."

"Here's hoping," I said. Everything I knew about football, I'd learned from Mara while hanging out at the pub during matches. That and rugby, another game I didn't understand, were huge here.

"To keep your family off your back, I thought I might check you out after that fall."

He waved a hand at me. "Fine. Tripped on a rug and lost my balance a wee bit. Nothing more than that."

"And those blood sugars? How have those been doing? Any dizziness?"

"I'm fine, I tell ya. No need to fuss, Doc. But I dinnae like being a bloody pin cushion."

"Right. I hear you, Mr. Guilford. The thing is, it's my job to fuss a bit, and it's your job to keep a check on those blood sugars. You fell, so I'm here. Don't make it a waste of a trip for me. Let me check a few things. You keep watching your match, and you won't even know I'm here."

He grumbled but then sighed. I carried my stethoscope in my purse, along with a few other medical essentials. I had a small kit that I normally had with me when I did house calls, but I hadn't been planning on that today.

"I need his glucose monitor," I said.

Pauline brought it, along with some test strips. He wasn't my only patient who was diabetic. I had quite a few elderly men and women who were dealing with diabetes.

After pricking his finger, I used the test strip. He was up in the two hundreds, not exactly deadly but enough to make him dizzy.

"Well, do you want the good news or the bad news?"

He glared at me. "Give it to me, Doc."

I smiled. "The bad news is those sugars are high enough to make you dizzy. Have you been taking the medication I prescribed?"

He shrugged.

"No," Pauline said from the kitchen.

"Well, you probably fell because of those sugars. And if you don't take the medicine and keep them down, then the next time you fall, you might get gangrene and lose a limb."

He peered at me over the rim of his glasses. "What? Rubbish."

"No, it isn't rubbish. It can happen in just a few days. Maybe it's a stubbed toe, or you come down wrong on a knee, and it just doesn't heal properly because of the diabetes."

"You're trying to put a scare into me," he said.

"I'm not one for that sort of thing," I said. "You know that. I'm always honest with you. I'm going to send Abigail up here to do some blood work. Or you can come down to the practice tomorrow. Either way, it's happening."

"Bloody vampires. No one is going anywhere tomorrow. There's a storm coming."

I smiled. He hadn't exactly said no. Nothing like the threat of gangrene to get someone moving in the right direction.

"We'll see about that. Promise me you will take the prescribed meds and that you'll stay away from the sweets and watch those carbs. Proteins and veggies are your friends."

He smirked and then nodded.

"Now, tell me how and where you fell."

By the time we left, my stomach was growling. Pauline had given Ewan and I a loaf each of Bannock, which was a skillet bread. I broke off a piece of the one she'd given me. I offered it to Ewan, and he took it. Then I pulled another piece off for me and ate it.

She'd also given me a group of sticks with a ribbon around the bundle. "I'm curious about this." I held up the sticks.

"Aye, that's a rowan twig," he said.

"And?"

"They are hung above the doors of a home or barn and are thought to ward off evil spirits. As a gift, it's to get rid of any bad feelings between friends or family. A peace offering of sorts."

"But I have no ill feelings toward the Guilfords. They are a lovely family."

Ewan chuckled. "Probably because their granddad is a bit of a grump. But it may also be part of their family traditions to give a small token to everyone who crosses their door."

"I'd read that Scots don't really celebrate the holidays, but I'm finding that not to be true."

"Aye, for centuries anything to do with Christmas was banned, even the baking. But that's no longer the case. Around 1958, the day became a public holiday again. I guess you could say we are making up for lost time. And our town has always been different. We never let go of our old traditions."

Just as he said that, we came over a rise in the road. The part of the town that was on the mountain came into view. The sky, even though it was only two in the afternoon, was darkening, and lights twinkled all around the town. Every building had been decorated, and the same had happened to the shops along the seawall in my part of Sea Isle. The whole thing was magical.

"It's beautiful," I said softly.

Ewan grinned. "Aye, 'tis."

"I don't think I've ever said this, but thank you for recruiting me."

He chuckled. "I sometimes wonder if you want to curse me for bringing you here."

"No. It isn't always easy, especially with cases like we have today, but I'll never regret moving here."

"Good to hear."

"What's your take on the band?" I asked Ewan as he drove back down the mountain. The wind whipped around his SUV, rocking it back and forth.

"I'm not sure what you mean."

I shrugged. "There's something up with them," I said. "Some of them seemed upset, but others, I'm not so sure."

"Well, it has to have been a bit of a shock," he said. "They've been together for years, and it's probably like losing a family member. You heard Davy. They were his only family."

"I did. But they seemed to throw a great deal of animosity Bram's way. In my experience, when speaking about the dead, most people tend to see only the positives. Right? That's a part of the healing process. But they were wondering if he was back on drugs.

"And from what we can tell from the tests so far, he wasn't a regular user. In fact, he seemed quite healthy in all regards, except for the clot in his brain. But then, it was almost like a bomb went off in his head. It's hard to tell if there was further deterioration."

"Why would there be? He was young."

"Yes, but they said he was manic and acting out of character the last few months. I wonder . . ."

We hit a big hole in the road, and my bread tumbled to the floor. At least the loaf was wrapped.

"Wonder what?" he asked.

"If there was more going on with Bram's health than we've seen so far," I said. And I wonder if we might have more than one killer. What if the whole band had ganged up on him and were covering up for each other. They all mentioned he'd been off in some way.

Something weird was going on with them.

Chapter Five

S ea Isle was full of holiday spirit, and one of the first big events was
the lighting of the town tree. I should have said trees. One would
grace the entrance to the library up the mountain, and the other was
at the end of the pier in front of my friend Jasper's bakery. While
most of the shops along the seawall had closed hours ago, he had a
table out on the sidewalk where he served coffee, tea, and some of the
best hot chocolate I'd ever had in my life.

And, because it was Jasper, he had an assortment of cakes and
treats people could buy.

I'd agreed to help him. Even though my hands and nose were
beyond frozen, we were having fun.

"I hear you've been hanging with the band," he said when things
quieted down a bit just before the big ceremony. "I can't believe we
heard Bram and the Stokers for the last time. It's strange."

"I don't disagree with you," I said. "It's weird and unsettling in
so many ways. Do you remember anything unusual from that night?
You stayed later than I did, and I heard they closed down the bar."

Someone walked up and asked for a hot chocolate. I poured
them some into a paper cup. Then they went off.

"Angie stayed at mine and had to catch an early train back to
Edinburgh this morning," he said. "We left soon after the last set. I

thought they sounded better than they had in years. Not that they've ever been bad. It was just their new songs were great, and most of the time I've heard them in big arenas. They were even better in a small venue. And it made for the perfect evening. Even their voices were on top."

"What do you mean?"

"Destinee's voice, for one. She'd been having trouble off and on the last few years. Something to do with her vocal cords being tired. You'd know more about that than me. But as you heard, she sounded grand. They also seemed to be getting along really well."

"Isn't that a cliché that some bands don't?"

He shrugged. "There are videos of them fighting onstage with one another. Nothing physical, just words. You can check it out online. But they could get a bit nasty. In Paris, I was there when Bram walked off stage in the middle of a set. He came back, but it was awkward the rest of the night. They were so incredibly tense. It was uncomfortable to watch."

"Do you think there are videos of that?"

He nodded. "Aye, all over the internet."

I'd have to check those out later. "What were the fights about?"

He shrugged. "Sometimes it was creative differences. Other times, it was more personal. The drummer, Liam, and the bass player, Boscoe, get into a lot with Bram. But then they all have a laugh. I wondered, at times, if maybe some of it was staged to create headlines or something. What is that saying: There's no such thing as bad PR?"

I had no idea and understood the dynamics of a rock band even less.

"I'm curious if there were interactions that might lead you to believe that one of them might try to kill Bram," I said in a hushed voice as several people walked by.

His eyes went wide.

"He was murdered?" he whispered back.

"I can't say," I said.

He gave me a look.

"It's in the realm of possibility," I said. "But don't say anything. I mean it. This is me telling you that it absolutely has to stay under wraps. Can you imagine what would happen if the press got wind of it? From what I understand, they are some sort of national treasure."

His shop, along with the pub, were ripe with village gossip most days, but I trusted him. I trusted all my friends. They'd been more than helpful with the few cases I'd worked on, and I couldn't have solved those without them.

"You are right, they are. But my lips are sealed." He made the universal sign of a zipper across his mouth. "And there were a lot of creative differences with songs and tone. But they've always been honest about that in the press. A lot of folks think that push and pull are what make them so great." He shook his head.

"What?"

"You saw him," he said. "Who would want to kill him? He was so beloved, especially by his fans. And that voice, there will never be another like it."

I didn't disagree with him. I hadn't known Bram, or his music, for very long, but I'd enjoyed their set the night before. And they had a distinctive sound, one that I quite enjoyed.

"As usual, there were lots of women around him," Jasper said. "And even a few men. I noticed some young women pointing and talking from a corner booth. One of them didn't look too happy. But I couldn't tell you who they were, other than possible groupies."

I was about to ask Jasper another question when a group of men and women walked by with a miniature-sized Viking longboat. They were all dressed in Viking garb, though some of them wore Santa hats.

"Uh, I need an explanation for that."

He laughed. "There are all sorts of holiday celebrations in this part of the world, and Sea Isle likes to be inclusive," he said. "The boat will be lit on fire as part of the Viking Yule, which technically isn't until the twenty-first, but they, like the Christians, like to make it a monthlong celebration.

"There are a lot of Viking descendants in the area. But there will also be events that celebrate Hanukkah and Kwanzaa, and even Krampus makes an appearance. There are traditions from Iceland, Norway, Switzerland, France, and all points in between. And we can't forget the Celts, druids, and pagans."

"I had no idea there were so many cultures represented in our small village."

He smiled. "Aye, and the celebrations began with Ewan's great-granddad. He wanted everyone to understand the cultures of the people they lived with here in Sea Isle, and so he gathered the holiday council. They designated several days in December and January for the various events, and it's been that way ever since. And we all participate in everything." He laughed. "It's our way of being inclusive."

"It sounds tiring." I'd signed up to help with some of the celebrations while I was on vacation. I thought it might help me integrate into the town and get to know the people better.

"We Scots love a party, and you have to admit, it's fun learning about other cultures."

"True."

"Hey, Doc," someone called out from the crowd. "Hurry, or you'll miss the fun."

I waved to the crowd, not really knowing who had greeted me, but I was pleased that they cared enough to do so. I loved this town and the people who lived here.

"We should get the table inside or we'll miss the tree lighting and the burning boat."

I helped him move everything into the tea shop, and then we headed down the pier with the rest of the crowd.

The tree at the end of the pier was enormous, and when we arrived, the large crowd sang a song in Gaelic. Even though I didn't understand the words, the blending of voices was beyond beautiful.

There had been a few lights on, but then everything went dark.

"Welcome," Ewan said from somewhere in the darkness. "Tonight, we launch our festive season in much the same way we did years ago. Neither the government, nor kings, have ever told Sea Isle what they could and could not celebrate."

Cheers went up.

"With the lighting of the tree—Laethanta saoire sona."

Everyone else said the Gaelic words back, and the tree blossomed with lights. It was huge, gorgeous, and then the songs began again.

"What was that last bit Ewan said in Gaelic?" I asked Mara, who had joined Jasper and me. Abigail and Tommy stood on the periphery behind us, but I heard the young man's sweet voice ringing out. He was quite the singer.

"It means happy holidays," she said. "What do you think about all of this?"

For someone who didn't really do much for the holidays, this was a lot, but I loved the sense of community and everyone coming together. "It's lovely," I said. "Thank you for suggesting I help out."

"You are welcome." She hooked her arm into mine and sang the Gaelic song. Then some small children went up on a platform and sang, "O Christmas Tree." Their sweet voices tugged at my heart. I knew many of them, as there'd been a flu outbreak earlier in the school year.

It was strange for me to know so many of my patients and to have relationships with their whole families. While we had repeats in the ER, it wasn't like I had a long-lasting relationship with anyone who came in for treatment.

But I cared about the people who lived here, and it had happened quickly. I was protective of them like they were my extended family.

After the children finished, there were some readings of short Scottish Christmas stories.

The Viking crowd came forward with their boat. The children clapped and cheered as the wooden boat went up in flames. There was a chant and then another song as the structure burned to ashes. Even I thought it was kind of cool.

"What is the significance?" I asked Jasper.

"It's the beginning of their twelve days of feasting, drinking, and celebrations."

"I sense a party theme with all these celebrations." I grinned.

"You would not be wrong, Doc," he said. "As always, any excuse for we Scots to party is welcome."

Around seven, the crowd broke up.

I'd been planning to head home and sit by the fire, but Mara and Abigail had other ideas.

"Chippies is open, and Abigail promised Tommy we'd all go," Mara said.

I smiled. Chippies was the local fish and chips shop, and it was Tommy's favorite place in the world. If he could eat there every day, he would. But health-conscious Abigail would never let that happen.

Jasper and I followed them to the shop, which was just down the way from his bakery. There was a long line, but we'd all do anything for Tommy, so we waited.

"Any word about the case?" Mara whispered.

Jasper's eyes went wide. He really was terrible with secrets, at least when it came to hiding them from our friends.

"What?" Mara asked as she glanced from our favorite baker to me.

"Jasper mentioned there were fights among the band members. What do you know about that?" I asked. "I mean, you are friends with Destinee, right?"

Mara pursed her lips and nodded. "More acquaintances these days when it comes to Destinee. They don't call them fights. They say

46

it's creative differences. Bram is—I mean, was—a strong personality. And it turns out he was right. For a while some of the band wanted to go more on the rock side of things. But their blend of indie rock is what distinguished them from everyone else. Most of the fans sided with Bram.

"There was a big feud online, and the media picked it up. But that was a few years ago."

"I didn't even know they used the term 'indie rock' here. I thought that was an American thing."

She nodded. "He never wanted to be like everyone else, and that turned out to be the best decision for the band. While he always said that they were a democratic society, he was most definitely the leader."

"I asked you this before, but do you remember them arguing that night over anything?"

"No. They truly seemed happy to be together. Destinee had a couple of health scares, and the nerves stole her voice for a few months. But she's fine now, and as you heard, as lovely as ever."

"Did she ever mention anything that might have upset her about Bram?"

Mara sighed. "I think she fancied him a bit, so the womanizing got on her nerves. But she never let him know her true feelings. In fact, I think she and Liam dated for a bit. And there was a thing with Render at some point. She told me that it wasn't easy meeting people outside the band when they were always on the road. But dating in a band never goes well.

"I think, like most people who spend that much time together, they're going to have their differences every once in a while."

Dating members of the band had to create some conflict, but I didn't see how that might be related to Bram's death.

"Is there any chance you found a notebook in the pub?"

"No. And Ewan's men came back for a second look. The scene has been cleared. Why?"

"The last time anyone saw Bram, he was working on some songs. The band said they left him with his notebook and guitar. We found the guitar, but we haven't seen the notebook, and it wasn't in his things."

We ordered, and as we did, the snow started coming down. At least it held off until after the event.

"Let's run to mine," I said after our order came up. There was a small path between two of the shops that led straight up the hill to my home and practice. We were drenched by the time we made it up and stopped under the portico. I pulled out my keys but then stopped.

The door was slightly ajar.

"Call Ewan," I whispered. Then I took the pepper spray out of my purse and held it in front of me.

"I want to eat my chippies," Tommy said.

"I hope they didn't steal the body again," Abigail whispered.

We all stared at the front door.

"Me too," I whispered.

"I'm the man. I should go first," Jasper said bravely.

"I've got the pepper spray."

"Okay," he said, sounding relieved.

I opened the door and stepped inside.

Chapter Six

My friends followed me in, and I flipped on the lights in the waiting area of the practice. We stood frozen in our spots, and it had nothing to do with the snow that had drenched us.

Someone had been going through our files. They were strewn about the office in a haphazard way. The good news was, my office was still locked, so they hadn't gone in there. All our current files were on encrypted software on the computer. There wouldn't have been anything personal to our patients in the drawers for someone to find.

"Well, I guess I didn't forget to lock up," I whispered. "Abigail, you stay here with Tommy."

"I want to eat my chippies," Tommy said. Then he sat down in one of the chairs and opened his box of fish.

"I'm not letting you go alone," she said.

"I'll go with her," Jasper said.

"We should wait for Ewan," Mara added.

Jasper gave her a look, and I couldn't help but smile.

"Who knows when he can get here," I said. "There is a famous music star in my freezer. I need to make sure everything is all right." I sounded much braver than I actually was.

"What's going on?" Ewan's voice boomed as he slid into the entryway.

We all screamed, including Jasper. Tommy put his hands over his ears. "Shush," he said. "Too loud."

I would have laughed had I not been so frightened.

"The door was open," I said. "We're going to check on the body."

Henry ran in behind Ewan. "We lost him up the hill, sir."

Ewan grumbled.

"Lost who?" I asked.

"The person who broke into your practice," he said. "One of my men saw a hooded figure going up the mountain from the back of your place. At first, he thought the person might just be taking a shortcut, but then he started running."

The last time something like this happened, the locks had been changed and security cameras put in.

"We need to check the body," I said.

I followed Ewan and Henry as they flipped on lights.

"No one touch anything," Ewan called out. "We may be able to pull some fingerprints."

We raced through the kitchen, but when we got to the door that hid the freezer, it was still locked. I pushed in the numbers on the keycode. The door shifted open.

Then I carefully unzipped the body bag. Bram was still there.

I blew out a breath I didn't know I'd been holding. The back door was also unlocked. So, the burglar had come in the front and gone out the back.

"I don't understand why someone would even try to break in here," I said. "How would they know where he was?"

Ewan and Henry followed me out. I locked the freezer door again.

"Word is out," Ewan said. "The story broke about an hour ago that Bram died in Sea Isle. All they would have had to do was ask around a bit to find out you are the coroner."

Great. That meant the press would most likely be descending on my doorstep soon.

"It's trending," Henry said as he held up his phone. All the men who worked with Ewan were great, but I had a soft spot in my heart for Henry. He was sweet on Abigail, and he already treated Tommy like a little brother.

"The town will be swarming with fans by morning," Ewan said. "It could have been our killer who broke in looking for something, or it could have been a journalist trying to get a bit of information. Either way, I'll put a man outside to watch the place.

"You need better doors," he said. "The locks should have kept them out."

"The four-hundred-year-old doors are staying," I said. They were old and intricately carved. And nearly impossible to keep closed properly because they'd warped slightly through the ages.

"Why don't we check the security cameras," I said.

I opened my phone and pulled up the feed. The two men stood behind me as the video loaded.

In the video, the person busted the lock on the front door using a crowbar. They wore a mac, much like most of the population in Scotland, along with some dark gloves. Unfortunately, the criminal was smart enough to keep his or her head down, and they wore gloves, so no skin showed. We had no hope of making any sort of identification. Well, it was probably a man because of the person's height and slim build.

The man never looked up. Since I only had cameras on the outside and in the autopsy freezer, there wasn't much else for us to see.

"Get me some stills," he said to Henry. "We'll send it to the experts to see if they can at least give us an exact height and weight."

"On it," Henry said.

"Doc, do you have everything you need from the victim?"

I frowned. "What do you mean?"

He sighed. "I had a request from the higher-ups. Seems the band's manager reached out to some of his friends in high places, and now they want the body moved to Edinburgh. It might save you a lot of trouble given what's just happened." He didn't seem happy about the situation.

Ewan probably wasn't used to being told what to do by higher-ups, but he seemed to be taking it well, despite his unhappiness.

"Yes. I can make sure we have everything we need. But as you know, the more we learn, things can come up. I'd rather keep him here just in case. Any chance you guys found his notebook somewhere?"

He shook his head. "Which notebook?"

"The band said he'd been writing new songs. It wasn't on his person or in his room. I was just curious where it ended up."

"Right. We'll investigate it," Ewan said. "I'll be escorting the body to Edinburgh with my team," he said. Again, he didn't sound happy about it at all.

"Did something else happen?" I asked.

He crossed his arms. "Henry, get someone to fix the front door for the doc. She'll need another lock. Maybe get one of those with a combination as well."

Great, more numbers for me to remember.

"Yes, sir."

While Ewan and I didn't always get along, I'd spent enough time with the constable to know when he was upset about something, even though he'd never let it show outwardly.

"Hey," I said. "Tell me what's going on, please."

He sighed. "The manager, Davy, didn't trust our force to give the investigation the attention it deserved."

"What a jerk," I said. "No one is better than you."

The side of his mouth quirked up in a grin. "Thanks for that, Doc."

"I mean it. You're always professional. They couldn't find someone better to investigate the case."

The grin spread across his face. "Well, technically, we'll be working with a special team at SPA."

"Spa? I don't understand that acronym."

"Scottish Police Authority," he said. "We will keep point on the investigation since it happened in our jurisdiction, but they will be overseeing it, as well as the on-the-ground footwork in Edinburgh and Glasgow.

"As it was explained to me, this death is of a national hero. They want boots on the ground, and that means checking out his places in Edinburgh and Glasgow, as well as his emails and such. My men are good, but my superiors are correct. We need more help."

"So, they don't think it's someone from here who killed him?"

"We don't know yet. Having boots on the ground, as you yanks say, in the bigger cities where he lived and worked will be helpful. They also have more technological resources than we do. They'll be going through his social media accounts and emails looking for clues."

I nodded. "It's odd he was killed here, right? I mean, they've been on the road and were getting ready to go back out. It just feels strange that it happened right now. Maybe that means something that we don't understand quite yet."

"I agree. It seems as if there was some kind of time element," he said. "Any idea about the murder weapon?"

I made a funny face. "Your guess is as good as mine," I said. "Abigail and I will focus in on that tomorrow. It's small and was able to . . ." I turned around and headed for the kitchen.

"What is it?" he asked.

I opened the drawer where Abigail had organized all the big kitchen utensils. A few months ago, Mara had given me a gift. I pulled it out and held it in my hand.

"I think this is the murder weapon," I said.

Ewan's eyes went wide.

Chapter Seven

I held out the air-pressured corkscrew Mara had given me. We drank a lot of wine during our girls' nights, and she was tired of cork pieces ending up in the bottle when it was my turn to open the wine.

"I need to measure the interior. I mean, it may not be the exact model used, but close enough," I said.

Then I was back in the autopsy room.

Abigail came in and pulled on a gown and gloves. "Ewan said you think you might have found the murder weapon."

"Well, not exactly the one, but something like it," I said. "Help me flip him over so we can get a better picture."

It took us nearly an hour to measure everything and for me to compare what we'd found to the model of corkscrew I had.

"You're right, Doc. It's a nearly perfect match. But why? And how would someone know that it could create an embolism. And why would they have a corkscrew out on the beach in the middle of the night?"

"And where is it?" I added. "Those are all great questions. I think the murder weapon is probably in the sea somewhere. That's what anyone with half a brain would do to get rid of it. As for your questions, our killer had to have planned this or had been very lucky in the moment. Compressing that air into his brain would have created exactly what we saw. Well, maybe not exactly, but close enough."

"Right. But also, the angle is weird."

I looked at the pictures she'd taken and the images of how the sharp implement had forced air into the brain.

"If he was sitting when he died, it would have been an awkward way of killing him, and there weren't any other footprints or marks around him," Abigail said. "But someone smart would have made a minimal mess. The snow had started falling and the wet ground . . ."

I nodded.

Ewan came back in but stayed near the entry.

"Any news?" he asked.

"It's definitely a corkscrew." I showed him the jagged edges on the photo, and how the measurements were nearly perfect. "Probably not this model, but one very close to it. The actual weapon doesn't have a smooth cylinder like this," I pointed to the plastic surrounding the opener. "That's what created the raised edges on the skin."

"Brilliant," he said. "It's more than we had this morning. If we can get photos, I can have someone do a sketch and maybe we can find the make and model. If we have that, we may be able to find out where it was purchased and by whom."

I nodded. I didn't understand why the SPA felt it necessary to oversee the investigation. Ewan was quite good at detective work.

"Abigail made an excellent point about the angle and the lack of forensic evidence of there being another person involved, but I have an idea about that," I said.

"What's that?" Ewan asked. He took out the notebook that he wrote everything down in, which was where I picked up the habit.

"There's a possibility that he might not have even felt the injection when it happened. I mean, it looks painful, but he had been drinking and had an almost toxic amount of alcohol running through his system. From what I understand, he wasn't usually such a big drinker, which means he wouldn't have tolerated it that well."

"Okay," Ewan said.

"The embolism may have taken a bit to kill him. It could have taken up to an hour or so before it traveled to the brain. He would have suffered stroke-like symptoms. Maybe he, or the others who were around him, thought he was drunk. Maybe he needed some fresh air and decided to walk down to the beach. He may have stumbled forward in the sand and felt like he had to sit down. That might be why we didn't see footprints or anything else around him."

"So, he stumbled onto the beach, and just sat down and died?"

"Most likely he had no idea what was going on," I said. "He would have been very confused, and again, with that much alcohol in his system—"

"And there were other drugs in his system," Abigail said. "We just haven't identified them yet. They may not have mixed well with the alcohol."

I pointed my pen at her. "That's a good point. I feel like we're still missing a big piece of the puzzle, but, like Ewan says, we have more than we did an hour ago."

"Do you think, perhaps, someone in his group was trying to get him drunk so they could kill him?" Abigail asked.

"Also a great question I don't have an answer to, except that perhaps they wanted him off his guard so he wouldn't notice the corkscrew plowing into his brain."

Abigail and I shivered. It was an awful way to die.

"Do you realize what you're saying?" he said.

I nodded. "We may have a premeditated murder on our hands. I don't know how or where the corkscrew comes in, but someone definitely planned to do something to him last night."

Ewan frowned. "Wait." He thumbed through his notebook. "That's it."

"What?" Abigail asked.

"My men found a full bottle of wine, an expensive one, in the trash near the crime scene. It hadn't been opened. We didn't think much about it."

"Well, now that is interesting," I said. "We'll need to do a check for fingerprints. The big question is, did the killer take the wine and corkscrew? Or did the victim take it down to the beach? If it was the victim, then it wasn't so premeditated.

"I feel like the killer had to know what would happen. Ugh. There are so many easier ways to kill someone. This is so confusing."

"We will figure it out, Doc," Abigail said. "We always do."

I smiled. I loved that she had such faith. I wasn't so sure about that.

"You need to check their rooms for that notebook," I said to Ewan. "I feel like that is a key, though don't ask me to explain it. It's just strange that it has disappeared. And check the B and B for the corkscrew too. Maybe the killer was dumb and kept it."

But I had my doubts.

"And possibly their phones and laptops for their search histories. I have a feeling if the killer knew what they were doing, they would have had to do some searches. What I can't figure out is why last night was so important. That was their last gig until after the holidays. It has to do with opportunity, right? That's what you're always talking about. Motive and opportunity."

"Aye," he said.

"Do you think it was someone in the band?" Abigail asked. "I don't understand why since they were about to go out on tour. It would have been good for all of them. I mean, they are well loved here, but wouldn't that have been great for all their careers?"

I nodded. "All good ideas to explore. We also know he was a bit of a womanizer." I glanced at Ewan. Mara had sworn me to secrecy about Ewan's past, and I wouldn't say anything. "Could it have been an angry husband or boyfriend? Or a former lover?"

"Once again, we would have too many suspects," Abigail said. "That is, if we're to believe everything the media says. He had a different woman every night."

"True," I said. "But we do have some idea of who might have been in town. And Mara has security cameras at the pub. If he was approached by someone there, maybe we can find it." I zipped the body back in the bag.

"Are you heading back to the B and B?" I asked. "I think I'd like to go with you, if you don't mind, that is."

"Aye, come on, then."

* * *

"When can we go home?" Davy, the band's manager, asked as soon as we walked through the door. "I need to make arrangements, and I've no idea what we're going to do about the tour." He threw his hands up in the air and stomped around the front room of the B and B like a child.

"How can you even worry about that right now?" Destinee asked. She was curled up on one of the cushy sofas with a book. "Bram is—gone." She took a tissue from her pocket and touched her nose. Her eyes watered. Without any makeup on, she appeared much younger than she had with the kohl eyeliner and red lipstick she normally wore.

She waved the tissue. "I can't seem to keep it together," she said.

I nodded toward Ewan, and he took Davy away.

"Grief isn't something that can necessarily be controlled," I said. "We all experience it in different ways. He was your friend, and it's understandable that you feel his loss deeply. You spent a great deal of time together."

She shook her head. "Some friend I am."

"Why do you say that?"

She sighed. "We've been arguing the last few weeks. I couldn't stand to be in the same room with him most days. Whatever I said, he would say the opposite. It was like he was trying to make me angry."

"Has that happened before?"

"We've had creative differences through the years. If I'm honest, lots of them. But not like the last couple of months. He's been—I mean, he was agitated, more so than usual. It was almost like he was trying to make us angry with him, and it was not just me."

"Was there something that triggered him. Anything you can think of that maybe upset him?"

"It started around the time the new tour was announced. At first, I thought maybe it was the pressure of a world tour, and especially with us going to America. We've done a few television appearances over there, and played some gigs, but not an actual tour.

"But he loved being onstage. You saw him last night. Imagine that, except in a much larger arena. We were all excited about it. Maybe a little nervous.

"But it was like none of us could do anything right where he was concerned. He was always a perfectionist. But we were all ready to kill—sorry, you know what I mean. Our rehearsals have been crap, and most of that was his fault. He'd storm out. Sometimes he forgot lyrics. It was all very erratic and unlike him.

"Then, last night everything seemed to come together. Even the new songs. And I couldn't believe he threw in some Christmas carols. It was like the early days for all of us. We had fun for the first time in forever. Afterward, we hung out and drank like the old days.

"Maybe a bit too much. My head still throbs."

She sniffed, and then glanced down at her book. It was poems by Kathleen Jamie. I had the same book on my to-be-read pile at home.

"I know you are grieving, but any information you can give us to help us understand what happened will help. Was there anyone angry enough to want to hurt him?"

She stared at the book without saying anything for more than a minute.

"Name the day, really. Aye, he was charming, but he could be a bully. I can't imagine—we've all been together so long. It really is like family. People say that, but it's true. We spend more time together than we do with our families. And we butt heads and hearts at times.

"But to murder him? I don't know. I'm sure we've all thought about it at one time or another." Her eyes went wide. "I didn't kill him, if that's what you're asking. Did I want to sometimes? Aye. But he was like a brother to me. An annoying big brother who always thought he knew best—and usually did."

I smiled at her. Odd, though, that she said big brother when there had been rumors that she was in love with him.

"I'm a doctor, so I've never worked with creatives like you. I'm sure it can get very emotional."

"Aye, it does. And we're all Scottish, so we're likely to cause a row then and there. And we'd been rowing for weeks on end, like I said. But last night . . ."

"You keep saying that as if you're surprised."

She gave me a watery smile. "In a way, it was magical for all of us. We thought maybe it was the town. The people are so kind, and we felt comfortable here. Bram even said that it was a magical place with the sea view, and it's so picturesque. That was when I mentioned that Mara asked us to play here. I thought for sure he'd say no, but I'd forgotten he grew up here. He was looking forward to staying through the holidays and hanging out with Render and his family. They're really close. But it was this town that excited him to play here last night."

"It's one of the reasons I moved here from America," I said. "Well, not to play but to work. I've never been in a place where the people are so kind and giving."

"It's funny. You yanks all want to come to the UK, and we are all trying to get to America."

"The-grass-is-greener syndrome," I said.

She nodded. "But with music, if we hit big there—I guess there's no reason to even think about it now. We can't go on without him."

"Really? But you're all so talented." I didn't know a great deal about the music world. Okay, I knew nothing. But lead singers were often replaced. I had seen that on the news. That's how Queen was still touring.

"Thank you for that. He was the heart though. I can't see us replacing him or going forward without him. The band is done."

I frowned. I hadn't really thought about that. I guessed I'd assumed one of the other band members might step up.

"So, outside of the band, do you remember anything strange from last night or the last few weeks?"

She sighed. "The constable's men have grilled us over and over."

"Sorry," I said.

She shrugged. "Other than his stalkers sabotaging the bus? Or that crazy one from last night who followed him into the bathroom?"

"Oh?"

"Yes. It was a constant with him. We usually travel with a couple of guys who act as security guards. But he wasn't worried about all of that here. And really, Davy was able to handle her. I think she was a wee bit wrecked."

I'd have Ewan investigate the woman. More than likely, Mara's security cameras would have picked that up. But usually murder was committed by someone the victim knew well.

Nevertheless, the stalker avenue was a valid one. It had happened before with celebrities. People with mental health problems who latched on to others could behave unpredictably.

But as I kept repeating to myself: murderers were normally someone the victim knew well.

"You mentioned some of the songs were new. Did Bram write all your songs?"

"Aye, he did. It has been about a year since he's had the bug to write, but it hit him hard the last few months. He's been working nonstop."

"He doesn't work with the rest of you?"

"Yes and no. Sometimes we sit around and write together. That's what we'd been doing most of the month. Some of our biggest hits, and we all admit it, came from stuff he wrote on his own, which we then tweaked when he brought it to us.

"Like I said, he was being an arse the last few months, but he was also writing some of the best songs of his career." She hiccupped a sob. "Sorry. It just comes in waves."

"Don't be sorry. You have every right to be sad. About the music, though. We haven't been able to find his notebook. It wasn't on him when—We haven't found it in his things." I corrected myself.

"Really? Did you check his coat? He had a pocket inside just big enough for his notebook."

Bram had been wearing a coat, but there hadn't been anything in the pockets. However, I hadn't been the one to examine it. I texted Abigail and asked her to check for an inside pocket.

I still didn't understand how he'd ended up at the beach. He hadn't driven himself. There wasn't a vehicle, and he didn't have one. If he'd come down from the B and B, it was a half mile walk at least, and the wind coming off the sea was freezing.

"I know you are like family, but was there maybe someone in the band who was a little angrier with Bram than the rest?" I didn't like the idea of trying to make her turn on her friends, but I had to know.

She glanced up from her book and then blinked. "What do you mean?"

I just sat there.

She shook her head. "Oh. No, it wasn't one of us. That I can tell you. Yes, we fought, but we loved one another. I told you, we're family. No matter how angry you might get, you don't murder your family."

It happened all the time. In fact, most murder victims were killed by family or people who were closest to them. The statistics didn't lie.

I held up a hand. "I didn't want to upset you. I'm just trying to find out the truth. The more we know, the quicker we can find a solution."

"You're a doctor, I don't understand why you need to ask so many questions."

She had a good point.

"I'm also the local coroner, and speaking for the dead is part of my responsibilities to the town—medically, that is. I want to do that for Bram. While I didn't know him like you and his fans did, I do appreciate that the world has lost a great artist. I loved your music, and it makes me sad that you won't be able to perform together anymore. I want to help all of you make sense of what has happened."

A tear slid down her cheek. "It's never going to make sense to me," she said.

"That I can understand. I've lost the people I love most. It always leaves us in a mess. But if there is a way you can steer me, even if it seems inconsequential, it might help."

"Talk to Davy about the fan mail. I heard them arguing about it a few days ago. Davy was pretty upset about something that came for Bram, but he told him not to worry about it. He was great with the fans. Even if someone was upset with him or said something on social media, he always turned it around to his favor."

"Do you know what it was exactly?"

She shook her head. "Those two kept us insulated so we could concentrate on the music. If Davy had a problem with something, or someone, though, it always went through Bram. In his way, he protected us. He could be an arsehole, but he cared about us."

"And you'd say his mental state was a bit, off, right? Just the last few months."

She shrugged. "Bram hadn't been himself since we came back together for rehearsals."

"Came back together?"

"Aye. We had three weeks off after the last tour. Then we started rehearsing for the new one. We were doing gigs off and on, usually private ones like the one we did last night."

She half coughed and half sobbed. "Oh. My. God."

"What?" I asked softly.

"That was it. That was our last time playing together. And it was nearly perfect." The tears began in earnest then. I handed her a box of tissues from nearby and patted her shoulder.

Something had changed in Bram's demeanor. She'd said he was forgetting lines and was testier than usual.

What if there had been something wrong with him medically. Had I missed it?

I needed to check the body again.

Chapter Eight

B leary-eyed the next morning, I stumbled toward my coffee maker. I started with an espresso. Shivering, I found a big turtleneck to throw over my flannel pajamas and stuck my feet into a pair of Uggs. Then I pulled a knit cap over my head, and I was much warmer.

There was a knock on the back door, and I sighed. It was way too early for company. I glanced at my watch. It was nearly nine in the morning. Okay, well, it was way too early for someone who didn't go to bed until five.

I peeked through the small window in the door and found Ewan deep in thought. I was surprised he knocked. Most of the time, since he owns the place, he just walks right in whenever he wants.

"Are you here to collect the body?"

"Nay. I called in a favor. We'll not be moving the body for a few more days or until we finish the investigation."

"How did you manage that?"

"Like I said, I called in a favor. I need some coffee."

After shutting the door behind him, I followed him into the kitchen. He handed me the cup that had been brewing and began another one for himself. It's like the people around me understood how much I needed my coffee to be even the tiniest bit civil.

We sat down at the kitchen table and stared at our cups for a bit.

"You told me Davy had called someone in Edinburgh to take over the investigation," I said after a few sips.

"Aye. He implied that I might not be impartial because I had a history with Bram."

I frowned. The fog hadn't quite cleared from my brain. And then it hit me.

"Davy knew about that?"

He shrugged. "Bram must have said something to him the night he died. He even implied I had reason to kill him."

I nearly choked on my coffee. "What?" I sputtered.

"I don't know how much Mara told you, and I assume she's the one who did. Years ago, he slept with my fiancée. We were all young. I had no business being engaged at that age. He probably saved me from a huge mistake. Well, I know he did. But it did create some bad blood between us."

"That's understandable," I said.

"Not enough to want him dead, mind you," he said. "Maybe back then. I'm long over that situation and had no reason to wish him dead."

Ewan as a murder suspect was laughable. As much as we butted heads, he was as forthright as they came. He cared about people too much to harm anyone.

"Then why were you so upset with Mara?"

"Well, I'm over it. But I don't necessarily like seeing his ugly mug in my town. I've never been a big fan of his music."

I laughed and then threw a hand over my mouth. "Sorry."

He shrugged.

"He wasn't ugly, but I can understand that. So, exactly how long do I have with the body?"

"As long as you need, or until the end of the week. That's all I could get. Still, they're sending someone down to help investigate."

"Did you guys find anything on their phones and laptops?"

He shook his head. "No search histories for anything related to what we suspected happened."

I frowned. "Are they really that worried about you being a suspect?"

"Nay. But with a celebrity like Bram, everything must be in order. We must go by the book. Since someone has made a complaint, then we must comply and follow the rules." It sounded like words from someone else coming through his voice. I never thought about Ewan having a boss when it came to law enforcement. He was always so in control of every situation, but it made sense.

"Do you know who they are sending?"

"Aye, that's why—"

The front door buzzed. I frowned. "I shouldn't have any patients today."

"That will be her. The detective they've sent."

I chugged the small bit of espresso I had left and headed toward the front reception where my practice was.

When I opened the door, I blinked. There in front of me was a beautiful woman who would have given Halle Berry a run for her money. She was supermodel gorgeous and did not in any way look like a policewoman.

She held out her hand. "Doctor McRoy, I'm Detective Inspector Bethany Thomson."

I shook her hand. She glanced over my shoulder and frowned.

"Ewan. I wasn't expecting you to be here so early." She glanced from my disheveled look to him.

"He just stopped in to tell me you were on your way. Please come in," I said. I didn't want to start out on the wrong foot with the inspector.

"You shouldn't be here," she said to him. "You are in observation mode only per the Chief Constable."

"Aye. And that's what I'm doing. Observing. As the doc says, I was only here to let her know you'd be taking over for the time being.

I'm here as a courtesy to our doctor, and I thought we might go over the case notes together."

There was an edge to his voice I'd never heard before. These two had a past, and it didn't look like a pleasant one.

"Did you now? Why would I need schooling from a man who is one of the main suspects?"

Ewan ran a hand through his hair. That meant he was frustrated and angry. "You can't possibly think I had anything to do with his death," he said. His voice was low, but the edge was still there.

"I'm not sure how you investigate, but I tend to look at facts first. Fact: you had a reason to want the victim dead. That's the motive. Fact: you were near him the night he died. There are several witnesses who corroborate that information. Opportunity."

Ewan huffed. "Along with two hundred others who were much closer to him than I was. Besides, I have an alibi. I was working another case when he died."

"Says you and your very loyal men. Besides, the doctor's report said that because of the temperatures it was impossible to say exactly when the victim died. Time of death could be off from three to five hours."

She was correct. But there was no way I'd get in the middle of these two arguing. My interest was piqued, though. She had it in for Ewan. Her evidence against him was flimsy at best, and Ewan had an incredible reputation in law enforcement. Plus, he was a pillar of the town.

Of course, I would never say that out loud in front of him.

"Bethany, you know I didn't kill him," Ewan said. He ran a hand through his hair again.

I almost smiled but covered my mouth as if I had to cough.

"That's Detective Inspector Thomson to you, Constable. Please remember that. Doctor, do you have time to go over your findings with me? I need to go over everything before I re-interview the suspects."

"Re-interview." He huffed. "I cannae believe you. Those interviews are as thorough as they come, and you know it."

Her eyebrows went up, then she focused her attention on me. What had she asked?

"I—uh, of course," I said. "Let's go to my kitchen. It's the warmest room." I motioned her through my offices and into the house.

Ewan huffed but followed.

"Would you like some coffee?" I asked.

"She's a tea drinker," Ewan said.

Yep. They had some sort of past.

"I'll put the kettle on," I said.

The two of them sat down at my kitchen table and stared at each other.

I cleared my throat as I put water in the kettle and turned it on.

"Is Scottish Breakfast tea okay? Cream and sugar?"

"Perfect," she said.

"Did you drive in this morning?" I asked as I put cream and sugar on the table in front of her.

"Aye," she said.

So she was one of those people who answered only the direct question. Ewan could be that way at times. Must have been a cop thing.

"Right, so feel free to ask me whatever you want. I was up running a few more tests on the victim last night. Didn't get to sleep until this morning. I'd just woken up when Ewan knocked on the door."

"What kind of tests? From what our medical examiner says, you've been more thorough than they would have been. And that's not easy for him to admit."

I smiled. "I don't have as much experience as your ME, but from the little I do, I feel you can't be too careful. It's best to run a full battery so there are fewer surprises later. We are still waiting for a few results from your labs in Edinburgh and Glasgow."

"Right. I've spoken with them. Because of the priority of the case, the tests you need will be fast-tracked. You should have answers in the next twenty-four to forty-eight hours. Is that why you decided to keep the victim here?"

I glanced at Ewan, who stared down at his cup. Had he used me as an excuse?

"Yes. As your ME said, I like to be thorough. When I was speaking with one of the band members last night, she made me curious about something. I'm grateful everyone has given me some extra time to run more tests."

I wasn't in the business of covering for Ewan, but I had a feeling he'd been trying to exert some sort of control over the situation. I couldn't blame him.

One thing was certain: he wasn't guilty. And second, they were lucky he conducted those interviews. He was able to get people to open up in a way I'd never seen before, not even on my favorite television shows.

"Wait, you were interviewing suspects?"

"From a medical standpoint, yes," I said. That was the truth. "I wanted to know about Bram's behaviors and how he was feeling before his death."

"What did you discover? Did you put your findings in the report?" She pulled a file out of her messenger bag.

"No. I went to bed. I'd planned on typing up my findings first thing this morning. But since I didn't go to bed until five, this is first thing in the morning."

The detective glanced at her watch and then at Ewan. "Would you like me to come back later?"

I smiled. "No. It's fine. I just need another cup of espresso, and then I can go over everything with the, uh, both of you."

The kettle popped off, and I went to make the tea. Without asking, I picked up Ewan's mug along with mine to make some more coffee.

When I had everything settled back on the table. I stood back up again. "I forgot about the biscuits." I found an unopened package of the chocolate and raspberry ones I liked. I'd just set them down when the back door opened.

Abigail and Tommy came in and stopped short when they saw us.

"Oh. You have company." She glanced from Ewan to Bethany, the shock on her face evident.

"This is Detective Inspector Bethany Thomson," I said. "She's here to help with the case. I wasn't expecting you two today."

"Tommy says there's a storm coming, and he wanted to cover some of the plants in the back garden. And I still had some tests running in the lab. Also, Mara called me and said she hadn't seen you for breakfast, so I brought you down some blueberry scones I made. There should be enough for all of you." She put a box with about a dozen scones on the table.

She grabbed the cream and jam from the fridge, and then put some small plates down. She did it all before I could even think about moving from the table.

It was just the way Abigail was made. She could anticipate needs better than anyone I'd ever met.

Meanwhile, Tommy stood in the corner.

"It's okay, Tommy," I said gently. "You can do whatever you need to in the garden."

He didn't look at me, but he nodded. "Thank you, Doc." He turned and swiftly went out. He never liked being around people, especially strangers.

Bethany watched him carefully but didn't say anything.

"I'll check on the tests," Abigail said. She walked out.

"As you were saying"—Bethany nodded toward me—"you had more tests to run last night."

"Right. Destinee had mentioned that Bram, our victim, had been agitated lately. She said he'd forgotten words to some of the songs they'd been singing for years. So, I wanted to check and see if there was any indication of trauma to his brain—I mean, other than the embolism."

"And?"

"Inconclusive," I said. "The brain was pretty destroyed by the embolism. It's tough to tell what blood vessels might have been damaged before or after."

"Are you saying you think he had brain damage before?"

I shook my head. "No. But perhaps early onset Alzheimer's or something. Autoimmune disease can also cause those symptoms. I have to run more tests. But like I said, even though we did an MRI before I cut into the brain, it's tough for me to tell. That air bubble was like a bomb that went off in his brain."

Ewan had been about to take a bite of scone but put it back on the plate.

"Are you thinking he did this to himself?" She pointed to the autopsy picture where we showed the puncture wound.

"No. It would be a terrible way to commit suicide. I just thought the memory loss might be indicative of something else."

"What can we do to help?" Ewan asked.

I put clotted cream and jam on my scone. "I need his medical history as soon as humanly possible," I said. "I reached out through medical records last night, but it said it could be up to a week before I receive access."

Ewan jumped up. "I'll take care of that now." He went through the back door with his cell phone to his ear. It was almost as if he couldn't get away fast enough.

I suppressed a smile.

Bethany watched him with a glare.

I so wanted to ask what that was about, but I just took a bite of my scone instead.

"I had a few questions," she said.

So, do I.

"Ask me anything."

"The angle of the murder weapon. Is there any way to get an approximate height of our unsub?"

"It's impossible with the information that we have from the scene," I said. "He most likely was standing when it happened and then stumbled forward to the beach."

She frowned. "But he was found in a seated position."

"Right. But there were no other footsteps around him. So, he was stabbed and then wandered down to where he was found." I described the stroke-like symptoms he likely suffered before he died.

"I read that. But the odd angle. Wouldn't the killer have to be shorter than Bram?"

I pursed my lips. "He was very tall. I'd say just about everyone was shorter."

"Except maybe the constable."

I laughed, then snorted.

She glared at me.

"Oh, you're serious. Ewan's clever, but I don't see him using a corkscrew to kill someone. And he'd do a much better job at hiding the body. He would have made certain we never found Bram." I'd been joking, but she seemed to ponder this. "You can't seriously think he had anything to do with this."

"As I said to the constable, I'm not ruling anything out. And we know Bram didn't try to kill himself? As you said before, he may have already been having mental problems."

"Well, we didn't find the murder weapon, which would have most likely been around him somewhere or still in his hand. As I said in my initial report, it would have taken some forethought and research, even by a medical professional, to know how to do that with a corkscrew."

She nodded and wrote something down in the notebook she'd opened.

"One thing I've been wondering, and I forgot about it last night," I said.

"What's that?"

"Did anyone ask Mrs. Beatty if she was missing a corkscrew?"

Bethany thumbed through some papers. "Yes, but she was uncertain. She keeps several for guests' rooms plus some extras. She had no idea how many she actually had. You'd think she'd keep some kind of inventory. That would be helpful to know and would put the weapon at a scene." She sounded more exasperated than angry at poor Mrs. Beatty.

I had a feeling it was just her personality.

I nodded. "Destinee also mentioned something about fan mail that was out of control. The manager, Davy, had been worried about it, but Bram didn't think it was a big deal. From what I understood, Destinee said it wasn't good. She even thought it had been one of Bram's stalkers who sabotaged their bus on the way here. She mentioned that several times, actually."

"Yes. I have my team in Edinburgh following up on some of the emails and letters that came in, and they will do on the ground interviews there and in Glasgow. Hopefully, they can narrow down that line of questioning for us."

"Did you happen to see any of the letters or emails? If so, did you notice anything about the intention in them? I mean, he was so beloved. I don't understand why one of his stalkers or fans might want to kill him, but that sort of thing has happened in America more than once."

"Maybe they took issue with one of the songs or the lyrics," Bethany said. "It happens. And you are correct. Celebrities are quite often in danger from people they don't even know about. This murder feels personal. Like I said, I go by the facts. But I also trust my gut instincts to a degree. "

"Well, I'm glad to know Ewan isn't your only suspect," I said, and then realized what had just come out of my mouth.

She smirked. "He did have motive, means, and opportunity. A stronger one than anyone else we've found so far."

I sighed. "Look, Inspector, I'm very much a cards-on-the-table kind of person. Ewan didn't do this. I have only known him a few months, but I can't see him killing someone. No matter how much he might not have liked him. Ewan is about as straight an arrow as one will find these days in the male species."

"Noted," she said. "Now, what can you tell me about the mix of drugs in his system?"

"Abigail is still testing for those." We spent the next hour going over the findings. It was easy to see she was smart and thoughtful. Except for her extreme dislike of Ewan, I found her easy to speak with and to understand.

Abigail came back with some more reports. "I saw some of your notes from last night," she said. "So, I ran a test to look for amyloids in the blood."

I perked up. That might save me some time getting his medical records.

"What's that?" Bethany asked.

"Proteins," Abigail said.

"Ones that might suggest early Alzheimer's. And?"

"Since the majority of the vessels in the brain were destroyed, I thought maybe there might be something—and there was."

"He had Alzheimer's?" Bethany leaned back in the booth. She frowned. "He was so young."

"Aye. The test won't show what stage, but the protein is in higher quantities than one might expect for a man his age," Abigail said.

Our rock star had early onset Alzheimer's. That put a different spin on things.

"Do you think he hired someone to kill him?" I asked. It was the first thing that came to my mind. A man as strong and virile as Bram wouldn't have done well with that kind of news.

Bethany and Abigail's eyes widened.

Chapter Nine

After going through Abigail's findings and giving the inspector the information she needed, I headed upstairs to take a shower. Well, I texted Ewan the findings, and then I took a shower. I had another long day ahead. Trying to solve a murder didn't feel very holiday-like. And it hadn't been much of a vacation so far. But I still wouldn't have traded this life for the one I had back in Seattle.

My phone dinged. It was Mara texting.

Liam's here.

I'd asked her to keep an eye out for any of the band members who might show up for a meal or a drink.

On my way, I texted back.

I quickly threw on my winter uniform, consisting of a fuzzy sweater, dark jeans, and boots. Downstairs, the inspector was gone. She seemed very professional and thorough, but other than that, I couldn't really get a read on her.

I just hoped she'd leave Ewan out of her investigation.

I went to search for Abigail. She was on the computer at her desk.

"You're supposed to be on holiday too," I said.

She scrunched up her face. "There are things that need doing, and you know how much it bothers me."

I did. She and our friend Jasper both had OCD, though it expressed itself in different ways. He was a perfectionist with pastries and desserts. She was a perfectionist in just about everything from house cleaning and record-keeping to her schooling.

"And it can't wait until we come back?"

"No," she said, and then sighed. "Tommy gets restless in the house. Here, he can work in the greenhouse with his plants and he's so much happier. We need to keep with his routines. It makes it easier on me, as well."

She was such a good sister and mother figure for Tommy.

"Have you bought your textbooks for next semester?"

She grinned. "Of course." She pointed to a stack of books on her desk. "Those are next on my list."

She'd had a 4.5 GPA this last semester, taking difficult medical classes. Like I said, she was a perfectionist and quite brilliant.

"I'm headed to the pub. I'll pick you both up some early lunch."

She frowned. "Were the scones not enough?"

I laughed. "I'm not eating. One of the band members is down there. I thought I might try to see if he feels like chatting."

She nodded. "Be careful," she said.

"I always am."

She snorted and then covered her mouth. We laughed.

"Well, I'm more careful than I used to be," I said.

After grabbing my white, puffy coat and reminding myself to buy myself a black coat so I didn't look like a giant marshmallow floating around, I walked down the cobblestones to the pub on the corner.

The wind had died down a bit, but it was still bone-chilling cold. The warmth of the pub and the delicious smells were welcome. Even though the journey from my house to the pub only took about three minutes, my teeth chattered.

I hung my puffy coat on one of the hooks near the bar and went to sit down. I spotted Liam and took a leather stool two spaces away from him.

A cup of coffee warmed one hand while he stared at his phone with the other.

"Morning, Doc," Mrs. Wilson said as she came out of the kitchen with a tray of food.

"Good morning," I said. "You have a crowd this morning."

"Aye," she said. "This lot's fans have discovered the sad news." She nodded toward Liam, who looked up. "Been a steady stream since this morning."

"I'm surprised they aren't harassing you," I said to Liam, hoping to open a dialogue.

"Davy asked that they give us our privacy to grieve in peace," he grumbled.

"Oh, I'm glad they are respecting that sentiment," I said. "You deserve it."

He glanced behind him, and I followed his gaze. There were several people watching, but when they saw him turn, they put their heads down.

"How is everyone feeling? I was worried about Destinee after talking with her yesterday."

"Aye. It's hard on all of us, but especially her. She was asleep when I left this morning. Or at least, I assume so. No one was around. Any idea when we can go home?"

I shrugged. "You'll have to speak to the constable or the inspector," I said.

"I just met her," he said. "I don't think she's a fan of the band. She didn't seem to like me or my mates very much."

"I've only just met her, but I wouldn't take it personally. I think she's that way with everyone."

He smirked.

"I'm sure you're all questioned out, but something—" I realized everyone in the pub had gone quiet.

I paused and turned around. Everyone cut their eyes down to their food or drinks again. There was no sense questioning him here.

"Is there any chance you could come up to my office?" I whispered. "I'd like to ask you some questions about Bram's health before—well, before everything happened."

He shrugged.

"Tell Mara I'll chat with her later," I said to Mr. Wilson. He'd been stacking glasses nearby. Most likely trying to hear every word we said.

I grabbed my coat, and Liam put on his, along with a beanie. He was tall and lanky, though not as tall as Bram had been.

When we walked outside, it was like putting my face in a freezer. I wrapped my scarf around the lower half the way Mara had taught me.

"What is it you wanted to ask?" he said as we rounded the corner.

"It was mentioned in some of the interviews that Bram's behavior had changed the last few months. Do you agree?"

He shrugged. "He had a lot on his mind with the tour and creating so many songs. As soon as the tour was locked in, he started writing more new music. He was just in one of his manic phases and he could be an arsehole. I know we are not supposed to say bad things about the dead, but he could be when he was like that. The pressure was definitely getting to him, though."

"In my past life as an ER doctor, I had to make life-and-death decisions in an instant. I still can't imagine the kind of pressure you all are under onstage in front of thousands of people. The need for everyone to work together must be intense at times."

He grinned. "Truth is, we all love that part of it," he said. "There's not a shy one among us. We live for the fans and their reactions. Bram taught us all to be appreciative of them. They have always kept us going through the hard times."

"And were you going through hard times before his death?"

It was as if a mask slid over his face. There was strain around his eyes. "Like I said, he could be a bloody arsehole when he was manic," he said.

"Talk to me about what you mean by manic."

He gave me a look.

"I'm a doctor. I know what it means, but it manifests differently with every person. There can be depressive manic phases, or ones where someone can't sit still or sleep for days."

He nodded. "Staying up all hours and writing. Making us rehearse the same things repeatedly until we met his ideal of perfection. But the last few weeks, he'd reached a new level of insanity. I dinnae use that word lightly. He was way off.

"Like I said before, we all thought it was because of the tour. I don't know, though. He was definitely different. And it wasn't like him to forget anything, especially lyrics. And he was always forgetting where he left his bloody notebook. He'd accuse us of hiding it from him so we didn't have to practice the new songs he wrote. Things like that. I guess that was the difference this time. He seemed paranoid."

That wasn't unusual for people with Alzheimer's, even in the early stages of the disease. Misplacing things and paranoia were just a couple of the terrible side effects people suffered. While I had medical tests to back up this new theory of mine, I still needed more facts.

For instance, why would he plan an international tour if he knew what was happening to him?

"Off the record, if you had to identify someone who might've killed Bram, who would be your first guess?"

He gave me a sharp look and narrowed his eyes. "No one in the band," he said. "Think about it. Without him, there is no tour. There is no money. Sure, we'll be able to live off the residuals for the rest of our lives, but what we had is gone. It had been the best part of all our lives.

"We can never be Bram and the Stokers again." He seemed genuinely traumatized by that fact. He choked up, which surprised me. But when he turned back, he stiffened. "You didn't tell me there would be press."

I glanced up to see several people outside my practice with microphones and cameras.

"They weren't here when I went down."

He sighed. "The fans might give us a break, but the press never will. I can't handle this right now." He turned and headed back down. I didn't blame him.

However, he still hadn't answered my question about who might want to kill Bram. I'd have to ask him again when there weren't so many peering eyes around.

There was a bloodcurdling scream, and then I heard Tommy shouting. That was something he never did. He hated all sorts of loud noises.

I took off running.

There was a small gap in the crowd of media, and I took advantage of it. I raced inside, running through the practice and my house. The only way to access the garden was around the back.

Tommy was still shouting, but I could also hear Abigail very calmly telling him to put the shovel down.

"No. Bad people in the garden. Bad people," he said as I made it through the long pathway going from the cemetery at the back of the house to the garden.

"Bloody idiot could have killed me," a man said. He was on the ground holding his hand. Abigail knelt beside him wrapping a kitchen cloth around his bloody appendage.

"You're trespassing, and he has every right to protect the premises," I said sharply. "Did you climb over the stone wall? Who are you?"

"I was just having a look around," he said. "I thought it was a church."

"Lies," I said. He'd scared Tommy, and the calm demeanor I was known for went out the window when it came to that kid. I'd protect him with my life.

"You're here with the rest of them trying to get a story."

Lucy Connelly

I pulled my phone from my pocket and dialed Ewan.

"Doc?" he answered.

"We have a reporter who trespassed onto our property," I said. "Tommy hit him with a shovel."

"Are they alive? Because I'm going to kill them for scaring the boy."

It was all I could do not to smile. He was every bit as protective of Tommy as I was.

"Unfortunately, yes. He's still alive. Though wounded."

"I'll be there in ten."

"There's a whole slew of them out front," I said.

I swear he growled. "I'll take care of it."

"Is he going to lose any fingers?" I asked Abigail.

That made the guy turn white. His eyes rounded. Served him right.

"I dinnae think so, Doc. But best we treat him quickly."

"I'll put that crazy boy in jail if you've damaged my hands."

"I think you have much more to worry about in that regard. The constable is protective of that boy, and you're trespassing."

"Is everything okay?" Henry said from behind me.

I may have jumped, and only Tommy holding that shovel kept me from screaming.

"Are you hurt?" He ran to Abigail. He'd been sweet on her for months and while their relationship developed at a snail's pace, it was what was best for her. And sweet Henry seemed perfectly willing to wait for as long as it took.

She whispered something to him.

"Tommy, let's go get some hot chocolate," Henry said softly.

"There's a bad man in the garden," Tommy said.

"I know. And you caught him. Good job. He can't hurt anyone. The doc needs to look at his hand. Now, let's go get some hot chocolate."

The shovel clattered to the ground.

Obediently, Tommy followed Henry into my house.

There were some shouts over the wall as Ewan's men cleared the area.

And then he was barreling into the garden.

"Everyone okay? Where's Tommy?"

"He's with Henry."

"What do you think you were doing?" He sneered at the reporter. He grabbed the man by the elbow and hauled him up to his feet.

"Like I told them"—he pointed at me and Abigail—"I was just having a look around."

"On private property?" Ewan's voice was low. The reporter didn't seem to be as afraid of him as he should have been. "You're trespassing, and you attacked one of my residents. You'll be doing time for this one."

"Me attack? Do you see this?" He held up his bloody hand. "I should sue."

"Please try," I said. "I don't know much about the Scottish court system, but I have a feeling they don't look kindly upon men who trespass and harass special needs teens. You've caused that poor boy too much grief. And as the good constable and I have said, you were trespassing."

The guy's eyes went wide. "I didn't know he—special needs?" It was the first time he appeared even a little bit sorry for what he'd done.

"Let's go," Ewan said.

"Should I look at his hand?" I asked.

"We have ice at the station," he said.

Then he hauled him through the cemetery and took him the long way around the mountain and down.

"You better check on Tommy," I said to Abigail. She was pale.

"He's never been violent like that," she said softly.

"He was doing nothing more than protecting his turf," I said. "God knows what I would have hit that guy with if it had been me out here. You've met me. I grab whatever is nearest and swing."

That made her smile. "Come on. I think we could all do with some hot chocolate. Oh, darn."

"What?"

"I forgot to grab your lunch. I was talking to the drummer from the band, and . . . I'll go get us something."

"No," she said sharply. Then she held up a hand. "Sorry. I'd like to take a walk. I'll get us something," she said. "If you don't mind. I need to work off some nervous energy. When I heard Tommy scream . . ."

"Oh, I know," I said. "I was out front. I thought I swallowed my heart there for a minute. And don't be upset with him, Abigail. He had the forethought to protect himself and us. He's a highly intelligent kid, and he just hit the man's hand . . . though I would've been happier if he'd given him a whack on the head. Might be the only thing that makes him think twice about trespassing again."

She blew out a breath. "I've seen him upset, but I think if I hadn't showed up, he might have bludgeoned him."

"But he didn't. If anything, I feel like he showed great restraint. And that idiot deserved whatever he got."

"You may be right about that," she said.

*   *   *

An hour and a half later, Henry, Abigail, Tommy, and myself had full bellies and were on the way to buy some Christmas trees for my house and the office. While I should have been trying to deduce who killed poor Bram, we all needed a distraction after the earlier events. Henry was there as protection, per Ewan. We were all crowded into his truck, but we didn't have far to go. The greenhouse and tree farm were just up the coast a bit.

Tommy had convinced me to buy living trees that he could plant in the garden after the holidays, and I thought that was a terrific idea.

When we arrived at the tree farm, I was surprised by how big it was. There was a huge greenhouse, and we followed Tommy inside.

He went straight to a gray-haired man who wore overalls over his thick sweater.

"Tommy, I'm so glad to see you," the man said softly. Then he nodded toward us. "What can I help you with today?"

"Two Nordmann fir trees," Tommy said. "Nine feet and six feet. Only containers please. Those are for the doc."

"Ah, I see. It's good you came early," the man said. "We sell out of the container trees early every year."

"Yes," Tommy said. "I'm here now. I will pick the best of the lot."

I smiled. He wasn't the easiest person to chat with, but he always got his point across. Even after eating lunch, he'd been agitated by the reporter's trespassing. I hadn't planned on getting a tree until closer to Christmas Day, but he'd asked Abigail if they could get their tree today, and I thought I'd go along to help. Then he'd convinced me to get trees as well.

As I said, he always gets his point across.

I agreed to two trees, though I had no idea if there might be holiday decorations stored somewhere around the house. There were secret rooms and broom closets all over the place, so I hoped to find some. Otherwise, I'd just buy what I needed.

The elderly gentleman held out his hand. "I know Abigail and Henry and Tommy, of course. Are you the new doc?"

I smiled. "I am. And you must be Mr. Galloway."

"Aye."

"Tommy said this was the best place to find my live Christmas trees. You have a beautiful farm."

His cheeks were ruddy, but I swear he blushed. "Thank you, Tommy. I can always use the business. And what size will you be needing?" he asked Abigail. "Same as always?"

She smiled at him. "Aye, five feet, please. I don't have soaring ceilings like the doc does."

We followed Tommy and Mr. Galloway down the aisles of trees. Occasionally, Tommy would stop and check one out. Then he would shake his head. "No, that isn't right," he'd say, and we'd be on to the next one.

Abigail glanced back at me and mouthed, "Sorry."

I shook my head. They were as close as any family I'd ever had, and I liked hanging out with them. Especially here in a place that was so gorgeous and smelled like the holidays.

It took more than half an hour to find all the trees we needed, and it had been worth every second to watch Tommy in his element.

"That boy knows more about plants than I ever will," Mr. Galloway said as I was paying him for my trees. "He has no idea of his brilliance or his talent."

I smiled. "I love that he's so passionate about living things," I said. "And I'm grateful he's taking care of my gardens."

"Aye, you're lucky, lass. That boy can grow just about anything. Amazing he is."

"Very true."

By the time we were headed back to my place, we'd bought three trees and so many green garlands I had no idea where I'd put them all. But Abigail assured me we needed them.

The pub was crowded as we turned the corner. People who none of us recognized waited to get inside. There was a police barricade at the bottom of the hill going up to my place. Henry waved, and two of his fellow officers moved the wooden gates back so he could drive through.

We were just about to pull in front of the office when my phone rang. I glanced down and saw it was Ewan.

I pushed the button to answer the phone.

"What's up?

"We have a problem," he said. "And I need your help."

Chapter Ten

A short time later, I was at the B and B. I'd left Henry with Abigail and Tommy, and I'd given them carte blanche to do whatever kind of decorating they desired. Or they could just dump the trees and go decorate their own place.

Abigail had wanted to come with me since I was headed to a medical emergency, but I convinced her to stay with Tommy. He still seemed a bit agitated, and I didn't want to add to his distress.

Ewan opened the door as I climbed the steps on the front porch, then grabbed my rolling kit from me. "We found her passed out in her bathtub," he said as I followed him upstairs. "She was completely dressed but unresponsive. Her breathing is fine, but we can't wake her up. I can't tell if it's drugs or something else."

They'd put her on top of the huge canopied bed in her room. She appeared dead, she was so pale.

Davy was pacing back and forth on the other side of the room.

"Did she eat or drink anything? Is she on any kind of medication?" I asked him as I checked her vitals. Her pulse was strong, as was her breath. Ewan had been right about that. It was as if she was just in a deep sleep.

"I've no idea. I've been working all morning trying to deal with the press. When she didn't come down for breakfast or lunch—I thought she was bloody dead in that bath. Why would she be in an empty tub with all her clothes on? I dinnae understand."

That was a good question.

"Ewan, look around for anything that might indicate she took something."

"Why do you just assume it's drugs? Someone killed our mate. Maybe they tried to kill her."

"Ewan?"

"Davy, let's head outside."

"What happened?" That was Bethany.

"Unresponsive," Ewan said as if that answered everything.

"What are you doing here?" Bethany asked him.

"My job. Responding to an emergency call."

"Inspector, can you help me a minute?" I waved her over. I had no desire to listen to the pair of them bicker.

"Do you know what happened?"

"Not yet. Heart rate and breathing seem normal, but we can't wake her up."

When I pushed up Destinee's sleeves, I noticed the skin was extremely dry and crinkled under my touch. That wasn't unusual in Scotland. The wind and cold were persistent in these winter months, but this was something more.

"Check with Davy, the band manager, and see if they've seen her eat or drink anything the last few days," I said. "I'd have Ewan do it, but I need him to do something else. Then, if you could keep that manager and her friends out of here, I'd be grateful."

"I've got it," she said.

When she left, she shut the door behind her.

"Thank you, Doc," Ewan said.

"I didn't do it for you. I think she may be severely dehydrated. I'm going to set up an IV and pump fluids into her. But I need you to fetch the larger kit from my car."

"On it," he said.

"Destinee, can you hear me? It's Doctor McRoy. Can you tell me if you've taken anything? Maybe something to help you sleep?"

Her eyes twitched as if she were in REM. That was actually a good sign. Her veins were nearly nonexistent, though. Another sign of dehydration.

Ewan had helped me enough over the last few months on emergency calls—not that we had that many—that he understood what needed to happen. He opened the big kit, took out the pieces of the IV pole, and snapped them together. After pulling out the saline solution, I started the IV. It wasn't easy since her veins were definitely not popping.

"I'd get the helicopter to transport her to Edinburgh, but the winds are too high. We can get emergency services to take her into the hospital."

I shook my head. "If she showed any other symptoms, I'd say yes. I think she's just dehydrated. And I'd bet buckets of money she's taken something to help her sleep."

"I didn't see anything," he said.

After finishing with the IV, I drew some blood. When I shifted my position, I noticed something under her pillow. I pulled it out and held it up to the light next to the bed.

The package appeared to be lozenges, and then it clicked. I'd seen these before in Seattle.

"What is that?" he asked.

"CBD gummies," I said. "Depending on how many she took, that could be why we can't wake her." I checked the THC levels. "Yeah, that might do it. And before you ask, no, they aren't legal here in Scotland."

He shook his head.

"I dinnae know that much about them, but I didn't think they were that strong. Does she need her stomach pumped? Do you think she tried to kill herself?"

I shook my head. "With CBD gummies? Not likely. But I will ask her when she wakes up. She'll be fine once she sleeps them off. Those combined with the fact that she's dehydrated was a bad mix."

It took two bags, but toward the end of the second one, she began to rouse a bit. She blinked when she saw me. And then squinted.

"Doc?" Her voice was raspy. "What happened?"

"Your bandmates couldn't wake you, so they gave me a call."

"Whhaat?" She seemed confused. "How long was I out?"

"Almost fourteen hours total. You were severely dehydrated, and I think that combined with your gummies had an adverse effect."

"Dehydrated?" She blinked.

"When was the last time you ate or drank anything?"

She couldn't seem to place the memory. She shrugged.

"Right. Do you remember how many of these you chewed?" I held up the package.

She grimaced. "I haven't been able to sleep. I took one, and nothing happened after about an hour. I took two more."

"They are delayed release," I said. "And not exactly legal here."

I glanced up at Ewan.

He sighed. "You have been through enough, lass. I see nothing."

She smiled, and so did I. I had a feeling if that had been Bethany, she'd be handcuffed to the bed.

"So, you need to eat and drink plenty of fluids. And don't take more than one of these in a twelve-hour period," I said as I held up the package. "Or better yet, don't take them at all. I can prescribe you something if you need to rest."

"They are more natural," she said.

I gave her a look.

"I get it, Doc. I won't take them again. That was scary. I kept trying to wake up. It was like I could hear you, but I just couldn't get my eyes to open. So, never again."

I didn't believe her. "No more than one," I said. "And whatever you do, don't let the detective inspector see the package. Ewan may be understanding, but she's very much by the book. Not that I'm condoning the use of any type of recreational drugs. I'm just trying to protect my patient.

"You'll be fine once you start replacing the fluids and eating some food. I have to ask you something, though."

She frowned. "Okay."

"Did you mean yourself harm?"

Her eyes went wide. "Nay. I promise. I was just after a good night's sleep. Ever since Bram died—I have been in some kind of weird haze. I couldn't sleep or eat. But I was exhausted. I dinnae mean to cause trouble."

For a music star, she was very contrite. Most of the ones I'd run into at the hospital in Seattle were entitled and not very sorry about anything. Especially when overdosing on drugs. For them, it was some kind of dumb badge of honor.

"It was no trouble, just be careful in the future." I took the IV out. Then I put my kit back together. When I opened the door to see about getting her a tray, Liam, Render, and Boscoe were just outside the door.

"Is she going to be okay?" Boscoe asked.

"Yes, she's fine. Liam, could you talk to Mrs. Beatty about a tray with some broth and tea and a pitcher of water? We need to keep those fluids going. You guys need to make sure she's taking in fluids every hour."

"Can you tell us what happened?" Render asked.

"That's between doctor and patient. You'll have to ask her. But she will be fine."

"I'll get that tray for her," Liam said.

"I'll help," Boscoe said.

Render was about to follow them.

"Can I speak to you?" I asked.

He frowned. He was thin and fit and reminded me of a skinny Chris Hemsworth, in a way. No man would ever be as handsome as Chris, but he came close with his long blond hair and square jaw.

"What is it?" he asked.

"I've heard from just about everyone in the band about their thoughts concerning Bram, but you haven't been around much."

He sniffed. "Aye. I'm not much for drama," he said. "They've been fighting, and it's easier to just walk away. I've been staying with me mum. She lives here. So, that's why I haven't been around much."

"Oh? I didn't know you were from Sea Isle."

He nodded. "Bram and I both were," he said.

My eyes must have gone wide. "What?" Then I remembered something one of the band members said about him coming back here.

"Aye. His family passed years ago, but we used to hang out as kids until he went to university. Then we started the band."

"No one has mentioned much about his ties to the place. Not even him when we first arrived."

"Right, that would be him keeping the past private. He's always had this goth thing going like he was born of vampires or something. But we grew up together, and his parents were as normal as they come." He grinned.

"Did he have things to hide?" I asked.

"Don't we all?" He cleared his throat. "Humble beginnings. His dad was a fisherman who died at sea. His mom raised him and was a cleaner. They had a good relationship until the cancer took her a decade or so ago. They were close, and her death wrecked him for a while. I can't know for sure, but I think this place brought back all those memories."

"He acted like he loved it here."

"Aye, he did. I think he'd dealt with a lot of his demons. He'd planned on staying with me and mum for the holidays and writing. Well, he was staying here at the B and B after they all left. But he was coming over for the holidays."

"You were still close, then."

He chuckled. "I know what you've heard about the fighting. And yes, he could be a bloody arsehole, but he was good to his core. My mom loved him like another son, and he was one of our family. And he was born musically brilliant. He's been writing songs our whole lives."

"Was his behavior always so erratic?"

He leaned against the wall and crossed his arms. "Not always. He did go through episodes at times that only seemed to get worse as we got older. I don't think anyone knows, but he'd just gone in for a bunch of tests." He whispered the last sentence.

"Was that because he forgot some lyrics?"

"Aye. And he told me everything agitated him lately. Like someone would say, 'Good day,' and he'd want to bite their head off. He also seemed more tired than usual. He's always been the most energetic of us, but not lately. I was truly worried about him."

"Did he tell you what the doctors said?" I still hadn't received all his medical files. But knowing he had tests meant I very much needed those records.

"Nay. Just that he'd gone. He seemed much more himself the last week. Especially when we got here. I thought he must have received some good news. We all seemed to be back on track. That last set . . ."

"Was one of your best from what the rest of the band says."

"It was. Nights like that are golden. He even said it at the pub after the set. We had a few pints like the good old days. Told stories about the early times when things were just getting going. It was a great time."

"And did you come back with them to the B and B?"

"For a bit. It was late, and I knew me mum would be waiting up. So, I headed home. I keep thinking if I had stayed, maybe I could have stopped whatever happened." He frowned, and his eyes watered. "I still cannae believe he's gone." He choked up, then cleared his throat.

"Did you ever know him to take drugs or anything like that? And no judgments. I'm just trying to get a complete medical history and get an idea of what he was truly like beyond the headlines."

"No drugs. He had a hard rule against them. I think that's how we've all lasted as long as we have. We had regular drug tests. He didn't care about a bit of weed. But nothing else. He was health-conscious when it came to that.

"I mean, in the early days, after his mum passed, we, uh . . . In university, he went down the rabbit hole with molly and weed, but he cleaned himself up when we all threatened to quit the band. That's when he came up with all the rules about drugs."

"Did he drink a lot?"

"Nay. A few pints here and there. He wasn't like the big music stars you read about in the tabloids. He lived a clean life and didn't like it when he wasn't clearheaded. Always said he wanted to be aware when the words came."

"I heard that he was on a writing spree."

He grinned. "Aye. Some of the best music of his life—that's why this is bollocks, him dying now. The words were flowing like they never had before. And we will not be able to record those songs without him."

I nodded. "Do you have any idea where his notebook might be?"

He frowned at the floor. "Davy asked me the same thing. No. I haven't seen it, but I'll keep an eye out."

I heard teacups rattling on a tray coming up the stairs.

"One last question. Is there anyone who might have wanted to hurt him?"

He shook his head. "Our Bram was an odd duck. But we all have our things that drive others crazy. He was like my brother." He frowned. "Like I said, I still can't believe he's gone. It feels like some kind of hoax."

It was no hoax. The popular music star was very much dead in my autopsy room.

I opened the door so Liam could take the tray in.

"Hey, luv," he said. "Brought you tea."

"I need to get back to my office," I said. "I know you're fine, Destinee, but it might be best if someone was with you for the next twenty-four hours. Just to make sure you keep those fluids going."

She shook her head. "I'm better, Doc. I don't need babysitters."

"Nonsense," Render said. "Mum's bringing us up some clootie dumplings and other treats. We'll have a grand time."

"Yum," she said. "Our Render's mum sends us all care packages with her baked goods all over the world. It's like a taste of home wherever we are. She's the best."

"I'll check on you a bit later," I said. "Here's my card." I left it on the nightstand. "My cell phone number is on there if you need me." I'd left her one before, but I didn't trust she hadn't put it in the bin.

"Thanks, Doc," she said. "Sorry for the worry."

"It's fine. Just take care of yourself. One of you should light a fire, I hear there is a storm coming. You'll want to stay warm, Destinee. And hydrated." I gave her a look.

She smiled and then saluted me. "Promise, Doc. No more drama from me."

Her friends seemed calmer than they had been earlier. That was probably the shock wearing off. Now they'd have to figure out a new normal, if that was even possible with a rock band.

As I was leaving, I saw Davy talking to Boscoe. He hadn't been around much either. The discussion seemed heated, and I paused. But they must have sensed me. They both turned to stare at me, and then Davy slammed the door.

Well, now. That wasn't suspicious at all.

Chapter Eleven

Since I didn't relish the idea of walking down the mountain in the cold, even though it wasn't that far, I went in search of Ewan. He was in the kitchen with Mrs. Beatty. They stopped talking when I walked through the doorway.

"How is she?" Ewan asked.

"Awake and doing fine. Thank you, Mrs. Beatty, for sending up a tray."

"I'm just glad she's alive," she said. She was busy mixing something in a large bowl. She was one of my patients, and she always seemed to have a smile on her face. Until today. "The sooner you two can figure out what happened, the better. I want these people out of my house. All they do is argue and try to kill themselves. I'm not certain how much more my nerves can take."

"I can move them to one of my holiday rentals if you have other bookings coming in," Ewan offered.

"Nay. That isn't necessary. I'm just frustrated. Besides, Bram booked the entire house through the New Year. I think he was planning on staying and writing when the others left, and he didn't want to be disturbed. I wouldn't have minded the company for the holidays. He was always a good boy."

"So, you knew him when he lived here before?"

"Aye." She smiled. "His ma was my cleaner, and a good one at that. He helped her even when he was a teen. Always a good lad, that one. Cannae say the same for that lot he hangs out with."

She paused her mixing and peered over her glasses at us. "Should I give the money back? He paid in advance. I didn't even think about it."

"I wouldn't worry," Ewan said. "I'll speak with the band's manager. Besides, they're all still here and renting multiple rooms. It will all even out in the end."

"Are they still fighting?" I asked.

She glanced at Ewan, and he nodded at her.

"I was just telling the constable, it's been nonstop. For the last forty-eight hours. I can't imagine how sad they must be. I'm certain they are all upset. I should be more kindly toward them."

"You have a right to your feelings," I said, "but I'm sure you're also right about them being a bit emotional. They've lost a dear friend, though it may not feel like it at times from your perspective. Can you give us any indication what the fights might be about?"

"I'm not one to eavesdrop and gossip," she said.

I bit my lip to keep from laughing. She was exactly the type.

"I just thought any information you might be able to share could help with the investigation or, perhaps, give us a motive."

She started stirring again. "Before he died, Bram and Davy were fighting about something that was supposed to happen in America. Bram dinnae like whatever Davy had planned, and he'd threatened to tell the rest of the band."

Well, that was interesting. Something about Davy didn't sit right with me. He was one of those guys who was a bit too smooth. He was at the top of my list, though I had no real reason as to why. Bram was his cash cow, so why would he kill him?

"And after Bram's death?"

"Whether the band should carry on with the tour," she said. "Davy's been talking with all of them. Some of them want to find

Lucy Connelly

some kind of work-around, or at least postpone. Others think it's time to end the band for good."

"Can you tell us who is leaning which way?"

"The young man who just came down to grab tea and Destinee think the band is done for good. I think. I get the young men confused sometimes. The others want to continue as The Stokers. I may have misheard. I'm really trying very hard not to listen, but they are sometimes quite loud."

"You are the sole of discretion, Mrs. Beatty," Ewan said.

She nodded. "Mind you, I didn't tell that woman trying to take your job any of that. I don't like outsiders coming in and messing about with our business. I'm on your side, Constable."

Ewan cleared his throat. "The detective inspector is just trying to do her job. And we are sharing information we gather with her to help the investigation."

Mrs. Beatty huffed. "Still, I prefer to speak with you and the doctor."

I grinned. I hadn't been in Sea Isle long, but at least she didn't see me as one of the outsiders.

After gathering my bags and checking on Destinee one more time, we headed down the mountain.

I told Ewan what I'd seen.

"I know you like facts, but there's something about Davy. Why would he think they could continue with the tour? Wasn't Bram the soul of the band like everyone says? I mean, he wrote most of their songs and he was the lead."

"Aye, it is difficult to imagine them moving forward without him, although Destinee is equally strong on vocals."

"She does have an amazing voice. But it wouldn't be the same, right? They could move forward as something different. Maybe that was the plan all along."

"What do you mean?"

"You like facts, and all I have right now is theory. I mean, I have some medical facts."

"Tell me."

"You know most of it. I want to see his medical files before saying anything conclusive."

"But . . ."

I sighed. He wasn't going to let it go.

"Maybe the plan all along was to do something different with the band. If—and it's a big if because none of them have mentioned it—someone knew that he was going to grow progressively worse mentally, then perhaps they decided to end things.

"Maybe, before the big American tour happened, someone wanted to change things up."

"So, they killed Bram in order to create something new with the band before they launched."

"Right," I said. "It's just a theory."

"'Tis a very plausible theory."

I was surprised he even considered it.

"It's a motive," I continued. "Greed is one of the big ones when it comes to a good motive. I mean, the band, for all their troubles, seem to have respected him in their own way, but this is also their livelihood and has been for years."

"True. Who else do you consider suspects?"

Even though it was early afternoon, Scotland grew dark quickly in the winter months. As we pulled up in front of my practice, I grinned. Someone, most likely Abigail, had wrapped lights around the topiaries on either side of the entrance.

"I have no real reason to suspect him, but Davy seems to be involved in the majority of the arguments," I said. "So, he's at the top. And I know I've said it before, but there is just something about him that doesn't sit right with me. He seems crafty. Like, if someone was going to look up how to commit murder with a wine opener, I'd put my bets on him."

Ewan nodded. "Who else?"

"Everyone else in the band," I said. "Think about it. His behavior had been erratic. They all said it. Maybe one of them had had enough of his antics and killed him." I thought for a moment. "And then, though we haven't talked to any of them, maybe a few of the stalkers they've been talking about."

"You think Destinee could have done it? I didn't think she was tall enough given your profile of how much force was needed to stick that thing in his brain."

I pursed my lips. "I need to test that idea to see if I can get an approximate idea of the height, weight, and force needed. But this isn't an episode of *CSI* or *Bones*. I can do some calculations, but with so many variables, it's hard to figure it out."

"So, how will you do that?"

I grinned. "Science, Constable. Always science. As much as I can do. It may be a waste of time, but I can at least try. Bram was tall, but if the killer had managed to get him to sit down . . . that's what I mean by so many variables."

He chuckled. "Let me know if you need any help."

"Thanks."

"Are you going to the caroling event at the library?"

I laughed. "I think I'm required by law to go to every event this month, at least according to Mara, because I volunteered for the holiday committee. When I signed up, I thought I'd be bored sitting around. I had no idea we'd have another murder to solve."

"Remember, Doc, you are on the medical side of things. 'Tis up to Bethany and myself to solve the case."

I cleared my throat. "Of course."

He chuckled. "Why don't I believe you?"

I shrugged. "I'm completely trustworthy. I have no idea what you're talking about."

"I'll see you there tonight," he said. Then he grinned.

If he could bottle that grin, he'd make a fortune selling it to women. Not that I thought of him that way.

Okay, sometimes I did. But the constable was well out of my league. Handsome, wealthy, and intelligent, he never lacked for a beautiful woman on his arm. Still, he had appeared in my dreams now and again.

Which did nothing but embarrass me when I saw him in person and one of those fake memories popped up.

Once I was inside, I hung up my coat and stored my kits in my office. Then, remembering someone had broken in, I decided to lock my office.

While I could have started the experiment with the corkscrew, my mind needed time to figure out the particulars. I needed a distraction.

One of the trees had been set up in the reception room but hadn't been decorated. That was the next thing on my list. I needed to see if the former doctor had stored holiday decorations somewhere in the house.

I'd hit a few of the shops in Sea Isle as well. For a small village, I'd been able to find nearly everything I needed for the house when I'd first arrived. Not that I'd needed much. Ewan and Abigail had made certain the place was well appointed.

I was just about to head down the hallway when there was a knock on the front door. I almost opened it without checking the camera on my phone, but I stopped. I'd learned that as safe as Sea Isle might be, one couldn't always believe that when there was a murderer about.

Once I saw who it was, I opened the door. "Detective Inspector, how can I help you?"

"I wanted to know how your patient is doing," she said. "And if she tried to kill herself."

"I—uh. I can't discuss her condition with you," I said. "I believe in doctor-patient confidentiality."

She sighed. "I understand that, Doc. Unfortunately, if she tried to kill herself, it could show she feels guilt over murdering the victim."

"Have you tried to speak to her about it?"

"Her manager called in his legal team. They won't let me anywhere near any of the band members unless I make an official request.

I was instructed to leave the B and B because the manager said I was harassing the band.

"But I understand from Mrs. Beatty that you and Ewan just left there. I get that you and the constable aren't happy about my joining the investigation, but I thought we were going to share information." She seemed quite cross about something.

I did wonder why we'd been allowed access when she wasn't. I had a feeling I had something to do with her attitude. That, and she hadn't given the band a ride when they'd been in desperate need.

And I'd cared for Destinee, so I had a reason to be there.

"I can assure you, she didn't try to kill herself," I said. "I will make an official report if that helps you. She was dehydrated and took something to help her sleep. That's why they couldn't wake her."

She frowned. Then she punched some buttons on her phone. She held it up for me to read. It was a news story about Destinee.

The headline read, "Singer So Distraught She Tries to Kill Herself."

I shook my head. "Why would they say that if it isn't true? And no one there would be talking to the press."

"So, you and Ewan didn't leak it to the press?"

I crossed my arms. "No. We are professionals, and I don't believe in lying, which is what that is. All lies. I don't understand what I've done to give you such a low opinion of me, Detective Inspector, but I would never speak to the press about a patient."

She huffed. "I didn't say you weren't professional. The media can be tricky at times. Maybe you inadvertently said something to someone. And Ewan was asked to step away from the case."

"The only people I've talked to today are the band members, and . . . oh." I stopped.

She jumped to conclusions at my pause in speech. "What? Was it Ewan?"

I rolled my eyes. "No. But Mrs. Beatty is known for, uh, sharing stories."

"Gossiping, you mean," she said.

"Yes. But it wasn't Ewan or me. While we asked her a few questions, we didn't tell her anything other than Destinee would be fine."

"Are you sure?" The woman was absolutely frustrating.

"If you and I are going to work together, I feel like we need to get a few things straight," I said.

"As in . . ."

"I'm a professional and I have ethics. So does Ewan, whether you are blinded to that with him or not. He was only there to help me. It was an emergency situation, or at least we thought it was at the time. The last I heard, he was still the constable, and he answered the call."

She sat down in one of the chairs in the reception room, and her body sagged.

"Look, I understand why you are hesitant to think he had something to do with this, but he did have a motive. You don't know about his past."

Now who is gossiping?

"I do. He had history with Bram. Years ago, when everyone was still in college. That is *ancient* history. To question his ethics twenty years later is ridiculous. I haven't known you long, Inspector, but I feel you are better than this."

She leaned back and appeared weary for someone so young.

"I worked under him the first few years when I was just out of training. I know all about his ethics. He'd let some criminals slide, and others he'd go after with the full force of the law. I think I know him better than you."

I didn't believe any of that. "Perhaps you do. But were those he let slide, as you say, juveniles or people who might have been down on their luck? Like, perhaps they stole some bread to feed their families, that sort of thing? Or kids who made a few mistakes?"

"I—a—" She frowned. "Yes. But they still broke the law."

I pursed my lips. "Right. But sometimes throwing the book at someone isn't what will help them be better citizens. My guess is he showed them compassion for a reason.

"The past is funny, Inspector, especially when we are young. We can form certain ideas about people and situations. But with a little maturity, we can begin to see those things in a new light.

"Ewan doesn't use his power in this town for bad. He's one of the best men I've ever met. I understand why that might be difficult for you to believe, but it's true. He's as fair as they come, and a great leader."

She sighed. Then her stomach growled.

I grinned. "When was the last time you had something to eat?"

She blinked. "I can't remember."

"Well, I never think well on an empty stomach. Why don't we run down to the pub and grab a meal? I need to eat before heading to the caroling ceremony tonight."

She shrugged but then stood up.

"There is one thing I can tell you about what happened today," I said as I pulled my coat back on and grabbed my keys.

"What's that?"

"If I had to pick one suspect right now, it would be the band's manager."

"Why is that?"

I told her what Mrs. Beatty had said about the fights.

"He did seem to want to slam down any more interviews with the police," she said. "I find that highly suspicious."

So did I.

Chapter Twelve

It was near four in the afternoon, and thankfully, not all the pub's tables were crowded with newcomers. We put our coats on the hooks on the outside pole of one of the booths and then sat down. Mara came over to the table.

"I read that Destinee tried to kill herself. Is that true?" she asked.

"Uh, no," I said. "The media is making up stories. But it's an ongoing investigation . . ."

"And you can't talk about it." She rolled her eyes. "Fine."

This solicited a small grin from Bethany.

"What can I get you two?" Mara asked. From the smirk, I could tell she wasn't happy with me. But it was important I gained Bethany's trust since she was involved with the investigation, and I wanted her to leave poor Ewan alone.

"What's the special tonight?"

"Gran made a great stew, and I baked some brown bread. And we have cranachan for dessert."

"I'm good with all that," I said. "Though I have no idea what cranachan is."

The other women chuckled.

"Layered dessert with oats, raspberries, a bit of cream cheese, and malt whiskey," Mara said. "You'll love it. Do you want a couple of pints, or are you on duty, Inspector?" She eyed the other woman carefully.

"I'm always on duty. Do you have some cider?"

"Aye, we do."

"I'll take that as well," I said.

After Mara left, my phone buzzed. It was an email from the hospital in Edinburgh. "Do you mind, Inspector." I held up my phone. "It looks like the medical files have come in on Bram."

She leaned her elbows on the table. "What do they say?"

I thumbed through them. It was difficult to read MRIs on my phone, but I'd done it before. The doctors had found signs of early onset Alzheimer's.

I frowned.

"What is it?"

"It confirms what we found in the tests," I said, "but the disease had progressed quickly. I'm surprised he could function as much as he did." I frowned. This was the brain of someone who had significant lesions and plaque. It must have affected his cognitive abilities much more than forgetting a few lyrics.

And they all said he'd been writing songs.

"What are you not telling me?" she asked. "And please don't use doctor-patient confidentiality with me. He was a victim. He's dead, so it no longer applies."

"I'm just trying to reconcile the man I met and saw perform with this brain. It doesn't compute."

"Explain," she said.

"Like I said, the disease was progressing quickly. His ability to talk, sing, walk, all those things, would have been affected in some way. They possibly already were."

"But he was in his thirties," she said.

"According to his file, late thirties. Lots of celebrities lie about their ages," I said. "It's a game of youth in show business, at least from what I've learned from former patients."

"Are you saying he was a walking time bomb? Like, there was no way he'd make it through that tour they'd planned?"

"I don't see how," I said. "He'd been so charming and sexy. Not that Alzheimer's made him less so. No one could have imagined what was going on in his mind. Had he really been writing? How was that even possible? And his performance that night had been impeccable.

"The band had even performed some of the new songs. He hadn't made a single mistake. Unless someone had been helping him. But who? And how had they done it?"

"You are thinking hard," Bethany said. "Tell me."

I explained how difficult it would be to perform with such an advanced case.

"Was it possible he was lip-synching?"

I shook my head. "We were close enough that it wouldn't have been possible for us not to notice. He sang live that night. My eyes were almost always on him or Destinee. It could be that someone was feeding the lyrics in his ear. Or maybe they had some kind of teleprompter we couldn't see."

She scrunched up her face. "What do you think it has to do with the case."

I shrugged. "I'm not sure. But whatever they did that night, I can't see how it would have worked long-term for their tour."

"Maybe that is one of the reasons they agreed to do the smaller show here at the pub. To work out what they were going to do for their live shows."

I nodded. "At the very least, it is a reason to talk to the band again."

"I cannae get close to them without going through their lawyers."

I grinned. "See, this is why it's good to have me around," I said. "I don't have that problem. I can check in to see how they are all doing, and no one will suspect a thing. I have a patient there I need to check up on. But it will have to wait until later. I promised Mara I'd attend the event tonight."

* * *

A few hours later, I boarded one of the shuttles heading up the mountain to the caroling ceremony. Luckily for me, the van was at the bottom of the hill my home and practice were on.

"Evening, Doc," Mr. Wilson said as I climbed into one of the seats.

I smiled. "Let me guess. Mara roped you into driving tonight?"

He laughed. "Oh, there's a fair amount of us helping out tonight last minute. The rock stars have brought a few more visitors than usual into town."

"Hey, Em," Jasper said. "I saved you a seat next to me."

I grinned and then joined him.

"I haven't seen you much," I said.

"It's been busy. I had two wedding cakes and so many seasonal parties. I need to find some help. I'd probably be sleeping right now if Mara hadn't threatened my life if I didn't show up."

I laughed. "She is persuasive that way. I think I might know someone who can help you, though. She's been staying with her grandmother and is looking for a job in the area."

"Does she have any experience in a bakery?"

I shrugged. "She graduated from university, where she studied literature. She's smart and kind, and I have a feeling she would be easy to teach." I'd met her when she brought her gran in for a checkup.

"Why would she want to work at the bakery?" He seemed confused.

"I don't know that she does, but she is looking for temp work around town for the holidays. At the very least, you could teach her to run the front of the bakery so you can concentrate on your orders."

"Aye, that's true. Send her my way."

"I'll do that."

"I know you can't say much, but is there anything new with the investigation? And did Destinee try to kill herself like the paper said?

She doesn't seem the type. Not that I'm sure there is a type. I guess the type is sad people."

Everyone in the full van quieted down and listened.

I smiled. "That's a doctor-patient thing, but between us, the paper was full of untruths. She was just exhausted." I didn't normally discuss anyone's medical issues in public, but I felt a responsibility to clear up the idiocy the tabloids had printed. While I hadn't been certain at first, I believed what Destinee had said. She took one too many gummies and paid the price.

"Aye, that makes sense. I can't even imagine what they must all be going through. I'm beside myself and I'm just a fan. I found myself listening to their first album the other day and nearly weeping at the thought that they will never play music together again."

"Is that true?" someone from the back of the van asked.

"I've no idea," I said. "I don't think they've made a decision about the future of the band yet."

That set everyone talking about the pros and cons.

The van pulled away from the curb, and we headed up the mountain. It was only a half a mile or so, and it didn't take long. When we arrived, it was as if this part of town had been turned into a winter wonderland in the last few hours. Every building on the main square was decorated and lit up with a dazzling array of lights.

As we disembarked, Jasper crooked his arm in mine. He laughed.

"What is it?"

"All my complaining, and now I'm glad I'm here. When I was a kid, this used to be my favorite night." While he'd been away for years, Sea Isle was Jasper's hometown. He'd lived here until he'd gone off to school in France to become a pâtissier.

"Why is that?" I asked.

He grinned. "You'll see."

Most people were gathering in front of the stone library. The building had been decorated with lights, which shone down on the shadow of an enormous tree.

Someone cleared their throat, and we all turned our attention to the small podium next to the tree.

"Welcome to our second night of Sea Isle holiday celebrations," Ewan said. He was the mayor and was forced to officiate so many things it was laughable. "We are happy to have so many visitors join us tonight. Small songbooks will be passed out after we light the tree.

"For the benefit of the environment, we ask that you return the books to the table by the library door so that we may use them again next year.

"Now, on to our festivities. To help us begin the evening, we have some special guests. The Stokers."

There were cheers and some murmuring among the crowd. Destinee and the rest of the crew stood next to Ewan. He gestured her forward.

"Happy holidays, everyone," Destinee said. She cleared her throat. "We wanted to take a quick moment to give our heartfelt thanks for all your condolences and for sharing your sweet town with us while we pull ourselves back together. Bram loved Sea Isle and everything it had to offer, and we are grateful you included us in tonight's celebration.

"Now, enough of the sad. Let's get this party started!" She held up a fist, but the smile she had didn't quite meet her eyes. That said, she appeared in much better shape than she had just a few hours ago.

She and the others put their hands on a big button. There was a countdown and then blinding lights as the enormous tree came to life.

Everyone started singing "O Christmas Tree," and it was beautiful.

"That was interesting," Bethany Thomson, the inspector detective, whispered beside me.

"What do you mean?" I whispered back.

"My guess is it's a publicity stunt in response to the stories that have been running about her," she said. "Every online site has been running stories that she was either dead or near death. This has to be their way of setting the record straight in front of news crews." She pointed to the right near the small stage. There were news cameras as well as photographers yelling for photos.

She was probably right. I had a feeling Davy was behind it because Destinee hadn't been up to dealing with the public. Of that, I'd been certain. It would probably be a few days before she felt anywhere close to normal.

To the right, just off the podium, were several fans waiting with photos and pens for autographs. But the band was ushered off quickly to a waiting van. My guess was they were heading back to Mrs. Beatty's.

Part of me felt sorry for Destinee and the rest of the band, but I supposed that sort of thing went with the territory.

The song finished, and the crowd launched into a Gaelic one I didn't understand, but it sounded beautiful. I followed along with the songbook Jasper held. In my head, I added learning Gaelic to my list of things I wanted to do over the next year. However, the Gaelic language was tougher than any medical terminology I had to learn. There were a lot of guttural sounds.

Still when they sang in the language, it was gorgeous.

I had a weird sense that someone was watching me. It was a sensation I've learned to pay attention to, so I turned around.

The inspector, who had been watching the crowd carefully, turned as well.

"Is something wrong?" she asked.

In the glow of the Christmas lights, there was a hooded figure just outside of the crowd. I couldn't see the person's face, but they turned quickly and walked away.

"No. I just had a weird feeling," I said.

"What kind of feeling?"

I shrugged. "Like someone was watching me."

"I'll investigate that fellow with the hoodie. He's been circling the crowd since we arrived."

So she'd noticed him as well. I wasn't sure how she knew it was a guy. I hadn't seen his face, but he was tall.

The song changed. I found myself watching the crowd with a new interest and a bit of worry.

By the time we dispersed, my stomach was in knots.

"What's going on?" Jasper asked.

"I don't know. I got one of my weird feelings."

"You should tell Ewan."

I'm not sure what I would have said. I did want to check on Destinee, though.

"I need to take care of something. I'll see you later."

I headed two blocks off the main square toward the B and B. There was a guard at the door.

"The band and Mrs. Beatty only," he said.

"I'm a doctor," I said, flashing my medical badge. "I've come to check on a patient." He frowned and then said something into a walkie-talkie.

It took about a minute, but then he opened the front door. "You can go in," he said.

Destinee, Davy, and Render were in the front reception room. She had a large bottle of water, and the others were drinking what looked like a pale ale.

"Hi, Doc," she said.

"You look much better," I said. "I was surprised to see you at the event."

She nodded. "Davy thought it best to get out in front of the stories they've been running. I'm knackered, but I'm feeling a lot better thanks to you."

I smiled. "That's good to hear."

"I'm looking forward to going home soon and sleeping in my own bed," she said.

"Oh?"

"You seem surprised," Davy said. "We aren't criminals. We have a right to head back to our homes."

"I agree," I said. "You have the right to mourn wherever you want, and I'm sure you have the holidays to get ready for as well."

"And a tour, apparently," Render said. He didn't sound happy about it.

"What?" I asked, shocked that they'd already made a decision.

Davy gave him a cross look. "We're keeping that under wraps for the moment, remember." He said the words through gritted teeth.

"The doc won't say anything. Davy's decided for all of us that we're going to do a Farewell to Bram tour," Liam said. "Since we'd recorded the vocals already for the new album that's releasing at the first of the year, we're going to dub his voice in with Destinee's live."

"I—oh. I didn't know you could do that," I said. "I mean, at live events." I wondered if they'd somehow done that for the pub performance, but I didn't think so. I'd heard Bram singing into the microphone.

"Technology is a wonder these days," Davy said. "Besides, we owe it to Bram. He wanted this tour more than any of us. The fans will be blown away. We have footage of them taping the new album. It will be like a movie and live experience all in one. And we should, with a bit of practice, be able to blend their voices just as if they were singing live with each other."

Destinee frowned. I got the impression this was more about Davy, and perhaps money, than Bram.

"But it won't be the same as having him there with us," she said. "I'm not as confident as Davy that fans will be happy with a ghostly Bram."

Davy's face turned red. "He won't be a ghost. And it's been done with Elvis and Nat King Cole. There's no reason we can't do it for the tour. It will just take some practice to get things right."

Destinee's jaw tightened, and she threw a hand in the air. "It's weird and feels wrong."

"We did want to ask, when will you be releasing Bram's body?" Davy asked. "We're trying to put together a memorial, and we wanted his ashes there. I thought the body was supposed to be shipped to Edinburgh, but I was informed you hadn't released it yet. Why is that?"

Destinee's eyes brimmed with tears. "The way you talk is so cold sometimes, Davy. We want Bram there, not just his ashes."

"You know what I mean, luv."

"He can't help being an arse," Render said. He put his arm around her shoulders.

She nodded as if in agreement.

There was no love lost between the band members and Davy. I couldn't blame them. They all deserved time to mourn their friend.

"We're still waiting for tests to come back," I said. "The labs and police in Edinburgh and Glasgow are also involved. So, it isn't just me."

"I see," Davy said. But I didn't think he did. He looked at me suspiciously. "So, you're not holding on to him for publicity."

"Davy!" Destinee shouted. "Why would you even say something like that? She's a doctor. She doesn't care about publicity. All she's done is try to help us, from picking us up on the side of the road to taking care of me. You need to get it together, man. Not everyone is like you, looking for a quick buck." She sobbed out the last word. "Sorry to yell, Doc. And sorry for the arsehole here. He's mainly thinking about money. It's the only thing he really cares about."

I raised my eyebrows and stared at Davy. "She's right. I'm only trying to find out what happened to your friend. I have no reason to hold on to the body, except for the tests we are still running. That, and I've been waiting to receive his medical records from before his death."

Davy flinched. It was subtle, but I saw it. It was almost as if I could see the wheels turning in his brain as he tried to determine how much I knew about Bram's medical history. Now I wondered how much he knew.

I wanted to ask about the pub performance, but I had something more pressing I needed to know.

"Oh, there is one thing. Was Bram a big wine drinker?"

They all looked at one another.

"What do you mean?" Davy asked.

I couldn't tell them about the exact way he died. "We found some evidence of wine near the body, and I was just curious."

"Bram had the occasional pint," Destinee said, "and even those were few and far between. I don't think I've ever seen him touch a glass of wine."

"Maybe wine and champagne for celebrations," Render added. "He was more into that scene after spending some time in Italy and France. He'd even started a wine cellar at his home in Edinburgh."

Davy frowned.

Interesting.

Still, it didn't explain why those items were at the beach with Bram. Was he going to celebrate or meet with one of his adoring fans?

If he hadn't taken the corkscrew, then the killer did. Was all of it premeditated? I'd asked myself that more than once with this case.

Destinee yawned. "Sorry, Doc. I think I'll head to bed. And don't worry, I won't be taking any of my special tablets."

I smiled. "If you don't mind, stop and see me on the way out of town, please. I just want to double-check that you don't have anything else going on physically and that you're on the mend. I like to be thorough."

"Thanks. I'll do that."

"Well, good night," I said, and I left.

So, the band was going to continue without Bram, and they already had the tracks with his voice. There was something creepy about not needing his actual body for the performances.

If I were a fan, would I like that one last chance to see him? Creepy, yes, but it made sense that fans might jump at the chance, especially if they wanted to hear the band's new songs.

And Davy had a plan to make it all happen. Had it been his plan to get rid of the ailing Bram all along?

Funny. Even though he had an alibi, Davy kept going to the top of my list of suspects. That one big motive—greed—reared its ugly head.

When I left, big fat snowflakes started falling from the sky. Praying I hadn't missed the last shuttle down the mountain, I was just about to turn the corner onto the main square when I heard footsteps.

My stomach knotted, and my breath caught in my throat.

I turned to see a shadow just beyond the lamppost. The person had stopped as well. It was the tall guy with the hoodie.

Crud.

I took off as fast as my Uggs could take me.

Chapter Thirteen

Thankfully, there were still people milling around the well-lit square. I stopped jogging when I reached the queue for the shuttle. I was out of breath, but at least I was near humanity.

I turned back to look at the street.

No one was there.

Someone touched my shoulder. I didn't scream, though I did flinch and raise my purse to whack whoever it was.

"Everything all right, Doc?" Ewan asked. "You were running."

"I—needed to catch the shuttle," I said. I felt foolish when I glanced back and no one was there.

Ewan gave me a look. It was the one he gave when he knew there was more to the story. He wouldn't let it go.

"Fine. I'd gone to check on Destinee, and when I was coming back . . ."

"What?"

"Someone was following me. When I stopped, they stopped. That sort of thing. That's why I was hurrying."

He glanced over my shoulder, and so did I. There was no one there.

"Might be someone in the media following you. We've got our hands full with all the new fans in town. Unless you can get one of your friends to go with you, I'd rather you not go off on your own. 'Tis not safe."

I shook my head. "I'm fine. Really. I mean, why would they be following me?"

"Information. Ill intent. Maybe they think you know something about the murder that hasn't been shared. You and I both know you do. Did you find out any other information while you were there?"

There were other people around who seemed to be quite interested in our conversation.

"Uh. Yes. But maybe we could chat later?"

He glanced around. "Right. Why don't I give you a lift home?"

"I don't want you to go out of your way. You can call me when you're done here."

"It's not out of my way. I was headed down to the pub. Mara says they have an unusually large crowd. I promised to check in."

"Okay." I followed him to his SUV.

Once we were inside the SUV, he turned the heater on full blast. He was kind that way.

"Tell me."

"First, I was surprised the whole band showed up at the event," I said.

"Davy called Mara about a half hour before it started," he said. "Told her they'd heard about it and wondered if they could be involved. Mara put it all together at the last minute."

"Do you think it was a publicity stunt to stop the rumors about Destinee?"

"Aye. There was a whole slew of new stories this evening about her and the band."

"I thought so too. They asked me not to say anything, but the band is still going on tour."

"What?" He seemed as surprised as I'd been.

"Yep. I guess they'd already recorded the new album, which is weird because I thought Bram was still writing songs for it. And we still haven't found his notebook. Where is it? I have this sneaking suspicion that the killer took it for some reason."

"Go back to the tour."

"So, they have technology, I guess, that they can use to layer in Bram's voice with Destinee and the others. According to Davy, they can even do that in a live performance."

He frowned. "I've seen it before when an artist dies and they're doing tributes, but I've never seen it on a tour."

I shrugged. "Davy said it would work."

"How did the others seem to feel about it?"

"Only Render and Destinee were there. He didn't seem to like the idea, and she thinks Davy is a creep for even coming up with the idea. I will say this: I know he has an alibi, but Davy is at the top of my list. He seems greedy.

"I mean, at the very least, he should give the band and the fans time to mourn. The tour starts at the end of January. I don't know the music world at all, but it feels wrong."

"I don't disagree. Do me a favor, Doc."

"What's that?"

"Don't open the door to strangers, and if you do need to go out alone, call one of your friends. Or call me."

"I thought you were my friend," I joked.

He laughed. "I am, but I know I'm usually last on the list."

"Only because you're so busy with your many jobs. But I hear you, and I've learned my lesson about asking for help."

"Well, now. 'Tis the season for miracles."

I rolled my eyes. "You're so funny."

"I have my moments. But if you felt like someone was following you, then you need to be careful."

"I didn't *feel* it. They were. When I stopped, they did. And when I hurried along, so did they. I was definitely being followed. However, I have no idea whether the person was a bad guy or someone from the media."

"Which is why I need you to be careful, Doc. Sometimes, as we found with the fellow who jumped the stone wall and scared Tommy, the media can also be the bad guys."

"True. But don't worry. Careful is my middle name."

He laughed hard. "Right. Now who is being funny?"

*　*　*

By the time Ewan dropped me off and walked me inside, it was near ten. Still, I was antsy.

After dumping my stuff, I went to my office so I could read Bram's scans on a bigger screen.

I read over everything again. His doctor had agreed with me. He'd been just as surprised by Bram's cognitive abilities given the severe progression of the disease.

It was a testament to the rocker's strength, and probably a lot of clean living. That said, he couldn't have had long mentally or physically. I'd talked about it with the inspector, but I'd forgotten to mention that to Ewan.

I sent him a quick message about what I'd found.

Still feeling anxious, I went in search of holiday decor. After checking some of the closets in the office, I headed back to the storeroom off the lab. I was just about to go through the secret bookcase door when there was a loud bang.

I jumped, then listened.

There was more banging against the door to the practice. I took out my phone and turned on the video so I could see who it was. The person was hunched over, but it very much looked liked Ewan.

The man was wearing the same jacket, though there was something all over it.

I ran for the door and unlocked it quickly.

When I opened it, Ewan staggered inside like he was drunk. He was covered in blood.

"What happened?"

His eyes were unfocused, and he was so pale.

"Ewan, can you hear me?"

"I—hit me from behind," he said. Then he tilted to the left and hit the floor.

"Ewan!"

Chapter Fourteen

Ewan was much too large for me to even try and carry. After making sure he was still breathing, I gathered towels, blankets, and my kit. I was able to roll him so I could check the back of his head. I cleaned the blood off quickly. He had a goose egg, and a thumb sized gash, which was what had caused all the blood.

I desperately needed to get an MRI. After stemming the bleeding, I called Abigail.

"I'm sorry to bother you so late, but Ewan's been hurt."

"I'm on my way. Tell me what you need."

"Someone strong enough to help me get him off the floor, and we need to run an MRI. He was hit on the head pretty hard."

"I'll need to bring Tommy."

"That's fine. Maybe he can help us get him off the floor."

"We'll be there in five minutes."

I wasn't sure how that was possible since they lived about ten minutes up the mountain, but two minutes later, someone banged on my door.

"Doc, it's Henry."

I got off the floor and opened the door. When I did, a blustery wind blew inside. Snow had been falling. It hadn't been windy when Ewan brought me home, but that was Scotland.

"Abigail called. What happened?"

"About a half hour after he dropped me off, he showed up on my doorstep like this. He said someone hit him from behind, and then he passed out. He has a head wound, and I need to get him on a gurney so we can wheel him back to the lab and get an MRI."

I ran for the gurney. It was quicker than explaining where to find it.

There was more banging on the door, and Henry hopped up off the floor to open it for Ewan's men. Thank God Abigail thought to call Henry.

Working together, we were able to get him up on a gurney. As we wheeled him back, Abigail and Tommy came in through the front door.

"Tommy, go play your game in Doc's snug," Abigail ordered

"Is Ewan going to be okay?" he asked. He didn't look directly at me, but I knew I was the one he was asking.

"Yes, but I need to borrow your sister for a bit."

"I will play my game. Fix him, please."

"That's the plan, I promise, Tommy."

He left then with his gaming system in his hands.

Rushing ahead, Abigail opened the secret doors, which were the bookshelves that made the hallway look like it was the end of the room. There was another long hallway that led to a medical facility that was better equipped than most small hospitals in the States. There were recovery rooms, and I had the ability to do MRIs, CAT scans, and X-rays. I had everything I might need in an emergency. Ewan had outfitted the practice so that if any of the passes were closed into the cities with larger hospitals, we could treat patients with top-quality care.

All of this had been quite a surprise when I'd arrived five months ago, but having a facility like this in my office had come in handy more than once, including when Abigail used it to save my life.

"Henry, while we get set up, I need you and your men to get Ewan into this gown."

He frowned. "He won't like that."

"I'm trying to see if there is swelling on his brain. If he were conscious, it wouldn't be necessary, but he isn't."

"Do what she wants, Henry. We don't have time to argue." Abigail's orders seemed to get through to him.

"He can't have any sort of metal on him," I added. "That's why he has to wear the gown."

Ewan was his boss and a very proud man. I understood his hesitation. Still, they had him undressed in a few minutes.

While Abigail calibrated the machine from the other side of the windowed wall, I cleaned the head wound again, and butterflied the gash. I didn't want to risk sewing it up quite yet in case there was more swelling.

"Ready," Abigail said.

"Everyone out," I ordered. I followed them out.

"You guys head to reception," I said. "Feel free to make some coffee or tea in my kitchen or at the coffee bar in reception. I'll let you know when we're done. Oh, and Henry, keep an eye on Tommy."

"I will," he said. "And I've got this lot. You focus on the boss."

"Will do."

I went into the side room where Abigail had booted up the computers. She dabbed her eyes, then blew her nose.

"Are you okay?"

"Aye," she said. "I just had a moment. It's strange to see him like this. He's so strong and takes care of us all."

Ewan was pale and very still. She was right. He was so strong and virile. I didn't use that word very often, but it fit him. He was the strength of Sea Isle, and whether we wanted to admit it or not, we all relied on him.

She pushed a button, and Ewan gently slid into the machine. I watched the screens as it scanned his brain. Ten minutes later, the news wasn't good.

"We need to do ventriculostomy," I said.

"Do you want to try the hospital?"

I shook my head. "I've done them many times before, and I don't want to take the time. The faster we get the fluid off his brain, the better his chances of avoiding any sort of permanent damage."

"Tell me what you need."

*   *   *

Fifteen minutes later, we had him prepped for surgery. I gave him anesthesia to keep him from waking up during the procedure.

"What's that for?" Henry asked. He'd scrubbed in with me and Abigail to help.

"We don't want him waking up while I've got a needle in his brain," I said.

He blanched. "Okay."

"I'm grateful you helped us get him ready, but you can wait outside with the others if you want. Abigail and I can handle it from here."

"I will not bother you again," he said. "But I'm staying."

I smiled. Henry was a great guy, and he was perfect for Abigail. I wasn't certain she'd quite clued in to exactly how perfect. He was patient and kind, two things she and Tommy desperately needed. And he was thoroughly in love with her, which was really the best thing about him.

"See that you don't," Abigail said sharply. "The doctor has enough to do without you nattering on and asking questions."

"Abigail." I shook my head.

She sighed.

"Sorry, Henry. I'm worried, and when that happens, I get cross. But we need to focus, okay?"

"Aye." He nodded, but it was obvious she'd hurt his feelings.

"Also, the needle I'm using is long, and that might be slightly disturbing to see. It's not an easy thing to watch."

"I'll stay," he said. "Just in case. But I'll be staring at my feet unless you need me. I'm not a big fan of needles of any sorts."

After rereading the scans, I took a deep breath. It was a fairly straightforward procedure, and I had done it many times, as I had told Abigail. But it didn't come without dangers. One wrong move, and there could be permanent damage.

I took a deep breath.

"Let's do this."

*　　*　　*

Twenty minutes later, I was done.

Henry was still staring at his feet.

"I'm finished," I said. "I just need to clean him up a bit more, and we can put him in one of the recovery rooms. We might want to transport him to one of the bigger hospitals now that the immediate danger is over."

"We cannot," Henry said. "A storm has rolled in. Passes are closed, and it's too windy to take the helicopter. I checked before you started."

I nodded. "That's fine. We can take care of him here. Once the anesthesia wears off, he should wake up."

Then we would know if there had been any damage. I didn't say that out loud, though. The pair of them were worried enough. Besides, Ewan was tough.

And hardheaded.

"We'll help," Henry said.

"I appreciate that, but why don't you all go home and get some rest?" I glanced at my watch. It was nearly three in the morning. I hadn't realized so much time had passed. "That is, after you help me load him into one of the recovery beds."

They helped me make him comfortable.

"You can go, I've got it from here," I said.

"No," Henry said. "None of us will be leaving until he wakes up and we know he's okay."

"I'm going to clean up the surgical suite," Abigail said.

"I can do that. You take Tommy home. I'm sure you're exhausted."

She shrugged. "He's probably asleep on the couch, and I'm too worried to rest."

I sighed. "Look, I appreciate your loyalty, and I know Ewan will as well, but it doesn't help anyone if everyone is exhausted. Henry, you have to protect the town. Start by trying to find out who whacked Ewan in the head."

He frowned. "I hadn't even thought—you are right. We should have already been investigating. He'll be angry that we didn't."

"Exactly. I'm grateful for your help. Take your men with you and rest up. For the next week or so, Ewan will need help. And you know him. He's not going to ask for it or want it."

Henry grinned and a bit of color came into his face.

"You know our constable well."

"I do. Abigail, I'll clean up and take the first watch, but I'll need you to rest so you can take the second. Okay? If you want to stay here, just sleep in my room or the guest room. Or put Tommy in there and take the couch."

She nodded.

It took another ten minutes to convince them to go, and then I quite literally shoved them out the door.

After cleaning up the surgical suite, I changed out of my scrubs. While the old stone building had great heaters, it was still chilly back here. We had to keep the equipment at a specific temperature.

I put on some sweats we normally kept for patients, and warm socks. After putting a cold wrap around his head, I checked his vitals again. Everything was fine. Even the goose egg on his head had gone down.

I sat down in the chair next to his bed with my laptop. I typed in my notes from the surgery.

I glanced up at Ewan. He seemed so peaceful. My heart lurched. Even though we more often than not butted heads, he was my friend.

More than that though, he was the reason I was here. He'd been the one to recruit me to Sea Isle with the help of Mr. and Mrs. Wilson. He was the one who had looked after me and made certain I had everything I needed. When I'd been hurt doing my first investigation, he'd moved heaven and earth to keep me alive.

I had a wonderful new life surrounded by people I loved and who loved me back. And it had all happened in such a short amount of time. Sea Isle had been the home my orphaned heart had always searched for, but I hadn't known that until I arrived.

I owed him so much.

He mumbled something.

"Ewan? Can you hear me?"

His eyes fluttered open, and then he winced.

"Bloody hell," he whispered hoarsely. "What have you done to me?"

I smiled. He really was going to be okay.

"How do you feel?"

"Like someone smashed my head with a cricket bat."

"I'm not sure if that was the weapon they used," I said, "but you aren't wrong. You were hit in the head by someone and stumbled into my office. There were wood shavings, so it could have been a cricket bat. Unfortunately, there was fluid on your brain, so I had to drain it off."

"I don't remember any of that."

"Do you have any idea who hit you?"

He tried to shake his head and winced.

"It's best if you don't move too much right now. We need to give that big brain of yours a chance to heal."

He reached an unsteady hand up and touched his head. We'd bandaged most of it. Although we'd only made a small puncture, I'd had to shave a small patch for the incision, and it was best we kept it clean.

"Don't worry. Even with your head shaved, you're still handsome."

He gave me a lopsided grin. "You think I'm handsome?"

I rolled my eyes, then handed him a cup and straw so he could sip some water.

Then he tried to sit up, and I gently pushed him back down.

"Unless you want to cause irreparable brain damage, you'll stay still for the next twenty-four hours. And take it easy for the next week."

His eyes went wide. "I can't take a week off. We have an investigation, and the boss is already trying to replace me."

"They would never do that. You'll do what I say, or I'll make them transfer you to Edinburgh and force you to stay in a hospital room."

"You can't do that," he grumbled.

"Oh, I can, and I will. You have one of the hardest heads of any man I've ever met. But you were seriously injured tonight. This town needs you to get well, so you will follow my orders."

He sighed. "Why are you always so bossy?"

I laughed. "I come by it naturally."

"I need to call Henry."

"He and your men already know what's happening. They were here, along with Abigail. They helped me look after you."

"They're a good lot."

"Yes. And they've got everything covered."

He frowned. He was strong and proud, and this wasn't easy for him. But I'd dealt with patients like him before.

"Think of it this way. The more you follow my orders, the faster you'll recover. Then you can get out there and do your thing."

He just stared at me. "Fine."

"What were you doing right before you were hit?"

"I'd been checking on the pub and making sure everything was all right. I'd left my car in front of your building, so I was headed back up here. And then everything—I don't remember anything."

"Do you remember showing up at my door?"

"No. The last thing I recall is leaving the pub."

That wasn't unusual. Short-term amnesia after a blow like that was more common than people believed.

"Seems we may have stirred the pot a little more than we thought when it comes to the investigation. Maybe I'm not the only one who needs to be careful," I said.

"You may be right about that, Doc. Are you thinking it has something to do with the current case and not someone else who wants me dead?"

I shook my head. "I think if they truly wanted you dead, you would be. Be grateful that didn't happen. But maybe they think you saw something on your way up, or someone."

He crinkled his brow. "I cannae remember anything after the pub."

"It will come to you." Or it wouldn't. The memory was never an exact science.

"Maybe your attack is unrelated, but we need to find our killer before they hurt anyone else."

"True words, Doc. True words."

Chapter Fifteen

After a few hours' sleep, I was feeling better about life. We did another scan of Ewan's head, and it was amazing how fast he'd already healed. Thankfully, the swelling was completely gone and there was no permanent damage.

I declared him fit enough to head home, though I insisted he take it easy the next few days. I also warned him not to bump his head.

Not long after Henry took him home, the detective inspector showed up at my door.

"One of the men at the station said Ewan was attacked last night."

"Yes, and it was quite serious. He could have died."

She frowned. "Is he here? I'd like to speak with him."

"I sent him home. He needs to rest. I'll tell you what I can, within the confines of doctor-patient privilege. But first, I need some coffee, and we can make you some tea."

"That sounds good," she said as she followed me into the kitchen.

I was surprised to find a note from Mara when we reached the kitchen: *Full Scottish warming in the hob. And some cranberry scones.*

I was lucky to have her as a friend. She was always looking out for me.

"It seems Mara has left me some breakfast. Would you like half of it?"

She shook her head. "I ate a few hours ago, but you go on. I'm sure you were up half the night."

"We were up *all* night," I said. I glanced at the clock above the door. It was about ten thirty in the morning. "Do you mind if I eat while we chat? Mara did leave some scones as well."

"Not at all," she said.

After making coffee and tea, I put the plates of food on the table. "What is it you'd like to know, Inspector?"

She took a piece of paper out of her messenger bag. "Just so you are aware, I have a warrant for all medical files pertaining to the case. That includes anything to do with Destinee."

I nodded. "Okay. I can put those together for you. What else do you need?"

"Do you believe what happened to the constable is related to the case?"

I put my fork down. "I don't know, but it's possible," I said. "I know your lot likes facts, but my gut says yes. There was someone following me from the B and B last night. I didn't get a good look at him because he was in the shadows."

She took out her notebook and a pen. "Can you give me any other details?"

"He was wearing a hooded coat, so I couldn't see his face. Kind of like the guy I saw the other night at the tree lighting. He was tall, though. If he hadn't stopped walking when I did, I wouldn't have thought much about it. But sometimes you get a sense for that sort of thing, and he was definitely following me. When I made it to the square where there were others around, I looked back, and he was gone. He didn't want to be seen."

"I'm going to recommend you travel with a companion until we get this case sorted," she said.

"Ewan mentioned that as well," I said.

"I'll be speaking to him later."

I sighed. "Maybe tomorrow. He really needs to get some rest."

"Can you give me some idea of what happened? At the very least, can you confirm he was bludgeoned from behind? That's what his men told me. And that he had swelling on the brain, and you had to perform a very delicate operation to relieve the pressure."

"Yes, all of that is true."

"Did he see who did it?"

"No. After he took me home last night, he left his SUV in front of the practice. Mara had needed his help with something at the pub. He was headed back up the hill when someone hit him."

"Do you have any idea what they hit him with?"

"No. He said a cricket bat, but I don't know. There were some wooden fragments in the wound. I have those in evidence. He was hit hard enough to make a small gash. He was lucky it wasn't worse." I frowned.

"What is it?"

"Spatially, the person would have to be fairly tall to hit him on the top and back of his head." I pointed to my skull. "The angle was odd."

"Just like the odd angle with the corkscrew."

I nodded. "But why? Why would someone risk attacking Ewan? Why would they be following me? It doesn't make sense. And who carries around a cricket bat?"

She shook her head. "There are so many things about this case that don't make sense. I read about some of the other cases you've worked on with the constable, and I was curious if you had any ideas about who might be behind all of this."

I finished the bite of egg I'd taken.

"I know we talked about this, but I find it odd that the band didn't know about the seriousness of Bram's condition. I don't think they're telling the truth because from what I saw on the scans and what they told me about the situation, it seems like they knew something was off."

"Do you think one of them is behind his murder?"

I smirked. "I keep asking myself the same thing over and over. There is a serious lack of clues when it comes to this case. I don't know. They are all hiding something. But then . . ."

"What?"

"I spoke with him and saw him perform. He was charming, and I saw no sign of the degenerative disease he had. I've read studies where patients who had a specific job continued to work for some time. They only exhibited symptoms when they were outside of their norm. But those cases were few and far between."

"Like some sort of muscle memory?"

"Yes. But I have no explanation as to how he was able to function at such a high level for so long. Medically, it shouldn't have been possible."

She thumbed through her notebook. "The band talked about his erratic behavior and said that he'd forget lyrics."

"Still," I said. "Do you have any ideas who might have killed him? Please tell me that you've taken Ewan off the list. I'm fairly certain he didn't hit himself on the head."

She smiled. "I'm keeping an open mind," she said. "I plan on speaking with the one they call Render in a bit. I have permission from the solicitors. He's been staying with his mother."

"Would it be okay if I come with you?"

She pulled a face.

"Please? I only had a chance to speak with him for a few minutes the other day. I'm trying to work up a full study of Bram's behavior before he died. And I'd like to get more medical history. From what I understand, they were great friends their whole lives. The more I know about Bram, the better I can do my job."

"I guess that would be all right." She didn't look happy about it, though.

I smiled. There might be hope for the inspector yet.

* * *

An hour later, we were in a part of Sea Isle I'd never been in before. The snowfall became heavier the farther up the mountain we went, and I was grateful Bethany had been the one driving. We were out past Ewan's estate on a rural farm that was filled with fuzzy sheep and an animal I didn't recognize.

They were furry, and several of them had a huge rack of horns. They didn't seem to mind the cold at all. They were munching on hedges along a fence line.

"Are those goats?"

"Aye," she said. "Some call them Scottish goats, others mountain goats."

"They have such long hair."

"I don't know much about them, but they are common in the highland areas."

We pulled up in front of a stone cottage that appeared to have been built on to through the years. There was a huge barn just behind it that was painted a dark green. With the snow falling and the multicolored lights in the window, it could have made a charming holiday card.

While the inspector knocked on the door, I looked around at the farm. There was a big tractor under a shed and several outbuildings past the barn, and it was all kept quite neat and orderly.

There were some fuzzy cows in a big corral whose fluffiness rivaled the sheep we'd seen in the field when coming up the road. It was obviously a working farm.

A young boy answered the door. I recognized Roddy from the early flu epidemic we'd had in November. He was one of my patients.

"Hi, Roddy," I said. I hadn't made the connection earlier, but Render must have been the big brother Roddy had talked about nonstop when he'd been so feverish. He'd mentioned his brother was in a band.

He looked around the inspector to me. "Doctor? Is someone sick?"

"No. Everyone is fine. I came with the inspector. She needs to speak with Render. Is he here?"

"Ma," he yelled. "The police and the doctor are here for Hamish."

Hamish must have been Render's real name.

Mrs. Lachlan came around the corner wiping her hands on an apron.

"Doctor, is everything okay?"

I smiled. "Yes. We were just trying to find Render, I mean, Hamish. The inspector needs to speak with him."

She gave the inspector a suspicious look. "What about?"

"I have inquiries about a death. I have permission from the band's solicitors to speak with him."

Mrs. Lachlan frowned. "My poor Bram. My heart hurts just thinking about him. He was supposed to spend Christmas with us. Did ya know that?" She spoke to me and completely ignored the inspector. While the people in Sea Isle were as friendly as they came, they didn't warm up easily to people poking around in their business.

"Hamish did mention that," I said. "I'm so sorry for your loss."

"Thank you, lass. I'm making some cheese, and I really can't stop. Follow me to the kitchen. Roddy, go wake your brother. Even when they aren't touring, he keeps those off hours and sleeps until noon."

"Yes, Mum." Roddy took off.

The kitchen was warm, and I slid off my coat, hat, and gloves. She showed us to a table near a window that overlooked the pasture where the cows were located.

"Would you like some tea or coffee?"

"I'm fine," the inspector said.

"Doctor?"

"I'm fine as well. Your farm is quite beautiful."

She smiled. "It keeps us going and gives us a living, though most of that is because of my Hamish. When the band first hit it big, he invested in the farm and hired help for me. I'm not sure what I would have done without him."

"Least I could do, Mum," Hamish said as he came into the kitchen looking a bit disheveled. He wore beat-up jeans and a cozy sweater. He went to the coffeepot and poured himself a big cup. "You've taken great care of all of us and every other lad or lass who needed a home around here. And it wasn't just me. Bram helped as well."

His mother was pouring something through cheese cloth. "That he did," she said. "He was a good boy. You both are."

Hamish threw an arm around her shoulders and kissed the top of her head. Their relationship was sweet and caring.

My relationship with my mom had been difficult. She hadn't been around much when I was a kid. But a few years before she died, we reconnected. I was grateful for that time with her, even though it wasn't always easy.

"We had a good role model," he said.

Then he turned to us. He frowned when he noticed the inspector.

"I gave my statement to Ewan," he said, "and we were told not to talk to you without the solicitors."

"Right," she said. "But I have some follow-up questions and permission from the solicitors. We can call them if you like. We can go to the station if you'd prefer privacy." There was an edge to her voice that hinted at a threat. Even I, with my lack of experience, knew that wasn't the way to play this.

"Do I need to call our personal solicitor?" Mrs. Lachlan asked. "I'll not have you going around accusing my boy of doing harm." She was angry.

"I'm not accusing anyone of . . ." The inspector appeared flustered. For such an important job, her people skills needed a bit of work.

I cleared my throat. "We're here more for me," I said.

The inspector shot me a look.

"I need more background on Bram's health. And I think the inspector was just trying to make Hamish comfortable," I said.

137

"Like, maybe he doesn't want to talk about his rock star ways in front of his mom."

Mother and son looked at each other and burst out laughing.

"We have no secrets," he said. "I tell her everything."

"Even things no mother wants to hear," she added.

"I didn't mean to offend you," the inspector said quickly. "I just want you to be comfortable, Mr. Lachlan. I, uh, thought since the doc needed a ride out here, I'd gather some background as well. Nothing too difficult or intrusive, I promise. And I did get permission for follow-up questions that were first presented to your solicitors."

He eyed her warily and then shrugged. "Mr. Lachlan was my dear departed Da. You can call me Render or Hamish, though I prefer Hamish."

"As do I," his mother said. He grinned at her.

"What is it you need to know?" he asked.

"Can you tell me the last time you saw the deceased?"

He sighed and sat down across from us at the worn wooden table. "Everyone went to Mrs. Beatty's after the pub," he said. "I headed home a half hour or so later. I knew Mum would be waiting up, and she has early chores here on the farm. I guess they carried on for a bit."

"Do you usually separate from the group?" she asked.

"I don't know what you mean," he said.

"You weren't staying at the B and B with them."

"Aye, because Mum would have my head if I didn't stay at home. She wasn't happy that Bram wasn't here with us. Maybe if he had been, then he wouldn't have been hurt. Usually, if we come home, we're here. Even him."

"I like having my boys here, especially during the holidays. And as far as I'm concerned, Bram was one of mine."

"Did he explain why he wanted to stay at the B and B?" I asked.

The inspector gave me a look. I might have forgotten this was her investigation.

"Since he was in town for the month, he didn't want to be an imposition to Mum," he said.

"As if," his mother said. "He's like a son. He would have been no bother."

"I think he also needed some peace and quiet, which isn't always possible here," he said. "Sorry, Mum, but it's true. He would have felt like he needed to do chores and hang out with us. He hadn't been feeling that great, and I think he wanted to just get away and rest before the big tour."

"Did he say anything to you before you parted ways?" the inspector asked.

"Just that he'd see me the next day. He was going to come and see Mum and Roddy. The rest of the band was supposed to be heading home for the holidays. But like I said, he was going to spend them with us."

"In the days leading up to his death, did he say anything about someone who might be threatening him?" she asked. "Did he exhibit any abnormal behavior?"

"Like I told the doc and Ewan, he hadn't been himself the last several months. His temper had been shorter than normal. He'd been edgy. But sometimes, when he was working on new stuff, that was the way."

"Would you say you were the closest to him?" she asked.

He shrugged. "I've known him longer, and he was more like family than the others."

"He was family," his mother said.

"True. I considered him a brother. We've been through just about everything together. To answer your other question, other than his stalkers, and he had a few, I don't know about any sort of threats."

She asked him a few more questions and then said we'd be leaving. Since the trek down the mountain would take a half hour, I asked if I could use the lavatory.

Mrs. Lachlan pointed down a long hallway to the last door.

As I was passing the various rooms, I glanced into what I thought might be Hamish's room. His guitar was in an open case in the corner. There were posters of The Cure on the walls. But it was the notebook on the wooden nightstand that caught my eye.

I glanced back down the hall to see if anyone was watching, then I went inside. The notebook was much like the one that had been described by the rest of the band. I picked it up.

I opened it and stared down at the disjointed writing. There were some complete sentences, but most of it was a jumble of words. The handwriting became progressively worse as it went along.

About halfway through the book, the handwriting was distinctly different. The words made sense, and the song lyrics were beautiful. I recognized a song as one they'd played that night at the pub.

This had to be Bram's notebook, but what was it doing here? The rest of the band said he'd had the notebook with him that night. But it hadn't been on the body. How did Hamish get it? Everyone had said Bram had the notebook when they went upstairs, and Hamish had been long gone by then.

There were footsteps out in the hallway, and I slid the notebook into my coat pocket. But before I could get to the doorway, Hamish appeared.

He glanced at the nightstand and then at me.

"What are you doing?" he asked angrily.

Chapter Sixteen

I straightened my shoulders and lifted my chin. "I could ask you the same question. You need to explain to me why you have Bram's notebook. The rest of the band saw him with it the night he died. You also keep saying you left long before they all went upstairs."

He glanced back down the hallway, then stepped inside. When he shut the door, I held my breath. Surely, he wouldn't kill me with the inspector just down the hall.

"I took it the next day," he said.

"From where? No one has been able to find it, and it wasn't on Bram's body."

His shoulders sagged.

"He'd stuck it in the bookcase in the lounge at Mrs. Beatty's. I saw it when I went to check on everyone."

"There are hundreds of books in there. How could you have known?"

He sighed. "Because I've been helping him," he said. He moved to sit on the edge of the bed. Then he put his head in his hands. "His mind . . . well, I'm sure you've seen his records. He was having a difficult time with everything. He wrote things down in the notebook, and then he'd talk about what he'd been thinking.

"I'd take the notes and write the songs for him. I was just helping him out."

I frowned. "Why keep it a secret that you were writing with him? Don't you want the credit?"

He shook his head. "You don't get it. No. I don't need credit. They are his ideas. He just couldn't write them down like he used to. I took the phrases and ideas and worked them up. Then we'd go over them and write the music for the band. But it was all him."

I had doubts about that.

"Why not tell us all that to begin with?"

"He did not want people to know about his condition," he said. "Not even the band. It was between us. This was his last . . . I wanted him to have all the glory he deserved. I was doing everything I could to keep him going. No one knows how hard we were trying to keep that secret, but we were making it work. "

Something clicked in my head. Render had been mouthing the words to the songs when he'd been playing that night at the pub. He often had his head down, but I'd noticed it during one of the ballads. I thought maybe he was doing it to keep time to the music.

"Were you singing in his ear that night at the pub?"

He went past me and sat on the edge of the bed. "You noticed?"

"It didn't click until just now."

"We had earpieces. He'd give me a hand signal if he couldn't think of something, and I'd whisper the words. We'd planned on using prompters on the tour. Lots of bands and artists use them these days. When you play as many songs as we do, it would be easy for anyone to forget."

"I don't understand why he wasn't just honest with everyone from the beginning," I said. "You all could have helped him."

"Bram wanted this last big tour for all of us. We're his family, and he wanted to go out in style. But someone took that from him."

He grimaced and looked like he might be tearing up.

I crossed my arms. "I saw his medical records," I said. "And his scans. He would have never made it, no matter how much you helped him. He had maybe a month, if that. He lasted longer than anyone I've ever seen with his condition."

Hamish rubbed his face with his hands. His eyes were rimmed red. "I knew it was bad, but . . . that night at the pub. I only had to help him with a few of the lyrics. I thought maybe it wasn't as bad as he thought. He'd really pulled it together for that performance. I thought maybe that live audience might be the thing that kept him going."

"But you'd seen his notebook and his writing, Hamish. You had to know his mind wasn't quite right anymore."

"I think when you love someone, you don't necessarily want to see the truth."

I understood that more than most. I'd gone through a situation where I hadn't wanted to accept or know the truth about my husband, who had been cheating on me. It was as if everything I'd known about him was a lie. It had nearly destroyed me.

But this was different.

"Hamish, I need to know if you have any idea who might have hurt him."

His shoulders sagged again, and he lifted his head. "I've no idea. I'll be honest, when I first heard he was dead, I assumed he killed himself. He'd talked about that a couple of times. When the time came, he didn't want to be a burden to anyone. I kept telling him it was nonsense and that I would always have his back. Mum and I would have taken care of him until the end. But he was a proud man."

I could imagine.

There was a knock on the door, and I may have jumped.

"The inspector is looking for the doctor," Roddy said.

"I'll be right there," I said.

"The notebook is evidence," I said. "I'm going to have to keep it, though I won't give it to the inspector right away or tell her where I found it for now." I'm not sure why I said that. It wasn't like me to withhold evidence, but I believed Hamish.

"Thank you. But I wasn't finished working on the songs. I know the writing doesn't make sense to most people, but since we talked about what he wanted to do, it does to me."

"I'll take pictures of it for you and print them out. Come by the office later in the week."

He nodded.

I said my goodbyes and then climbed into the inspector's car. The snow was thicker than it had been earlier. Again, I was grateful she was the one driving.

"Is everything okay?" she asked.

I nodded. I didn't like the idea of keeping evidence from her, but I wanted to talk to Ewan first. Nothing against the inspector, but I didn't trust she'd give poor Hamish the benefit of the doubt. She was determined to pin the murder on someone fast. I believed him, though. It had been his voice and the terrible grief I recognized there. He'd been heartbroken by his friend's death.

He'd loved Bram and had been doing everything in his power to help him get through the tour. That, and he hadn't wanted any credit for those songs. I'd seen what Bram wrote, and I didn't care how much the singer had explained to Hamish, he'd done wonders with those lyrics.

"You seem quiet," she said.

I laughed. "I was trying not to bug you while you drive in his mess."

"I'm used to it," she said. "Snow doesn't bother me."

"What did you think about Hamish?"

"I like his mum," she said. "She's a hard worker and she cares about her children and the rest of the kids in Sea Isle. She reminded me of my mum."

"Oh?"

She nodded. "Until she died, she was always taking in wayward souls. Our house sometimes felt like a youth hostel."

I grinned. "What did she do for a living?"

"Oh, she came by that naturally. She was a social worker. Not a better soul in the world. I miss her every day, especially this time of year. She loved the holidays."

"I'm sorry for your loss."

"And how about you, Doctor? Does your family in the States miss you?"

I cleared my throat. "I don't have anyone left," I said. "When my dad died, my mom had a tough time, so I went to live with my grandmother. When she died, I went into foster care and ended up with a great family. But now, they are gone as well."

"Did your mum ever come back?" She turned the corner by what I thought was Ewan's estate. It was hard to see the big mansion with the blinding snow, but I recognized some of the workers' cottages on the edge of the property.

"She did. And we were lucky enough to have some time together before she passed."

"I'm sorry. I seem to be asking all the wrong questions. I didn't mean to be so nosy. I guess it comes with the job."

"It's okay."

"I'm just curious how an American doctor ended up in Nowhere, Scotland."

I chuckled. "I was recruited. And I was looking for a big change. This is about as far from head of the ER at my old hospital as I could get. And while I haven't done as much research as I would like, my father's family came from this area, so it felt like I had ties to the place."

I'd meant to go down the genealogy path in a big way, but between my practice and my other commitments, I still hadn't done as much research as I would like. The town historian had found some documents about my ancestors, the McRaes. The name had changed to McRoy when some of them moved to the States.

But there were thousands of different lines of McRaes and a lot to sort through. It was one of my projects for this holiday. Well, before the murder.

The inspector's phone buzzed, and she pushed the button on the dashboard.

The voice was crackling because of a bad connection this high up on the mountain.

"What? I can't hear you," she said.

"Missing," came across. I thought it might be Henry, but it was hard to say.

"Who is missing?"

The line went dead.

"Do you mind if we stop by the station before I take you back down the mountain?"

"Not at all. If someone is missing, they may need medical attention."

But who could it be?

Chapter Seventeen

The stone building that housed the police station was several hundred years old. Even though I worked with Ewan on cases, I'd never actually been inside. The computers and monitors on the walls were juxtaposed with the medieval architecture, and the old building was surprisingly bright.

There was no reception desk. It was just a large room with several desks near the lobby area, which was situated with soft and comfortable sofas.

Henry was on the phone but waved to me when I walked in with the inspector.

"You were cutting out. Who is missing?" Bethany asked. Her tone was brusque, but I had a feeling that was just who she was.

"The band's manager, Davy, and Destinee," Ewan said from behind us. He wore a knit cap over the bandages on his head, but the white peaked through some of the edges. He was also much paler than normal.

"You should be in bed," I said. "In fact, I remember telling you to stay there for a week."

"I'm fine, and we are on a high weather alert. We need everyone we can get."

"You'll be no good to anyone if you pass out from the pain."

He frowned at me. "We also have two people missing. I dinnae have time to argue with you, Doc."

"Maybe they're just in town or down on the sea walk," I said. "How do you know they're missing?"

"Exactly what I was going to ask," the inspector said. Then she gave me side-eye. I always seemed to be stepping on her toes, but it wasn't on purpose. I'm just a naturally curious person.

"Liam, the drummer, reported them missing an hour ago," Henry said. "Says he hasn't seen them since late last night. The manager had rented a car, but it isn't at the B and B, and I have the agency who rented it out tracking it by satellite."

"My people can probably do it faster if you give me the information," the inspector said.

Henry handed her a printout, and she walked away.

"At the very least, you should sit down," I said to Ewan.

"Doc, I meant it. I'm fine."

"You'll sit, or I'll make Henry take you home. My orders."

Henry looked from Ewan to me, then pretended to go through a pile of papers on his desk. Poor guy. The last thing he wanted to do was get between Ewan and me. There probably weren't two people in all of Sea Isle more hardheaded than the pair of us.

"Fine. Follow me." I was surprised when he took a seat at one of the desks in the same room with his men. I'd assumed he'd at least have his own office.

"What do we know so far?" he asked Henry.

"The last time Liam or Mrs. Beatty saw the manager was around six last night. He'd headed down to the pub. Neither of them remembers him coming back. This morning, when Liam went to check on Destinee, she was gone. All her things were packed up, and the room was empty.

"He went to ask the manager where she was, and Davy's things were gone as well. We assume they headed back to Edinburgh. However, we had the police there check, and neither of them are at their homes. We've put out a bulletin for the car. On their end, they're checking hotels and hospitals."

"Good job," Ewan said. "The roads aren't passable in some areas, so maybe they were held up somewhere along the way."

"Yes, sir. I've got men out, but it's slow going. The weather isn't helping. The winds and the heavy snowfall are making it difficult."

Carl, one of his men, waved a hand. "Sir, we've found the vehicle." He was on the phone.

"Ten miles north. We have injuries. They're being transported to the doc's place now. Looks like we may have a fatality as well."

Ewan sighed. "Tell them to preserve the scene. Was it a crash?"

"Don't know, sir. Colson has put the victims in his lorry. He's headed to the doc's now. Looks like they tried to go through one of the highland passes, though, since the roads were blocked."

"I need to be prepared for whatever is coming," I said.

"Come on, Doc," Ewan said. He took his keys out of his pocket.

"I'll drive," I said.

"In this weather?" he asked.

"I'll drive," said the inspector.

"Fine," he said. Then he handed her the keys.

I was surprised when he didn't argue with her. The snow was heavy, and the wind was wild. It took about twenty minutes to make the five-minute drive down the mountain because we had to go so slowly.

No one spoke in the car, as it was obvious the inspector needed all her concentration to stay on the road. When she pulled up in front of my practice, I jumped out. After unlocking the door, I ushered Bethany and Ewan inside.

"I don't know what I'm preparing for, but I'm sure they'll need warmth," I said as I shivered. I loved living in an old church that was over four hundred years old, but sometimes it was a bit chilly indoors.

"I'll see to the heat," Ewan said. He went off toward the boiler.

"Tell me what I can do to help," said the inspector.

"There's a med supply storage just around the corner. Gather all the blankets and heating pads you can find."

I went to get the exam rooms ready when I heard someone at the back of the house.

"Who is that?" the inspector asked as I came into the hall.

"I don't know," I said. Picking up the bat I left behind the door that separated the practice from my living quarters, I moved forward. But the inspector tugged on my arm.

"Stay behind me," she said as she pulled her baton from her coat and extended it. Part of me wanted to run and get Ewan, but the last thing he needed was to be injured again.

Together, we peeked around the corner. There was Abigail making tea and setting out food on the long counter next to the hob.

"What are you doing?" the inspector asked sharply.

Abigail screamed and dropped the kettle on the hob. I don't know why, but when she screamed, so did I, and the large bat clattered to the floor.

"Bloody hell, what's going on?" Ewan roared as he came running.

"Why is everyone yelling?" Abigail asked. She breathed heavily, and her hand was on her chest.

I gently pushed the inspector to the side. "We didn't know anyone else was here, and you scared us," I said.

She frowned. "Sorry, Doc. Tommy wanted to move some of the plants to the greenhouse, so I decided to clean while I was here. Then Henry called and said there was an emergency, and I set about making tea for the patients and workers."

"That was kind of you," I said. "I worry about Tommy being out in the snow, though."

"He's not. I helped him get the plants into the greenhouse. He's in there, and he's warm. The heaters Ewan helped him install make it quite comfortable even on a day like today. It's warmer than our home. We're having trouble with the boiler again."

Ewan came in and started making himself a cup of coffee. "I'll have that looked at," he said. "You should have told me."

"I can handle my own home repairs, and we're on the list. The repairman is just busy this time of year."

Ewan turned and raised his eyebrows. "I have a personal staff who can take care of those things. Your home is on my estate. You know what that means." He sounded more like a big brother than a landlord, and it was everything I could do not to smile. He was quite protective of Abigail and Tommy.

"Right, well, for now you can just stay here with me," I said. "I'm still not used to these *occasional* blizzards you get." Everyone in town kept telling me that while it was quite often cold and damp in the winter months, they really didn't get that much snow. But in the last few months, there had been two blizzards, and it had snowed at least twice a week.

Their idea of what constituted a lot of snow and mine were two different things.

"I was just about to make some sandwiches. Any idea when the team will make it here?" Abigail asked.

"They are about a quarter of an hour out," Ewan said. "The plows are trying to clear the road for them, but it is slow."

"Any news on how Destinee and Davy are doing?" I asked.

"They had to sedate her," he said. "She was manic and suffering from hypothermia, according to my men."

"And Davy?"

"Unresponsive," he said.

"I should have gone with them," I said.

"No, Doc. I know what you're thinking. My men are well trained, but the last thing we need is for you to be out in this mess. From what I understand, there was nothing you could do for him."

"Do they have any idea what happened?"

"No. Destinee wasn't making any sense when they arrived. As I said, she was manic, and she tried to run away from them and into the snow. They found the car under several feet of snow. It had plowed into an embankment on the side of the road."

"Maybe he had a heart attack and crashed," Abigail said. "I wonder how long they've been out there."

"They tried to bring him back, but . . . it doesn't sound like he made it," Ewan said.

"Why would they even try to leave town?" the inspector asked. "It makes the manager and Destinee look extremely guilty. Maybe they were trying to leave the country."

I'd been wondering the same thing, and I didn't disagree with her. Davy's need for escape may have been the very thing that caused his death, though I wouldn't know until I examined him.

"Well, best we be ready for whatever is coming our way," I said. "I have a feeling this won't be the only emergency we'll be dealing with today." While most Sea Isle residents were smart enough to stay inside during crazy weather, we had a fair number of visitors because of what happened to Bram.

We divided and conquered what needed to be done, and I have to say I was quite impressed with how the inspector pitched in to help.

By the time the covered lorry rolled up in front of the clinic, we were ready.

"We lost him again," one of the men said. He was on top of Davy, administering CPR.

"In here," I said. I motioned to the exam room we'd set up as a temporary cardiac suite. "Abigail?"

"Clear," she said. And then she put the defibrillator pads on his chest.

Davy's back arched, and then he hit the table hard.

No sinus rhythm.

I shot epinephrine into his chest, but there was still no response. Abigail hit him with the pads again.

There was a small flicker and then nothing. We went back and forth for another twenty minutes, but it was useless.

Davy was dead.

Chapter Eighteen

By late that afternoon, the storm didn't seem to be abating any time soon. My practice had become a hub for medical emergencies and for those helping with search and rescue.

I had a postmortem to do, but with one emergency after another, there hadn't been time. Treating the living was priority one. Luckily, except for a broken leg, and an elbow, none of the patients had anything too seriously wrong with them.

Destinee was still asleep, and we needed answers about what had happened the night before. But first, I had to deal with the emergencies at hand.

In true Sea Isle fashion, those who lived here had the brains to stay indoors during storms, unlike the fans and press who had shown up for any sort of news about the band. They didn't seem to have the same good sense as our locals.

Roadblocks had been set up just outside of town. No one would be leaving any time soon, though the snow was expected to stop in a few hours. Still, it would be a day or more before the plows could clear everything, especially on the passes and higher up the mountain.

While I was looking at the elbow of a young woman who had slipped on some ice, Abigail came into the surgical suite. She glanced at the X-ray and pointed to the small fracture.

I nodded.

"I can take care of the arm. You're needed," she said. She glanced at the patient, then nodded toward the door.

"Abigail will put the cast on for you, and I'll be back to check on you in just a bit," I said to the woman.

Ewan stood just outside the door.

"Bethany says Destinee is awake, but she will only talk to you," he said. I'd left the inspector in one of our recovery suites with the singer so she could monitor her. The EMTs had given her a healthy dose of meds to knock her out.

That was my way of keeping the inspector happy and out of my way. She was good in an emergency, but she'd been trying to help a bit too much, throwing around orders to people who didn't appreciate what she had to say.

Keeping the constable off his feet was impossible, but I had convinced him to at least help me triage at the clinic. I argued that if he slipped or hurt himself again, he risked brain damage, and at the very least, he would be out of commission for much longer.

As we walked through the reception area, I found Mara and Jasper handing out food and hot drinks to the emergency workers.

"When did you guys get here?" I asked.

"We've been here about two hours," Mara said. "The grans have the pub covered, and Ewan needed more food for his teams, so here we are."

I really did have the most wonderful friends.

"I'm glad you're here, and thank you."

"Just doing what we should," Jasper said. "I closed my shop a wee bit early. I won't be responsible for some sugar addict slipping on ice because they need a fix. Besides, if someone was hurt, it would not be worth staying open. The last thing I need is someone suing me because they needed a croissant."

I laughed and felt my shoulders drop about two inches. Jasper was good at always making us smile.

"I need to see to another patient. Mara, could you help Abigail? She's working on a cast, and while I know she can handle it on her own, it's helpful to have another set of hands."

"Of course. Which room?"

"Exam room three," I said. "Jasper, if you don't mind handling the food and drinks on your own, I'd be grateful."

"Anything that has nothing to do with blood and gore is fine by me." He smiled.

Even Ewan chuckled at that.

Ewan and I went down the long hallway and past the bookcase door, which was already open. We'd been back and forth so much doing X-rays and scans the last several hours that it didn't make sense to shut it.

In the recovery suite, Destinee was pale, and her body shook under the pile of blankets. When I came in, the inspector looked up from the laptop she'd been typing on and closed it. "I'll wait outside," she said. Then she stepped out of the room.

Ewan cleared his throat. Destinee looked at him and then me. "Please," she said hoarsely. "Just the doc."

He gave a short nod and left, but I had a feeling he and Bethany hadn't gone far.

"How are you feeling?" I asked.

"Freezing," her teeth chattered. "Don't you have heat?"

"We do," I said. Then I checked the individual thermometer in the room. It was set on seventy, and it was warmer in here than anywhere else in my house.

"Yes, it's quite toasty in here. The shivering you feel may be the effects of the drugs you were given wearing off, and shock."

I went about checking her vitals. Everything was normal, though her blood pressure was a bit low. That wasn't unusual given the drugs in her system.

"Is Davy dead? No one will tell me the truth."

I glanced out the window of the suite to where Ewan and the inspector stood. They were watching us carefully. I stepped over and pulled the curtains closed.

"We couldn't revive him, Destinee. I'm sorry for your loss."

She sniffed, and then a small sob escaped. I handed her a box of tissues from the table next to her bed. Then I waited while she cried for quite a while. She took a long, shaky breathy.

"Can you tell me what happened? Why were you trying to leave during a storm like this?"

"Davy said it wouldn't be that bad, and that he'd driven through worse when we were on tour in Sweden," she said. "I didn't want to go with him, but the idea of sleeping in my own bed . . . I needed out of that B and B. Everywhere I looked made me think of Bram and what had happened. I felt like I was coming out of my skin."

"Why was he in such a hurry to leave, though?"

She turned her head toward the wall.

"Destinee?"

"I'm really thirsty," she said. I handed her a small glass with some water and a straw. She sipped it a couple of times and then handed it back to me. "Thanks."

"It might make you feel better to just tell me what happened," I said.

"We'd made it a few miles out of town, but the snow was thick, and it was dark. He couldn't see out of the window. He was so stressed. I begged him to turn the car around and go back."

She sniffed.

"We were screaming at each other, and then he grabbed his chest and fell forward. We were heading toward the sea, and I pulled on the steering wheel. I overcorrected, and we plowed into a snowbank."

"Was he conscious?"

A tear slid down her cheek. "Yes, but he was having trouble breathing. First, I pulled him to my side of the car. Then I put the car in reverse, but the wheels just spun. I didn't know what to do.

"I tried to use our phones, but we didn't have any service. He kept fading in and out," she said. "So, I just covered him up with a coat from the back seat, and we sat there in the dark. I'd turn the car on every so often for the heater, but I worried about running out of gas if I kept it running the whole time. Then we would have been in big trouble.

"I took one of my tablets, more to stay calm than anything. In hindsight that was a big mistake. My head was not very clear."

"Did Davy say anything to you?"

More tears streamed down her cheeks, and she nodded. "He came to, just an hour or so before the rescue team arrived. I thought that maybe he was better. He said there was something I needed to know. That he had a confession." She sobbed even harder.

It was all I could do not to scream "Tell me!" but I just stood there while she did her best to compose herself. When she'd stopped crying, I handed her the water again. She took a few more sips.

"What did he confess?"

"That he'd killed Bram," she said.

My mouth dropped open, and I forced it shut. Well, he had been at the top of my list. "I thought he had an alibi?"

She shrugged. "I said that wrong. He assisted him," she said. "But still, it's murder, right?" She sobbed again.

Davy really had been the one to kill Bram, but what did she mean by 'assisted'? Did she mean assisted suicide?

"Maybe just take a deep breath."

She did as I asked.

"Now, tell me exactly what he said."

She closed her eyes as if she were thinking hard.

"He said that Bram had been quite ill and that he wasn't going to be able to do the tour. I called him a liar. Yes, he'd been forgetful, but Bram wasn't that sick. He forgot things and was grumpy. But sick?"

Oh, but he was.

"And then what happened?"

She breathed deeply again. "He told me that Bram had done some research and that he'd found the way he wanted to die. That he'd read it in a book or online somewhere. He wanted to make it look like it was from natural causes so the band could get the insurance."

"But you don't believe that?"

She shook her head. "Bram didn't worry about things like insurance. That was Davy's job. That's what I'm trying to say. Nothing he said made sense."

"Why don't you tell me the rest," I said.

"Well, I told him that he wasn't making sense and that he just needed to rest and save his strength. But he insisted I listen to him. He said that Bram felt like that last concert was nearly perfect and that Bram believed it was time for him to go. He asked Davy to help him down to the sea so he could listen to the ocean like he did when he was boy."

She sobbed really hard then. And it took several minutes for her to calm down again.

"Davy said he didn't know what Bram had planned, but he didn't want to leave him alone. So, he followed him down the mountain. He said Bram had his guitar, and that even though it was freezing, every so often he'd start singing and playing as they walked."

She swallowed hard.

"When they made it to the beach, Bram started talking about all the things he'd wanted to do but never would. He made Davy promise to take care of all of us. Bram's biggest wish was for us to carry on without him. His greatest desire was to keep the band together.

"I feel bad because I dinnae believe Bram would ever say such a thing. I loved him, but the man had an ego. There was no way he'd want us to continue without him. I knew Davy had to be lying and that he had helped kill our friend. And then I was stuck in the car with him. I thought I might go there with him like that."

She grabbed her stomach. "I feel sick," she said. I handed her a kidney dish, which was what we used for patients. She waited, but nothing came up.

"I can get you something for the nausea," I said.

"Wait," she cried. "I have to get this out."

"Okay," I said.

She held on to the dish so hard her fingers turned white.

"Bram told Davy he didn't have the courage to live with the changes that were coming. He wanted to go out on his own terms. But if it looked like suicide . . ."

"Then no insurance."

She nodded. "Like I said, he'd done research. He asked Davy to hold his guitar. He was not certain what he was doing, but he must have done whatever it was." She shook her head. "It makes me sick to think about that."

"Did Davy give you specifics about how he stabbed himself?" That made no sense. Technically, it could have happened that way, but it would have been difficult.

Her eyes went wide.

Wait. Had I just given something away? Darn. I hoped Ewan and Bethany hadn't heard that. At least they couldn't see the reaction. But if Davy confessed to knowing what happened, wouldn't he have told her Bram stabbed himself?

Something didn't feel right.

She coughed. "Yes, but it was dark, and Davy didn't see exactly what happened. Bram grabbed his guitar and threw the bottle they'd brought down into the trash. He told Davy to go home and that he wanted to be alone.

"Davy argued with him, but . . . Sometimes when Bram wanted something, you couldn't deny him. He just walked away and left him there to die all alone.

"I was furious with Davy for leaving him. I was screaming at him, and then he passed out again. I dinnae know if I should be angry or scared. I just dinnae want to die in that car. I know I keep saying that. That's why I took another tablet to calm down. And before you say anything, remember that I was trapped in the car with the man who killed Bram."

Well, technically, Bram had killed himself. That is, if the story was true. I still wasn't sure how he'd managed that given the angle of the wound. In fact, I wasn't at all certain I believed any of this, but Destinee seemed to believe what she was saying.

I thought maybe Davy had killed Bram but didn't want to give a full confession in case he survived. But at the same time, he wanted someone to know what had happened. That made sense, in a weird way. But something big bothered me.

"It is understandable why you were so upset," I said.

"I thought we were going to die in that car," she said. "When they pulled us out and opened the door, I went a little crazy. I dinnae mean to scare anyone."

"Again, understandable. You were also in shock. Did he say anything else, like why he hit the constable with a cricket bat?"

Her eyes went wide. "What? No. He hurt the constable?"

I had no idea if Davy did or not. Davy may have confessed, but I didn't feel like we were any closer to the truth. Something wasn't right about this story.

But I didn't know why I felt that way. And then it hit me—there were no specifics to the story. Everything she said could have been easily denied by Davy if he'd lived. And she'd been absolutely surprised when I mentioned stabbing.

"Are you sure he didn't give you any specifics as to how he helped?"

She shook her head.

I sighed, though I covered it with a cough.

"We have doctor-patient confidentiality, but I need to let the authorities know what happened. Do I have your permission to tell them what you've said?"

She nodded. "Don't make me talk to them right now, please. I know I'll have to tell them everything, but I need some time. It has been . . ."

"A lot."

After making certain she was comfortable and letting her know I'd be sending some soup her way, I went out to speak to Ewan and the inspector.

The inspector's jaw dropped. Ewan frowned.

"Do you believe her?" he asked.

I shrugged. "She seemed truly upset by it all, and she was furious with Davy for helping Bram. That much was clear."

"I need to speak to her," the inspector said.

I held up a hand. "She's in no state to give you more details right now."

"She just talked to you."

"And she's in shock," I said. "She needs some time."

There was a hard set to the inspector's jaw. She opened her mouth, but Ewan put a hand on her arm.

"Bethany let's give her twenty-four hours. It will take that long to dig out from the snowfall. She isn't going anywhere."

"But she could change her story, and something doesn't add up," she said.

"I agree," I said, "but when her body has settled down and her mind is void of the drugs she's been given, not to mention what she'd already taken, we might get clearer answers."

She nodded tightly.

"Now, unless there are any other emergencies, I'd like to do the postmortem on Davy."

He was in his thirties and had seemed perfectly healthy.

I needed to make certain he hadn't been murdered.

Chapter Nineteen

Once the snow and wind died down, things around Sea Isle moved quickly back to normal. The plows had the streets clear in town, but it would be a day or so before the passes leading out of town would be open. Leaving the care of the rescue teams to Ewan, Mara, and Jasper, I headed toward the freezer where I did autopsies.

Abigail was with Tommy in the den. "I'm getting him set up with his games and headphones. I'll be there in a minute," she said.

"Take your time."

I was exhausted. It had been a wild couple of days. It was not at all the sleepy vacation I'd imagined. Today had reminded me more of working in the ER back in Seattle, one case after another. I didn't miss those hectic days or the lack of normalcy I had back then. At the time, I hadn't realized how much of a life beyond work I didn't have.

After grabbing some espresso to help me for a few hours, and eating some banana bread someone had dropped by, I headed into the room where we'd stored Davy's and Bram's bodies. I drew some blood for toxicology. Then I set about getting to work. A short time later, Abigail joined me. We worked as a team for the next few hours, weighing, measuring, and searching for medical clues.

Ewan opened the door. "Is everything going all right? Any answers?"

"Not yet."

"I need to help my team. Will you be okay?"

I smiled. "We'll muddle through without you," I joked.

He chuckled. "I'm certain you will. Let me know if you discover anything. Bethany as well."

"Will do."

Ewan left.

Once we reached Davy's heart, we found our answers.

"That's strange," Abigail said.

"I agree, and highly unusual." A large clot had formed, blocking a major artery.

"What do you think caused it?"

"Could have been from running into the snowbank. He had several contusions. But let's look for marks like we found on Bram," I said.

"Do you think . . ." Her eyes went wide.

"It's worth checking," I said. "They would have had to hit the right vein. But his heart is filled with plaque. His diet must have been terrible."

"Or he's Scottish," she said.

She wasn't one for making jokes. When she did, they were funny.

"You all are very fond of your fatty proteins."

"That we are."

"Hmm," I said.

"What is it?"

"It's faint, but there is a small puncture wound here on the thigh. Maybe it was made by a hypodermic needle. Let's get some measurements."

"I can't believe you found that," she said. It was a tiny hole.

"If I hadn't been looking for it specifically, I would have missed it. And if Bram hadn't died the way he did, I wouldn't have been looking for it in the first place."

"But it's not the corkscrew," she said.

"No, but same method of killing, and much easier to hide."

I'd been hunched over and stood up. My back spasmed from being in the same position for so long.

"Are you okay?"

"I'm old, and it's been a long day," I said.

"Do you think it's murder again?"

"Unfortunately, I believe it's too much of a coincidence not to be. We need to see if he was diabetic or used other types of drugs. That may not be it at all. Once again, it's difficult to know given how he died. Could have been from the accident or the puncture. My guess, even though it's not very scientific, is the latter."

"Any idea why Davy was murdered?"

"I have my suspicions, and it has to do with the original murder."

There was a knock on the door. Abigail opened it. Ewan and the inspector stood there.

"Any news?" he asked.

"It's possible he was killed in a similar way as Bram, though the clot ended up in his heart, and it was a different weapon. Most likely, it was a hypodermic needle of some kind."

He turned and glanced at the inspector.

"I told you her story didn't add up, and she was the only other person in the car," she said.

I held up a hand. "The problem is, I can't say for certain his death wasn't caused by contusions he received during the accident. He had bruises all over his body. But we did find a puncture, which makes me suspicious. I'll keep trying—"

"She was there. She's the killer," Bethany said.

"Bethany, we need proof." Ewan gave her a look. "Are you even listening?

"*Ewan*, he was murdered, and she was the only one there. She probably made up the whole story."

Abigail, who was never fond of any sort of conflict, turned to me. "I'll run these toxicology reports." Then she pushed past them carrying the vials she needed for the tests.

"I understand why you might think that," I said, "but he could have been stabbed with the hypodermic needle at any time. Clots can travel quite slowly. It's impossible to know exactly when the air entered his system. Like Bram, I'll need his medical history as soon as possible. It could have also been caused by the accident. I'm sorry that I don't have something more definitive for you. Get me those records, though. That will help."

Bethany sighed. "I will see what I can do."

"Wouldn't he have felt it, though?" Ewan asked. "They were in that car for hours before we found them. She had plenty of time."

"The needle was quite small. He may have been asleep when it happened."

He looked at me, and I continued. "I'm not saying she didn't do it, but the puncture could have happened at any time in the last twenty-four hours. What I can tell you is, the person who did this had to know exactly where to stab him with that needle. If it had been a bit to the right or left, the needle would have missed the vein."

They frowned.

"Do any of the suspects have some kind of medical training?"

"Just Davy," Ewan answered. "He had CPR training in their early days so he could help if something went wrong."

The inspector glanced at him, seemingly surprised.

He shrugged. "It was one of the first things I checked when Em told me how Bram died. It seemed oddly specific to cause an embolism like that."

"What I don't like is that if the story she's telling us is true, that means we possibly have two killers," the inspector said. "One of them is in that surgical suite."

She had a point. I hadn't thought of that.

"I don't think she's telling us the whole truth, but I don't see her as a murderer."

"Is this something someone could learn on the internet?" she asked.

I shrugged. "It's possible. You can find just about anything on the internet. But it would be difficult for a layman to hit it just right. With Bram, there was a bigger weapon, and the target was much closer. Either he or someone else blew air directly into the brain. This is different."

"The situation has become much more complicated," Ewan said.

I nodded. "We need to trace Davy's whereabouts over the last twenty-four hours and figure out who he saw and where he was. I know Destinee looks like the prime suspect, and I understand why that is, but I just don't see her killing someone that way."

"I'll get my men on it," Ewan said.

"I'll call my team and see if they can do a deep dive into any sort of medical education for any of our suspects." She held up a hand. "I know you've done that, Ewan, but it doesn't hurt to double-check. Maybe we need to widen the circle."

"Who else could it be?" I asked. "Most killers know their victims."

"We've run across four stalkers who have sent threatening messages to the band, two of which are in Sea Isle and staying near the B and B," the inspector said. "For the record, I agree that killers often know their victims, but we have to look at everything and everyone. It wouldn't be the first time a fan took things too far."

I thought about that as she continued. "But my money is on the woman in your back rooms. Like I said, her story doesn't add up, and she was with the victim, alone, for several hours. Doctor, I'd like to take her in for questioning. When will she be released?"

I shrugged. "First of all, you can call me Em. We'll have to play it by ear. I'm not certain when she'll be well enough. Honestly, I'm more worried about her mental state, which is fragile, than I am about her physical condition. But if she is the killer . . ."

"I'll keep someone posted outside her door until she can be moved," Ewan said. "I wouldn't do that to you, Em."

"Oh, you needn't worry," the inspector said. "I won't be leaving her side."

"Thanks, Bethany. I realize with you both on the case, you don't really need my help with the investigation, but I'd like to look at the background on the stalkers you keep mentioning. Maybe a fresh pair of eyes will help."

Bethany opened her mouth, but Ewan held up a hand. "The doc's point of view has been helpful in the past," he said. "She's helped solve more than one case. This is a confusing one, and I don't see the harm in looking at all our options."

She nodded. "Fine. I'll have the files sent over to you."

"Great. I also need Davy's medical files. You seem to have more pull in that regard. I'd appreciate if you pushed for them to be sent quickly."

"We'll take care of it," Ewan said.

"I need to finish the postmortem. I'll let you know if we find anything else," I said. I didn't disagree with the inspector. Destinee did seem to be the most likely suspect, but Ewan was right. Other than proximity, we had no proof.

She could have made up the story about Davy helping Bram. Maybe she was the one who killed him. However, the way Davy was possibly killed really made me wonder who it could be since it required specific knowledge about how to use the hypodermic needle. It was more than just jabbing air into someone's system.

Also, if Destinee was telling the truth and Davy did kill Bram, then who killed Davy? I had a feeling I'd be asking myself that same question over and over again.

* * *

After a full eight hours of sleep, I felt like a new person. I took a shower and dressed. When I went downstairs, I found my house still full of people. Abigail was in the kitchen making coffee. Tommy was headed out the back door, most likely going to the greenhouse.

"Mornin'," Abigail said.

"Good morning," I said. "Thanks for making some coffee. Have you checked on Destinee?"

"Aye. She's well enough to be complaining about the accommodations. I've taken her some tea. Mara's gone down to help with the breakfast crowd, but she'll be back later."

"Did she stay here all night?"

"Aye. We slept on the couch. I put Tommy in the guest room."

"You should go get some rest," I said. "Use my room."

"Oh, we slept fine. Besides, Ewan says we'll need a new boiler at our place. So, if you don't mind, we'll be staying on for a bit."

"You know I never mind company in this big old place," I said. "You're welcome for as long as you like."

"Thank you. We'll try not to be too much of a bother."

"Abigail, one thing you never are is a bother. I adore you and Tommy. I'm happy for you to stay here as long as you like. I'll go check on Destinee. You are supposed to be on vacation. Feel free to grab a nap if you need one."

She shrugged. "I'm good, but I might do some studying. I want to get ahead on next semester's classes."

I smiled. She wasn't one for letting grass grow under her feet. If she wasn't studying for her classes, she was taking care of her brother. She was one of the best humans I'd ever come across.

After inhaling some espresso, I went to check on Destinee. She was sitting up in bed, flipping through the channels on the television. There was a guard just outside her door, and I noticed the inspector curled up on one of the beds in another recovery suite. Bethany must have sensed me because she opened her eyes and nodded. I gave her a wave, then walked into Destinee's room.

"How are you feeling?" I asked.

"Better," Destinee said. "When can I leave?"

"Let's check your vitals," I said. "Mentally, how are you?"

She shrugged. "I feel like yesterday was some kind of weird nightmare. I don't know why I went so crazy last night. Maybe it was the stress of everything. I haven't been myself since we arrived in this town, and I just want to go home."

"I don't blame you," I said. "Do you remember anything else from the accident?"

"No, not really. Except . . ."

"What?"

"I don't know. It feels like I watched everything that happened on television. Like I was outside of myself. It's weird. I feel like I went slightly mad. But that isn't me, I promise. I'm usually the calm one in the group. The peacemaker. I've felt crazy since I arrived."

It dawned on me that while I'd collected blood samples when she'd passed out, we'd never actually run tests on them.

"Today is the first day in the last four or so that feel clearheaded."

"Well, there's that," I said. "I'm happy to release you medically, but I'm afraid you will probably be in Sea Isle a bit longer. They said it would be another day before the passes are clear."

She sighed. "I can't go back to the B and B, but I don't want to stay here."

"You don't need to worry about where you'll be staying," Bethany said from the doorway.

"Destinee Cameron, I'm arresting you for murder. You have the right . . ."

I'm not sure whose eyes were bigger, mine or the rocker's.

But she was in big trouble.

Chapter Twenty

A few hours later, the only people left at my practice were Tommy and Abigail. She was on the sofa studying, and he was still out in the greenhouse. Needing some fresh air, I offered to get them some treats from Jasper's patisserie.

I stopped in at the pub to see if Mara wanted to go with me, but Mrs. Wilson said she'd gone upstairs to take a nap.

The air was nippy, though the sun shone for the first time in what seemed like forever. That was something Scotland and Seattle had in common. Sunshine wasn't so abundant.

Jasper's place was full of people with shopping bags. It was weird to see so many strangers in town. After only a few months living in Sea Isle, I felt as though I knew most of the residents.

"Afternoon, Doc. How are you?" Jasper asked when I stepped up to the counter.

"You're busy today," I said.

He smiled. "Thanks to all the fans being trapped in town, we're all doing okay. I mean, sad business as to why, but . . ."

"I get it. In a way, it's a blessing this time of year."

He nodded. "Oh, looks like there's a table clear. Let me clean that off for you."

"I was just going to grab and go," I said.

"Right," he whispered, "except I think you may want to stay awhile and have a listen to those two young women in the corner."

I glanced behind me and saw two women dressed in Bram and the Stokers attire from head to toe. They were whispering to each other.

"Oh?"

"Let's just say I've heard some interesting snippets about Bram as I walked by."

"Noted," I said.

He quickly cleaned off the table, and I sat down with a cup of coffee.

"I'll bring you a chicken salad sandwich, then put your order together," he said.

"Thanks."

I pulled out my phone and scrolled through my emails.

As soon as I sat down, the women went silent. It figured. I was curious what Jasper had overheard. I'd have to ask him later. For now, I pretended to be more interested in my phone than in anyone around me.

"Is there anything on social media yet?" one woman asked the other.

"No. That's weird, right? Are you sure you heard the policeman right?"

"Yes. It was Davy who died."

"Good. That dobber got what he deserved," the other one said. "I can't believe he was so rude to us. I mean, I used to be the president of the fan club. He can't treat us like that."

I'd learned a few months ago that *dobber* was a curse word and had to do with a male appendage.

"Bram wasn't any better. What he did to you was just awful. After everything you'd done for him."

"True. They were both arseholes."

If they no longer cared for the band, why had they come to town?

Unless it was to kill them.

"When do you think we'll be able to get back to Glasgow? I've got to be at the hospital tomorrow for work."

I nearly choked on my coffee. When I'd been talking to the team, I'd said the killer had medical experience. I texted Ewan and told him what I'd heard. He texted back to keep them at the shop.

The other woman replied, "The man at the pub said they'd have the pass cleared by tomorrow."

"I've got to find a way out of here. I can't miss work again. I need that job."

Had I found the killers? If she was a nurse, she would have known exactly what to do, and they didn't sound very happy with Davy or Bram.

"You're a nurse, and you hate it there anyway. I bet you can find a better job somewhere else."

They were silent again.

"Oh, look, it's that handsome constable. Remember him from the pub the other night?"

"He could be a model in a magazine."

I smiled. They weren't wrong. Ewan was quite handsome in a rugged sort of way. But they were about to be surprised.

"Doctor," he said when he entered Jasper's shop.

"Afternoon, Constable." I nodded my head toward the women.

He nodded back.

"Ewan, did you want anything?" Jasper asked. He glanced from me to Ewan.

"No. I just need to speak to some of your customers." He turned toward the women. Their eyes widened, and their jaws dropped.

"I need you two to come with me," he said.

"I want my solicitor," one of them said.

"We didn't do anything," the other said at the same time.

"That can be arranged," he said. "But for now, I'd just like to chat down at the station."

He ushered them out.

The rest of the crowd was left googly-eyed by the turn of events, and the chatter grew louder.

Jasper brought over my order, and I finished my sandwich. They didn't seem like killers, but their behavior was suspicious. What I'd learned about murder the last few months had shown that one couldn't always predict the nature of a killer. When people were pushed, or just greedy or angry, they could go to extraordinary lengths.

"Hey, are you going to the forest festival tonight?" he asked.

With everything going on, I'd forgotten about that. "Explain to me exactly what that one is," I said.

"It's a short trail through the trees that's been cleared. It's lit by candles. Well, fake ones, but it is quite pretty. Everyone walks through and observes silence as they give praise to Mother Nature."

"Is it one of the Celtic celebrations?"

He shrugged. "Who knows? Most likely it is, since it has to do with nature. There's a big party with music and dancing at the end. The whole town will be there."

"I will be there because I promised, though I could do with a quiet evening and a good night's sleep."

He laughed. "You can sleep when it's the New Year. December is for partying."

I laughed with him.

"'Tis quite beautiful," he said. "You won't be sorry. I'll come by and get you. Starts near your house anyway."

"Okay, thanks. I'd appreciate it."

On the way back, the sidewalks were much more crowded than they had been the week before. People who had been trapped here by the weather seemed to be making the most of it by doing some holiday shopping.

All the shops had been decorated at the first of the month, and it reminded me that I still had bare trees waiting for ornaments. I'd hired a few workmen to put lights on the outside of the old church I lived in because it was expected. They were due the next day.

Abigail was running tests, and Tommy was outside somewhere. The sun was still shining, but it was bitterly cold. I went to check on him and found him repotting some plants in the warm greenhouse.

I knocked on the door before entering so that I didn't surprise him.

"I brought back some treats from Jasper's," I said.

"Tarts?" he asked. He loved the lemon tarts Jasper made.

"Yes. And some chicken salad sandwiches."

He nodded.

"I'll leave you to it."

Inside, I lit the fire in the den and turned on Christmas carols. Then I remembered that I'd never found the decorations. I started my hunt once again. I didn't find much, so I went back to the surgical suite. Abigail was still running tests.

"I know you're busy, but I wanted to let you know I brought back some sandwiches and treats from Jasper's." I told her about what had happened with the two women.

"Do you think they could have killed them?"

"I don't have any idea. I only know what I heard, which was enough to make me suspicious."

"What if you've solved the case by accident again?"

"Sheer dumb luck that would be, and Jasper would get the credit. He heard some of the things they'd been saying before I arrived. He was the one who steered me to them."

She smiled. "I like that our little gang is always looking out for the bad ones in the world."

I grinned. "Me too. I think I asked before, but I can't remember. You wouldn't happen to know if the former doctor had any Christmas decorations? I've gone through most of the storage rooms but haven't found any."

She shook her head. "He wasn't one for holidays. I used to keep a small fake tree on my desk. So, no. I don't think he left any behind."

"Well, I guess I'll have to go shopping. Too bad the roads are closed."

"Actually, Lulu just got a bunch in, and there's several shops by the library that carry all kinds of holiday things."

"Oh, that's a great idea. I'd rather shop local. I had no idea Lulu carried Christmas stuff." Her shop tended toward antiques and vintage clothing. "Would you like to go with me after you've had your lunch?"

She pursed her lips. "I haven't finished all the toxicology reports from the manager."

I shrugged. "They can wait a couple of hours. Go eat some lunch and then we'll head out. Would Tommy like to come?"

"He'd be happier staying here. Henry is due to swap out with the man watching your front door. He'll look after him."

I hadn't even noticed the guy outside.

"Okay. I'm going to make a list while you eat."

* * *

An hour later, we headed over to Lulu's. She was in her usual seventies garb. Her red pantsuit had a fake fur collar. She looked like a 1970s version of Mrs. Claus.

"Hi, Lulu," I said as we walked inside.

She indicated that she was on the phone but gave us a wave and a smile. Abigail steered me to the right side of the store, which was filled with holiday accoutrements. Lulu carried everything from vintage furniture and clocks to clothing and other antiques. She was our friend Angie's aunt. Like Angie, she had a signature style. She was also cooler than all of us put together.

We found several boxes of glass ornaments that looked like ice crystals. The shop also had sapphire glass balls that were quite extraordinary, as well as some in different colors. I gathered all the glass balls I could and put them on the counter, and then I went back for more.

"Do you want to do a color theme or mix them up?" Abigail said.

"Since I have two trees, let's do both. We can decorate the one in the front office window with the blue ones. Then we can mix things up with the one in the den."

We picked some more baubles, as Abigail called them.

Lulu hung up the phone as we approached the counter to pay for our stuff.

"You've picked some beautiful baubles," she said.

"Thank you for keeping so many in stock. I wasn't sure how I would decorate since the roads are closed."

She shook her head. "I don't mind so much. The shop has been busy with the out-of-towners, but my new shipments can't get in, which is troublesome. Also, the media keeps calling. Bloodhounds, the lot of them."

"Why are they calling you?" Abigail asked. I wanted to know the same thing.

"No idea. They seem to be calling all the businesses trying to find out information about the murder. The one I was just talking to says the police aren't saying anything.

"I heard some young women were arrested at Jasper's earlier this afternoon." She gave me the eye.

I shrugged. "I just overheard some gossip and thought the constable should know," I said. "But it's an—"

"Ongoing investigation," Lulu interrupted.

I smiled. "Yes."

"Well, I hope the whole mess is over soon. Here we are trying to bring holiday shoppers to Sea Isle, and we murder one of the most important musicians in Scotland."

"True, but it seems to have brought a lot of people into town. There are more people here now than there was on the night the band performed."

"There is that," she said. "He was in here, you know, on the day he performed. He and that woman who is in the band. They were arguing something fierce. In fact, she was so angry at him that she stormed out."

"Oh?" This was the first time I'd heard of it.

"Aye. He bought a notebook and a painting. The one of the old mill. He said it reminded him of his childhood. He paid to have it shipped to his house in Edinburgh but asked me to wait until after the holidays to send it. I don't know what to do with it now."

"Can I see it?"

She went to the back room and then came back out. The painting was quite beautiful, and there was something familiar about it.

"It's gorgeous," I said. It didn't look like something a musician might buy, but I supposed they could be just as varied with their art choices as the rest of us.

"Who painted it?" I tried to read the name in the corner.

"William Stoker," she said. "He was a local artist who lived here in the sixties and seventies. He died at sea years ago. Art was his hobby, but he was a fisherman by trade. Very sad story. The widow was a new mom who had a difficult time with her wee one. I think he ended up in care."

Had the painting been done by Bram's father? I'd also had no idea his real last name had been Stoker. Had kids given him a hard time in school? I never understood why parents gave kids odd names. It only made their lives more difficult growing up. Were they related to the Irish writer Bram Stoker? I remembered that some of his books were set in Scotland.

Abigail stared down at the painting and then at me. She must have been asking herself the same questions.

"I'll see if I can find out who will be handling his estate, and I'll let you know," I said. "My guess is it will end up going to a museum for the band. Unless there is a will and someone inherits everything." I was certain that Ewan and Bethany had thought of that. Who would inherit his estate since he had no family? That could also be a reason to kill him. People who murdered were often greedy. It was one of the most common motives.

"Oh, you are a dear. Thank you. I wouldn't feel right keeping it since he paid cash."

"No problem."

She rang up my items and put them in festive packages with ribbons and tulle. When we left, our arms were full.

As we headed back to the house, one question plagued me: If Bram had planned to kill himself in Sea Isle like Destinee said, why had he bought the painting?

Chapter
Twenty-One

The reporters who were supposed to stay down the hill had inched their way up again. With Tommy at the house alone, I worried one might have tried to jump the stone wall again and upset him. As Abigail and I hurried up, a barrage of questions followed us.

"Was Bram murdered by someone in the band?"

"Do the police have a suspect? Is it Destinee?"

"Who were the women in the patisserie who were arrested?"

"Was it stalkers?"

"Is there a conspiracy cover-up?"

It was all I could do not to smile after that last question.

We ignored them all.

Luckily, none of them had breached the wall, and Tommy was still ensconced in the greenhouse happily puttering away with his plants. Henry was keeping him company, but when I told him about the reporters getting a bit too close, he headed out front.

"I'd like to help you decorate," Abigail said. "I've always wanted to see the place done up."

"I'd love that," I said.

Her phone buzzed, and she frowned.

"What is it?"

"Nothing."

"Tell me, Abigail."

"It's about the boiler. Ewan says they can't get a new one in until the pass is cleared. It could be another two days before we can get back into the house."

"Well, you'll just have to stay here, then," I said.

"Are you sure? You've been so kind already. I don't want to take advantage of you. Ewan offered rooms at his place, but we're more comfortable here."

I shook my head. "Abigail, you do so much for me. Don't even think about it. You and Tommy are always welcome here. You've become family to me. I'm always sad when it's time for you to go home." That was true.

There were people who brought more to one's life than they took. Abigail and Tommy were those kinds of people. They really had become a surrogate family. I'd give my life for them, and I didn't say that lightly.

She gave me a shy smile. "Thank you, Doc. You have become family to us too."

After making some coffee and putting the kettle on for Abigail, we divided up the ornaments, or baubles, as she called them. I decided to use white lights on one tree and multicolored lights on the other tree. Then I turned on some old-fashioned Christmas carols, and it wasn't long before we were done. There were garlands and lights. My home had become magical.

The excitement of the last few days had worn on me more than I thought. I needed this respite. Still, I was curious what was going on with the investigation. So, while Abigail put together some dinner for us, I texted Ewan to see if there was any news. He didn't answer back. I assumed he was busy. He was usually pretty good about that sort of thing.

After we ate, we dressed warmly for the forest festival. Jasper and Mara met us outside, and we followed the crowd of people up the mountain.

The chilling cold had me pulling up the cowl on my sweater and wrapping my knit scarf around my face so that only my eyes appeared over the top. I wasn't sure I'd ever get used to the cold here. It went deep into the bones and stayed.

Still, trudging up the mountain helped keep me warm. It was quite beautiful and quiet. There were so many people, but no one made a sound as we went up the lighted path. The trunks of the trees had been wrapped in lights, and there was a sense of peace.

When we passed the bothy where I'd found my first dead body, as the coroner, I shivered a bit. It had only been August when I'd moved here, but it felt like years had passed since I'd accidentally ended up there with a dead body. So much had happened since then. As if she'd sensed my unease near the bothy, Mara crooked her arm in mine and winked.

When I first decided to move here, there was no way I could have understood or imagined how quickly I'd settle into this beautiful town. Most of that had to do with my dear, sweet friends. They were a group of people I didn't realize I needed in my life, and I was so grateful to know them now.

Walking with the crowd meant we had to go slowly, which I did happily, even though the cold stole one's breath while going up the mountain. At least the path had been cleared of snow so there was less chance of slipping and falling.

A half hour later, the path opened at an area just behind the library. Several booths had been set up with cider, hot chocolate, and all types of food. Still, people were more subdued than they had been the night of the tree lighting. It was as if no one wanted to let go of the quiet we'd all experienced together.

Someone bumped into me, but before I could turn to see who it was, they were gone.

That's weird.

I found Ewan talking with Bethany, and I went over.

"Any news?" I asked. Then I lowered my voice. One never knew when a reporter might be lurking around. "Are you still holding Destinee?"

"Yes," he said, "but she still hasn't been formally charged, and we put her up at another B and B. Her solicitor insisted."

"We were told the accommodations at the station weren't appropriate for someone who had been through so much *medically*," Bethany said sarcastically as she put air quotes around the last word.

"Do you have any news for us?" she asked.

"We're still running tests," I said. Maybe I should have done that instead of decorating, but I needed a break. My mind was already refreshed after taking an afternoon off work.

The peaceful walk tonight had helped as well. My shoulders had dropped at least an inch.

"Any idea when the passes will be open?" I asked.

"They're open now," Ewan said. "The crews just finished up about an hour ago."

I breathed deep. "That's good to hear. What about the young women in Jasper's place?"

"They were just attention-seekers," Bethany said. "One of them did have some good insight into the band, though. Seems there was a lot more animosity than we'd been told."

"Oh?"

"Before the tour had come about, there had been talk about them breaking up. Bram was going solo. That was the rumor the young women had heard," Bethany said.

"Davy was the one who kept the band together," Ewan said. "At least, that's what the former head of the fan club said."

"How did she become the former head?" I asked.

"She had a falling out with Davy," Bethany said. "She'd arrived at Bram's place to get some photos to sign for the fans. From what she says, it was something she did often, and she claims they had an appointment.

"But when she showed up, Davy told her that she had to stop bugging Bram. When she tried to tell him that she had an appointment, he became quite belligerent with her. He fired her for overstepping."

"Her friend backed her up, but we only know her side of the story," Ewan added.

"It does seem like an extreme reaction, though. Wait. Did she say when this happened?"

"About two months ago. Why?"

"Remember Bram's medical records? That was about the time that he found out what was happening to him. Perhaps Davy had been trying to protect him."

"Davy said he didn't know anything about Bram's condition at the beginning," Bethany said. "Well, when we first interviewed him."

"Well, we can't ask him, can we?" Ewan said.

"Oh, there's something I forgot to tell you," I said.

"What's that?" Ewan asked.

"When I was at Lulu's this morning, she said Bram had bought a painting. It's of an old mill somewhere here in town."

"And why is that relevant?" Bethany asked sharply.

She really needed to work on her tone.

"Because he bought it the day he died and asked that it be shipped to his home in Edinburgh."

They stared at me, and then Ewan cocked his head.

"What?" Bethany asked as she glanced from him to me.

"Why would he buy a painting to be shipped to his house if he'd planned to kill himself here?" he asked.

Her eyes went wide. "Why indeed? So, it wasn't suicide as Destinee said."

"She only knows what Davy told her," Ewan said. "Could be that Davy found out how sick he was and decided to do something about it before he could embarrass the band."

"But then who killed Davy?" I asked.

"Destinee is still our obvious suspect," the inspector said. "But how did she have the medical knowledge, and why do it when she was the only person there? That doesn't make sense. She might be a bit flaky, but she is not stupid."

"And like I said before, he could have been injected at any time," I added. "Why would she risk getting in a car with someone she knew might die along the way?"

"There is that," Ewan agreed.

I had the sense someone might be watching us, and I turned to look over my shoulder. Half the town was staring at us, but there also was a hooded figure near the back door of the library.

"Who is that?" I pointed at the door. When I did, the person moved. "Darn. Where did he go?"

"Who?" Ewan asked as he turned around.

"I don't see anyone," Bethany said.

"I swear it was the same man I saw the other night, but I still couldn't see his face. He's tall and lanky."

Ewan and Bethany moved toward the library. Without speaking, they split up and searched around the sides of the building. When they returned, both of them shrugged. Then they went to search through the crowd.

"Is everything okay?" Mara asked. She'd brought me a cup of hot chocolate.

"I think so," I said. "I thought I saw the person who followed me the other night, so Ewan and the inspector went to look for him."

"It's a man?" she asked.

"Or a very tall woman," I said.

"Did you see his face?" She glanced around at the crowd.

"No. He always seems to know how to stay in the shadows so I can't see his face. Or her face. I don't know. I'm starting to think maybe I'm paranoid. I'm just glad Abigail and Tommy are staying with me. It will be good to have company tonight."

She frowned. "You know I'm happy to come up anytime."

I smiled. "I do. I'm probably being paranoid."

"Not after everything you've been through with the cases you've worked on since you arrived here," Mara said. "It's good that you stay vigilant."

"Thanks. Speaking of Abigail, have you seen her?"

"Oh, I was supposed to tell you. She and Tommy have gone back down in one of the shuttles. Even though it's fairly quiet, there were a few too many people for him."

"That's understandable. He did seem to enjoy the walk though."

"That he did. That kid loves anything to do with nature."

"He does."

"I overheard some of the fans saying that there is going to be a memorial service on Saturday," Mara said.

That was news to me.

"And that it's going to be here. I thought for certain they'd do it in Edinburgh or Glasgow where Bram had homes."

"Me too. Who is setting that up? Bram didn't have any family. It seems like maybe that's something Davy would have done, but he's not here anymore. Maybe one of the other band members took charge."

"I don't know," Mara said, "but it might help the investigation if we find out."

That was a very good idea.

Chapter
Twenty-Two

The next morning, I woke up to the smell of coffee. It was one of my favorite scents. Since I didn't have to get up, I thought about snuggling in my blankets for a bit longer. The wind whipped around the building and through the window. I could see it was cloudy outside. I checked the clock. It was seven in the morning.

I sighed. It didn't take me long to shower and dress and head downstairs for my first cup. Abigail was in the kitchen making breakfast.

"Mornin'," she said.

"I could have picked us up breakfast at the pub," I said.

"No use. It's just as easy to cook at home," she said.

Maybe for some people. I mean, I could cook enough to take care of myself. But I preferred food made by others who were much more talented than me. Abigail was one of those people.

Abigail added, "Plus, Tommy wanted his special toast sandwich."

"Do I want to know what that is?"

She laughed. "Basically, it's an egg sandwich with crispy bacon, a tomato, and a slice of potato."

"It actually doesn't sound bad," I said.

"I'll make you one."

"You don't have to do that."

She shrugged. "Easy enough to make three as one."

I wasn't so sure about that. "Okay, thank you. Tell me what I can do to help."

"Actually, I put the reports from all the tests we've run over there." She pointed to a pile of papers on the kitchen table. "I haven't had a chance to go through them yet."

"I'll take a look," I said.

I started with the dead men. We'd already run several tests on Bram, and the repeats showed the same results.

So, I moved on to Davy. He had high levels of antidepressants as well as anxiety meds. And yet, he'd still seemed so agitated and nervous all the time. There didn't seem to be anything else unusual, except what one would expect in someone who had a heart attack.

The big thing was that none of the drugs in his system required any sort of hypodermic needle, so there was no real reason for a puncture—unless someone had wanted to kill him in the same way as Bram.

I needed to speak with the band members to see if any of them had seen something the day Davy died. I'd asked Destinee, but she hadn't remembered anything.

How could someone not feel a needle poking into their thigh? Maybe he hadn't been awake when it happened. Perhaps Davy had been distracted by something or someone. If he'd been super cold, he may not have felt it.

Someone knocked on the door, so I went to see who it was.

"Hello, Doc," Mr. Gregor said. He was one of my patients.

"Is everything okay?" I asked as I ushered him into the reception area. "How is your blood pressure?"

He smiled. "All good. I check it a few times a day like you said. The medicine works. My crew is here to hang your lights on the church."

"Oh." I'd completely forgotten about it. "I didn't realize I'd hired your company. I thought you owned a tree trimming service."

"Aye, but this time of year we make our money by doing decorations for homes and businesses. I just wanted to let you know before the boys go stomping around up there." He pointed to the ceiling.

I grinned. "I appreciate that. Wait, you aren't going up there, are you?"

He held up his hand. "I leave the climbing to the young ones now. The missus would have my head."

When we first learned he had high blood pressure, which was an epidemic in this small town, it was because he'd tumbled off a roof after feeling dizzy. He'd, thankfully, landed in some bushes.

"That's good to know. Let me know if you need anything from me."

"We'll be fine, but thank you. I'll email an invoice. Well, the missus handles the books, so it will be coming from her. Happy Christmas."

"Happy Christmas," I said.

I returned to the kitchen to find Tommy already wolfing down his breakfast, and mine was on the table. I told him and Abigail about the workmen.

"Oh, that's going to be so pretty when they are done."

"I like holiday lights," Tommy said.

Abigail and I smiled at him.

"Me too," I said.

After breakfast, Abigail wanted to study, and Tommy headed out to the greenhouse again. I couldn't imagine what he could find to do out there, but he always seemed so busy.

There was no way I could sit around the house when I had so many questions, so I decided to head up the hill to the B and B. With the roads open, the band might have gone back to Edinburgh, but maybe not. The memorial was in a few days, so they might have stuck around.

Even though it was cloudy, the roads were dry. I drove up through the old part of town and parked in front of the B and B.

When I stepped inside, Mrs. Beatty was at the front desk in the lobby area.

"Hi, Mrs. Beatty," I said.

"Welcome, Doctor. Can I help you with something?" Her usually coiffed hair was a bit mussed, and she appeared agitated.

"Is everything okay?"

She sighed. "Destinee decided to move back in," she said. "Decided her lodgings at my competition weren't up to snuff. I've been rushing around cleaning. Debra, the cleaner, doesn't come in until noon, so I had to ready her room to her specifications." She rolled her eyes. "I'll be so glad when they are gone," she whispered.

"From what I hear, that should be in only a few more days," I said.

"True. They mentioned they'd be heading out after the memorial. I know I should never speak ill of my guests, but not only are they up all hours, but they leave messes everywhere they go." She glanced at her watch. "I need to go make tea for them. They're in the front drawing room. Did you need something?"

I smiled. "You go on ahead. I'm here to ask them a few questions in an official capacity."

"Ah. Well, I'll be in the kitchen if you need me." She went down the hallway.

As I neared the closed pocket doors, I overheard them arguing.

"How do we know it isn't one of us?" Destinee asked. Her high-pitched voice sounded nervous.

"You're the one the police picked up," Liam said.

It sounded like she growled at him. "Only because I was in the car with him. What no one seems to realize is that I could have died as well. It was freezing out there, and I couldn't move the car."

"So you say," Liam replied.

"Hey, hey, guys," Hamish said. "She's right. Why would she try to kill him if she was getting in the car with him? Besides, we don't even know if he was murdered."

"That's what the police said when they arrested me," Destinee said. "I have no idea how he died. I swear it was a heart attack. One minute he was fine, and the next he was clutching his chest. I didn't kill him. I swear to you."

"We need to find out how he died," Boscoe said. "Maybe if we knew that, then we could help the police. Instead of sharing the information with us, they just toy with us. I can't wait for this memorial to be done, and then I'm going home and locking the door. They can talk to me through my solicitor." He didn't sound happy at all.

"I think we all feel that way. At least now we can get home," Liam said. I thought it was Liam. The voice was lowered, so it was hard to tell. I'd also only spoken to them a couple of times.

"I wish we'd never come to this place," Destinee said. "Sorry, Hamish. It's a cute town. I know it has special meaning for you and Bram. But we've had nothing but trouble since we arrived."

There seemed to be a lull in the conversation.

I knocked on the pocket doors before opening one side.

"Doctor," Destinee said. "Did you need something?"

Oh, I had so many questions, but I had to play this cool.

"Actually, I'm finalizing some paperwork. I must admit I'm surprised to see you all here. I thought with the pass open you'd be headed home."

"I'm not allowed to leave," Destinee bit out. "At least for now. I'm still under caution."

"The rest of us are hanging around for the memorial. Did you hear about that?" Boscoe asked.

"Except for me," Hamish said. "I'm staying with my mum for the holidays."

"I did hear about the memorial," I said. "I was wondering whose idea it was to hold it here."

"That would be my mum," Hamish said. "She doesn't like the idea of Bram not having a proper ceremony. The rest of the gang agreed. But now, the record company has sort of taken over. They think it's a great idea to have it in Bram's hometown."

The others nodded.

"We'll do something after the New Year for Davy," Liam said. "That is what his family in Glasgow want. They'll be doing a private service when they get the body back." He stared at me expectantly. "Any idea when that might be?"

I shrugged. "Soon," I said.

"But we're Bram's family," Hamish said. "So, we're going to do right by him."

They all nodded again. The animosity I'd heard through the door seemed to be gone. They were putting up a united front.

Interesting.

"I'm curious, given what you know now about Bram, do you have any new insight into what might have happened in the days leading up to his death?" I held up a hand. "I know the police have been all over it, and you're probably sick of answering questions. But I'm asking more from a medical perspective. I want to understand what Bram and Davy were going through before they died."

The band members all looked at one another.

Hamish, who had been pacing back and forth behind the couch, sat down in one of the wingback chairs. He still seemed fidgety, but who could blame him? "I told you what I know," he said.

"And what's that?" Liam asked.

"That he'd been helping Bram write the new songs, right?" Destinee asked.

Hamish stared at her in surprise. "You knew?"

She shrugged. "I had a feeling something was different. Bram was a great songwriter, but the new ones were . . ."

"More soulful," Boscoe said. "Deeper, in a way. That was you, man?" he asked Hamish.

He blushed and then nodded. "They were Bram's ideas. I just helped make them more coherent."

"So he really was losing his mind," Liam said. "Do you know why, Doc?"

I glanced at Hamish, who had tucked his chin to his chest. He just stared down at the floor.

"I'm not supposed to comment on an ongoing investigation."

They sighed collectively. I might have laughed if things hadn't been so serious.

"Davy told us all about the early Alzheimer's," Liam said. "And Destinee told us that's why Bram killed himself."

I glanced at her. She, too, was staring at her feet. Something was hinky about her story, but I just couldn't quite put my finger on it.

"We're not sure he did commit suicide." I don't know why I said it. Maybe it was to see how they'd react, and I wasn't disappointed.

They all glared at her.

"I only relayed what Davy told me in the car," she said. "I don't know if he killed him or not, but he was there. He told me that." She started to cry. Boscoe, who sat on the sofa with her, handed her a tissue.

"No one is blaming you," he said.

From the looks on the others' faces, I wasn't so sure about that.

"Right now, let's focus on the hours before Davy's death," I said. "Actually, the whole day. Can you tell me about his movements? Did he run into anyone unusual?" I thought about the hooded man. Was there a stranger out there who could be behind all of this?

"If he died of a heart attack, why does that matter?" Hamish asked.

He made a great point.

"I wanted to see if anything happened that might have triggered the episode. He wasn't on any sort of blood pressure medication that we could find. While heart attacks seemingly out of the blue aren't that unusual, I need to make certain I have all the facts before signing his death certificate. Also, the police have determined there was some sort of foul play."

There was no reason to tell them about the embolism.

"And they blame me," Destinee whispered.

I was certain Davy had been murdered, possibly by someone in this room. Whether it was Destinee . . . my gut said no, but I just wasn't sure.

"He spent most of the day on the phone," Boscoe said. "He was in his room. We did go out to the pub, though. Not the one on the corner, but the other one. The one on the corner with the good shepherd's pie was closed."

I smiled. That was Mara's Pig & Whistle. They had excellent shepherd's pie.

"Oh, I forgot about that," Liam said. "He's right. Davy had rented a car, just to get us out of the house. We went to the pub and walked around some of the shops. We signed a few autographs, but the fans kept their distance for the most part.

"We came back just as the forest walking thing was happening. We had to take a detour to get around the crowds so we could get back to the B and B. Davy had wondered if we should show our faces so the rumors would stop, but we talked him out of it."

It had been Davy who asked Destinee to say something to the crowd the night of the tree lighting. I wasn't surprised. That confirmed our theory that he had wanted to show the public that she didn't try to kill herself over grief.

And that he only cared about the band having decent PR.

I had a feeling that if had Davy survived, he'd be in jail as the most likely suspect, but he was no longer a factor. Still, it had to be someone in this room.

I shuddered and then cleared my throat.

"Did you go anywhere else during the day? Did anything happen at the pub?"

Boscoe frowned. "There were a few people at the pub, but they left us alone. Before that, we walked up and down a bit by the sea."

"It was freezing," Destinee said. "They went for a walk. I went on to the pub."

"Aye, that's right," Hamish said. "That's when he told us about his plan."

"His plan?" I asked.

"To scale down the tour but to continue on. It was going to be a memorial tour for Bram."

"What did you all think of that?"

They were quiet for a bit. I'd learned from Ewan to let the question hang.

"I wasn't happy," Boscoe said finally. "It all seemed too fast and not quite right. I get that Davy was worried about the money, but we loved Bram. We need more than a month to mourn him. The fans deserved that time as well."

The others nodded.

"Davy only cared about money and the band losing traction," Hamish said. "I know it's not kind to speak ill of the dead, but . . ."

"He's right," Liam said. "Bram was our friend. Yes, we had our arguments, but we were as close as any family. When we said all that to Davy, he reminded us we'd signed contracts. We were legally obligated to continue touring."

"Like it didn't matter that our friend was dead," Liam said. Out of all of them, he seemed the angriest at Davy.

I needed to investigate his background.

"How did you feel about all of that?" I asked Destinee.

She sighed again and then sniffed. "I don't care if I ever perform again," she said.

The guys jerked their heads back.

She shrugged. "I'm sorry. After everything that has happened, I just feel so lost. Like the world is never going to be right again." A tear slid down her cheek. She did not seem like someone who had committed murder.

But I'd been fooled before—well, more than once—by a killer.

"You might feel differently after a few months," Hamish said. "But we all need time to grieve. Hopefully, the new label guy will give us more time."

"Label guy?"

"Yeah," Boscoe said. "With Davy gone, the record company decided to send one of their own to look after us until we find a new manager." He sighed. "If we decide to find one. We're supposed to meet after the holidays with the label. They've also taken over everything to do with the memorial."

"Which is a blessing," Destinee said. "I can't even think straight right now. That one policewoman had me so confused. I was ready to confess to everything just to make her stop."

"Oh? I'm sure that was difficult." I pretended to be surprised. Bethany could be a bit aggressive at times, but I had a feeling she was great at her job.

"Aren't you with them?" she asked. "Are we even supposed to be talking to you? *They* have to go through the lawyers."

I shrugged. "I leave the cop stuff to them. I just investigate the medical side of things to see if I can figure out how it happened. They concentrate more on the who and why."

"I suppose that makes sense," Boscoe said. He didn't look like he believed me.

"I'd like to go back to Bram, even a few weeks ago. Did you have any idea about his condition?" I stared at Hamish. I was curious since he had known.

"No," he said as he stared back at me. "I don't think anyone but me and Davy knew."

"Like we've said a hundred times before, he was grouchier, maybe," Liam said.

"He never did have much patience," Boscoe said. "Now that we know he was having trouble, it makes sense. I feel bad that we argued so much. I wish he would have just confessed everything. We could have helped more."

"What about? I only ask to see if maybe he had some triggers."

"It was always about the music," Hamish said. "He knew exactly what he wanted, and sometimes we didn't meet his expectations—until that night at the pub when it all came together."

Destinee smiled. "I think we were all surprised. I remember Bram saying that maybe we just needed that live audience to make us work. I'm so glad we had that night."

"Me too," Boscoe said. "He was pleased—we all were—that everything had gone over so well. Especially the new songs."

"The ones that Hamish helped him write?"

They all turned to look at him. His eyes went wide.

"Render, how long had you been helping him?" Liam asked.

"And more to the point, why not tell us the truth about what was going on with him?" Boscoe asked. "We could have helped."

"I'd been helping Bram for the last few months," Hamish said. "When he started having trouble, I helped him out. He made me swear an oath. He dinnae want anyone treating him differently or thinking he wasn't able to do the tour."

"But Bram said he wrote all the songs," Destinee said. She seemed as confused as the rest of them.

"Right. He did. I just helped out a bit."

Why was he downplaying his contribution? I'd seen the handwriting. He'd done more than help.

I started to ask but then realized he probably didn't want to take anything away from Bram. He'd also made a pact.

"I'm curious as to how all of you met," I said. "I think I asked Bram in the car, but I don't think we talked about everyone."

"University," Destinee said. "Except for Hamish. They'd known each other since they were kids. Hamish was working on the farm but would come to Edinburgh for rehearsals and to play gigs on the weekend. I was friends with Liam and Boscoe, and Bram brought Hamish into the group."

They all nodded.

"It took about a year," Boscoe said, "but then we got on with the label, and we've been touring ever since."

"That seems fast," I said. "Not that I know anything about putting a band together."

"It was," Boscoe said. "We had a different sort of sound and that worked for us. We also got lucky one night when Davy came to one of our shows. He worked as a scout for the label back then. He discovered us."

"And this was your first time going to America?" They were international. I thought it odd that they hadn't toured in my home country.

"Oh, we've been there a couple of times," Boscoe said. "We had just never done the big arenas until now." He frowned. "Or rather, we were going to do them. Without Bram and Davy, I don't know what's going to happen with the label."

"That must be rough for all of you, I'm sure. You've been through so much. Oh, about Davy. That last day, are you sure you didn't run into anyone strange? Did you happen to see maybe someone in the shadows?"

The all looked at one another.

"What do you mean?" Boscoe asked. "Like a stalker?"

"Maybe, or just anyone who seemed to be hanging about that seemed suspicious."

Boscoe shrugged. "There are always people around. It comes with the territory."

That didn't surprise me.

"Well, thank you for speaking to me. If you think of anything else, let me know." I stood. "Oh, one more thing. Do any of you have any sort of medical training?"

Chapter
Twenty-Three

As I suspected, they all stared at me and shook their heads. If one of them was the killer, they would have known exactly why I'd asked if they had medical experience. That was going to take a deep dive into a background search, which I was certain the police had already done.

But that didn't mean I couldn't do one on my own.

"Doc, do you know exactly what happened to Davy?" Liam asked.

"About that, do you know if he had any previous medical conditions?"

"He took pills, but I didn't know what they were for," Hamish said. He glanced around at his fellow band members. They shrugged.

"Do you think he was murdered? I thought it was a heart attack?" Boscoe said.

Yes, he was definitely murdered. "That's why I'm here, to help fill out my report. I appreciate you talking to me today."

"Are you coming to the memorial?" Destinee asked.

I blinked. "I, uh, didn't know I was invited," I said.

"Everyone is," Hamish said.

"But we'll make sure you're on the list to get inside the church," Boscoe said. "You've helped Destinee and seem to be the only one in town who is genuinely interested in finding out what happened to our friends."

"Thank you for saying that. I am invested in knowing the truth."

I waved goodbye and then left. On my way through town, I stopped at the police station.

Henry greeted me as he was going out, his arms full of a basket of baked goods. "Oh, hi, Doc."

"Henry, can I help? You have your hands full."

He smiled. "I did some baking last night. I heard Abigail and Tommy were staying with you, and I thought I'd take them down some treats."

Henry was such a prince and so charming. I hoped Abigail clued in soon just how much he cared for her. She was sweet, smart, and pretty, but their relationship had to be the slowest burn ever. She also wasn't very trusting. He seemed to have the patience she needed, though, and the desire to see things through.

He was definitely one of the good guys, and Abigail deserved that.

"I could take them down for you. I just stopped in to see if Ewan was around."

He glanced down at the basket and then at me. "Oh. I, uh . . . I'm headed that way. I'll drop them off. The constable is inside. Bye, Doc."

I smiled as I watched him walk away. No way would he let me stop him from visiting Abigail. It was adorable.

Inside, Ewan was bent over his desk in the back staring at his computer.

Carl was at the front desk. "Doc? Is everything okay?" he asked.

Ewan stood when he heard him and then walked to the front.

Carl took a call and turned away from us.

"I, uh, just came from the B and B," I said. "I thought I'd stop in to see if you discovered anything about our suspects."

"You questioned them alone?" he asked.

I shrugged. "I was just getting some more background on Bram's and Davy's conditions. I was curious to know if you found out anything new about the band members' backgrounds."

"First of all, from now on, ask me or Bethany before you question them. They've already called their solicitors twice. We must get permission to speak to them." He seemed more surprised than angry.

I shrugged. "That's kind of why I didn't ask you. I told them I was there to ask about medical things, and they believed me. I don't think you'll get any complaints. They invited me to the memorial personally."

His eyes went wide. Then he cleared his throat. "Still. One of them might be a killer. It would be best if you had an escort in the future."

"Noted." The constable was always a bit overprotective, but I didn't bother pointing that out.

"What was your question?"

"I'm wondering how deep of a dive you've done into their history. Do any of them have any sort of medical training?"

"I was just going through their files, and I didn't see anything. Most of them were studying art or music at university, and they've all been in the band for years. Why?"

"Like I said before, the killer had to know what they were doing, and they had to be fast if Davy didn't notice what was happening. Or it happened when he was asleep."

"Right. I'm guessing none of them confessed to having medical training."

"Correct. So, if you didn't find anything in their background, then maybe it isn't them."

He sighed and then shoved a hand through his hair. He always did that when he was frustrated. "But you don't believe that, do you?"

"No. I know it was one of them." It was the first time I voiced that assertion out loud.

"I don't disagree."

"There's more to the story. Something we are missing. Destinee has to be lying about what Davy said, but we have no way to prove it. But I also don't think she was the one who killed Bram. Also, like we've said, it would make no sense for her to try and kill Davy before getting in a car with him."

"If you had to guess right now, who would you pick?"

I frowned. "I don't want to point fingers when I really don't have a clue. The three remaining men all seem to care deeply for Bram and Davy. That's why none of this makes sense. It feels like we're going in circles."

"We're just throwing things out there. Why would you pick them?"

I shrugged. "Normally, given the circumstances, Destinee would be my number one just because of her story about Davy and the fact she was with him in the car. But she would have been an idiot to kill someone and then sit in a car with them like that. I don't think it's her. I just wish she'd tell us the truth."

He nodded. "Who else?"

"I don't know," I said. "If Davy hadn't died, he would have been right up there where Bram was concerned. The other three—Liam, Boscoe, and Hamish—just don't seem the type. Hamish seems a bit protective of Destinee. Liam is the quietest of the group. Boscoe seems to be the one who is the most upset by all of this. Oh, and Hamish doesn't want to take credit for the songs he helped write."

"What are you talking about?"

My eyes went wide. I realized I'd forgotten to tell him about the notebook.

"Right. So, about that." I described what I'd discovered at Hamish's house.

He sighed. "Doc, that notebook is evidence. It should be here at the station. Do you have it with you?"

I shook my head. "It's locked in my office at the moment. I'll get it to you." But first, I was going to take pictures of everything. I don't know why, but I think I might find some sort of clues in the lyrics about Bram's state of mind.

He didn't seem the type to kill himself, and he'd bought that painting. I asked Ewan what he thought about the painting.

"Hmm. You're right. That is odd, though people in that sort of mental state can change their minds quickly. You'd know more about that than me."

"Yes. In a depressive state, people can do just about anything. His doctors should have been aware, though. I need to speak with his doctor. I'll call him when I get home."

"Let me know if you find out anything."

"How's your head?"

"It's fine."

He still wore a knit cap over the bandage. "If you come by later, I'll change out the dressing."

"Okay, Doc. Just be careful. Whoever did this hit me on the head and was following you. You asking those medical questions might give the killer the idea that you're on to them."

I sighed. I hadn't thought about that. "Unless it isn't one of them." I held up a hand. "But I hear you. I will be careful. You do the same."

He grinned. That didn't happen often, but it was heart-stopping when he did.

I waved goodbye and headed out.

Since I was close to Angie's tartan shop, I decided to stop in to see if she was there. After cleaning up some family business, she and her husband had finally taken their honeymoon. While I'd seen her on the night Bram and his band played at the pub, we hadn't had much time to talk the last month or so.

The bell clanged when I walked in, and I smiled when I saw her cutting some fabric on the long counter.

She threw down the scissors and opened her arms. "Hello, friend," she said.

"I've missed you." I hugged her hard. "How is married life?"

"Even more amazing than I thought it would be. I was coming down to see you after work today to tell you all about it." She seemed so happy, much more so than the last few times I'd seen her.

Her new father-in-law had been in on a plot with her stepmother to stop Angie and Damian's marriage. It was a huge mess that had taken a while to sort out, and it nearly killed me.

"I can't wait. I'll invite Mara, and we'll make a night of it."

"That sounds grand. How is the case going? I feel like I'm missing out on our snooping activities. I've been making the rounds at all the shops to catch up. Of course, I needn't have worried about this one. Granddad always has things in hand."

"Aye, I do," he said from the back room. "Been tending this business since before your papa was born."

We laughed.

"Is it true about Bram? Have you figured out what happened yet? I still can't believe he's dead and that we saw their last performance. It's weird."

"We're working on it. I was just headed down to my office to make some calls. I won't keep you from your work. If you don't have to get back to Edinburgh right away, let's have dinner tonight."

She nodded. "Damian has gone to London for business for a few days, and I'm staying with Granddad to help with holiday orders. I look forward to it."

"Great. There's another Viking holiday thing tonight, but maybe we can all go together."

"I'd like that. But it's not Viking. It's Swedish. It's St. Lucia Day. You will love it."

"I can't keep up," I said.

She smiled. "You get used to it. I kind of enjoy that the village likes to celebrate everything together and that they are so inclusive."

"I do too, but for someone who hasn't ever really celebrated the holidays, it can be a lot."

She laughed. "That I can understand. I'm guessing Mara volunteered you for everything so you wouldn't feel left out."

"You are correct. Oh, before I go, I'd like to get a new coat."

"What's wrong with the one you're wearing?"

I smiled. "I love it, but with all the layers I need for winter here, I sometimes feel like the Stay Puft Marshmallow Man."

"I have no idea who that is, but it doesn't sound good."

"It's fine if I'm not wearing three layers under it, but when I am, I feel like a giant marshmallow."

We laughed.

"Let's look at a more fitted one, then. I know just the thing."

She helped me pick out a very warm navy coat. While I thought it fit fine, she wanted to make a few alterations. She promised to bring it to me that night.

We hugged again, and I headed out. I was so lucky to have found Angie, Mara, and Abigail. They'd become wonderfully close friends, and I counted that blessing every day.

* * *

Back home, Abigail, Tommy, and Henry were hanging out in my kitchen. After grabbing a cup of coffee and one of the muffins Henry had brought, I went to my office and pulled up Bram's files.

The doctor treating his Alzheimer's was out on vacation, but I left a message for him to call me when he got a chance.

Then I called his GP.

"Dr. Helmbridge," he answered. I was surprised he'd answered his own phone.

"Hello, this is Dr. Emilia McRoy. I'm the coroner on Bram Stoker's case. I have a few questions for you, if you have the time."

"I have a few minutes," he said, "but I'm not sure how I can help. I haven't seen him since I sent him to the specialist for his condition."

"Right. I was just curious about a few things concerning his state of mind."

"Such as?"

"Did he ever have any suicidal tendencies?"

"Bram? No. He was upset when I told him what was happening, but he wouldn't have killed himself. He was more in a hurry for treatment so he could keep going. Told me he'd be working until he couldn't anymore." He paused. "It's sad, though, for a young man with so much talent to come to an end like that. Do you have any idea what happened to him?"

"The investigation is ongoing. I see from your notes that the last time you saw him was about three months ago?"

"That's correct. Like I said, that's when I sent him to the specialist."

"And he had no history of depression in the past? I'm not seeing anything in his records."

"No. He was full of fight and determination when I last saw him. Even with his condition, he'd be the last person I'd expect to take his own life. Why are you asking about his mental state?"

I pursed my lips. Even though I had only known Bram for a day, I would have thought the same thing. Bram was strong and capable, even with what was going on with his brain, but depression didn't always make sense. Those in extreme depressive states could become quite adept at hiding their condition.

Many patients put on happy faces for those around them, even though a chemical imbalance in their brain meant they felt something much different—and it was an imbalance. Most people could handle the ebb and flow of life, but when there was a disorder in the brain, everything became magnified and normal life was difficult to manage.

He could have been determined to end things before he was a burden to anyone. That I could understand.

"Is there anything else you can tell me about him that might help?"

"We did talk about the stress he'd been under with work. He was worried about putting a new tour together and keeping the band happy, all while dealing with a decreased mental capacity. But if any-one could find a way to cope, it would be Bram."

We talked for a short while longer and then hung up.

I realized I'd forgotten to tell Abigail about Angie coming for dinner, and I needed to check with Jasper and Mara to see if they could come over before the event later. Jasper was one of the girls in our book.

I sent a quick text to them. *Last-minute get-together at mine?* I asked.

Big order for tonight, but next time, Jasper texted back.

Then I went in search of Abigail. She and Henry were still in the kitchen talking softly. He was making googly eyes at her, and she was smiling.

I liked seeing her so happy. She deserved every bit of it. I couldn't think of two people more perfect for each other.

I cleared my throat, and they jumped as if I'd caught them at something. They were adults, but I didn't think either of them had much experience with relationships.

"Sorry to interrupt, but Abigail, Angie is coming over later for dinner. And I thought—" My phone dinged. I pulled it out of my pocket. Mara had texted back a thumbs-up emoji. "And Mara. I thought we could do one of our girls' nights before the event."

Henry frowned.

"Unless you have other plans, which is fine," I said quickly.

She shrugged. "Henry said he'd pick up Tommy and I for St. Lucia tonight, but we're free before that."

Henry smiled again.

"Will Tommy be okay with the crowds?" I asked.

"Actually, he's going to make cookies with Ewan's housekeeper," Henry said. "I set it up so Abigail could go tonight."

"Well, that was sweet of you," I said.

"Henry is very thoughtful," she said. I sometimes wondered if she noticed.

He seemed quite pleased by her admission. "I should get back to work," he said. "I'll see you at eight thirty."

Then he leaned down and kissed her cheek. They both blushed.

It was adorable.

Amid all the craziness with the investigation, it did my heart good to see these two making their way slowly toward each other.

* * *

Later that evening, I had our individual pizzas in the oven. I wasn't much of a cook, but I did know how to buy ready-made pizza dough and toppings.

"It feels like so long since we've done this," Mara said, and then sipped her wine.

"It was before my wedding," Angie said. "I'm so glad things are starting to get back to normal. Well, in a way. All Damian's business stuff is sorted, and his dad is in prison, so he can't harass us anymore. His mom is on a long vacation, and I'm not sure she'll be coming back. Caleb is in rehab, but he's doing much better. When he gets out, I think he might be joining his mom."

"How is your dad doing?" Angie's stepmom, the one currently married to her dad, had tried to kill her and had succeeded in murdering her ex.

She pursed her lips. "He started divorce proceedings, and from what I gather, he is off women for the moment. Can you believe that? My dad?" She shrugged. "Now, tell me what's happening with all of you. Abigail, are you still seeing Henry?"

Abigail blushed.

"Well, I guess I know that answer." Angie laughed as she said it. "You two are so good together."

Abigail took a deep breath. "He's patient with me and Tommy. For that, I'm grateful."

"Well, I'd say you're both very lucky," Mara added. "He's sweet, handsome, and kind. That is a difficult combination to find."

"She's right," Angie added.

"Ask him if he has an older brother," Mara joked.

We all laughed.

"I know I saw you at the pub, Mara, that night when the band played, but you were so busy we didn't get to catch up," Angie said.

Mara grinned. "It's been crazy busy with all the fans and press in town. I haven't had time to think or help much with Em's investigation."

"Hey, you have a pub to run," I said. "You don't need to worry about the investigation. Besides, between Ewan and Bethany, they have it handled."

"Who is Bethany?" Angie asked.

I explained the situation.

"But Ewan's surely been cleared, so why is she still hanging around?"

"The band was very popular, and the order came from the higher-ups," I said.

"Do you think they'll still be a band after all of this?"

I shrugged. "Honestly, without Bram and Davy to hold them together, I don't think so. I could be wrong. They talked about some person from their label coming to talk to them, but who knows?"

"They hired us to do the catering after the memorial," Mara said. "The record label, that is."

"How many do they expect?"

"We're catering for one hundred people. They just want to keep it to the band and their families and people from the label. No fans or press allowed."

"That makes sense," Abigail said.

I agreed.

"Can you at least tell us how the manager died?" Angie asked. "Maybe we can help."

I wasn't supposed to share details, but they all knew this town better than I did, and they'd helped before on cases.

I explained what happened.

"That's awful, and it could have happened at any time?" Angie asked.

I nodded.

"Someone is a very clever killer," Angie said. "You're sure it isn't Destinee? I mean, she was there."

Mara snorted.

We all looked at her.

"What?" I asked. "She's your friend, right?"

"I wouldn't say friend exactly," Mara said. "We ran in the same circles for a while. She has a gorgeous voice, but I can't see her as being bright enough to pull off something like this.

"And yes, I know how terrible that sounds. But you would need some sort of scientific knowledge, right? That was definitely not anything she was interested in when we were younger. Music has always been her life."

Abigail frowned.

"What is it?" I asked.

"I, uh . . ." She hesitated.

"We're just throwing things out. Feel free to say what's on your mind," I said.

"It didn't dawn on me at first, but then you mentioned someone would need access and medical knowledge."

"Right," I said. "Does one of the members have that? We haven't been able to find anything in their backgrounds. None of them was studying it when they were at university."

"No," she said. "But Hamish has worked on that farm his whole life, and his dad was a vet before he died. He knows his way around medicines and hypodermic needles. He's a sweetheart, though. He's always looked after his little brother and his ma. I just can't see it."

Lucy Connelly

"There is no good reason for killing someone, but maybe he had one," Mara said.

"It is certainly something to consider." She was right. Out of the group, he did seem the least likely.

But could Hamish, the young man who loved his family so much, be the killer?

Chapter
Twenty-Four

As the St. Lucia celebration came to a close, I smiled. I really loved this village and how they all pulled together. At least tonight's celebration was indoors. We were in the cathedral up the hill, and it was gorgeous. I'd never been inside, and the whole place was lit only by candlelight. The golden glow on the stained glass gave the space an ethereal feel.

Even though I didn't really know what was going on during the ceremony where a young girl walked up the center aisle in a crown lit by battery-operated candles, it was beautiful. Being with my friends made it even more special. Special breads, cookies, mulled wine, coffee, and tea were served afterward.

"I like the events that are inside," I said to Jasper when we made it to the table where his sweets were. He and the local bread baker had worked together to cater the event. Again, everyone was pitching in and working together.

"I'm a born Scotsman, but I agree, Doc," he said. "How is everything going? Did you see the band was here?"

"Were they?" I glanced around.

"They were up in the balcony but left right after it was over. I'm sure they're tired of being stuck in the B and B all the time."

It was odd that they'd risk being around so many people, though. Maybe they wanted the press to see them doing something normal.

"Did you hear about the memorial? I'm helping Mara with the catering."

"It's sad, but also good for business, right?"

He nodded. "I'm sorry I had to miss out tonight. I was baking until twenty minutes before the event."

"No worries. You know we'll do it again."

"So, did our Scooby gang come up with anything?" He whispered the question.

I smiled. "Maybe, but I can't talk about it here." There were way too many people around. "Do you by chance know the Lachlans? They have a sheep farm just outside of town."

He shook his head. "There's a lot of Lachlans in town."

"I'm talking about Render, from the band, and his family."

"Oh, yes. They were here. They sat in the balcony with the band, but I think they've left. Why?"

"Just curious if they were here," I said.

He narrowed his eyes.

"Do you know anything about them?"

He shook his head. "Years ago, when I was a kid, his da was our vet, but I don't know them. He was a few years ahead of me in school. And I'm gay." He said the last bit as if that explained why they didn't run in the same crowd.

"Then he missed out on having one of the most creative and best friends a person could have."

He grinned. "Aye, he did. So, is it, uh, him?" he whispered again.

I glanced around to see several people watching us.

He looked over my shoulder. "Oh. Got it. Make sure you try the ones with the cinnamon on top, Doc." He said it loudly so that it sounded like we'd been talking about his desserts.

I winked at him. He'd confirmed Abigail's story about Hamish's father. That said, Hamish wasn't a vet. Still, working on a farm and vaccinating animals did make him a more likely suspect.

Abigail waved me over.

"I think that's my signal to go." I gave Jasper a quick hug and then went to meet her. "What's up?"

"Henry has to get back to work, but he offered to take us all back down to your place."

"We could take the shuttles," I said. "I don't want him to have to go out of his way."

"He said he's heading that way for a call. But we need to hurry."

I followed her out. We climbed into Henry's police cruiser. It didn't go unnoticed that half the town watched us with curiosity. I was grateful we didn't have to stand out in the cold and wait for a shuttle.

"This is kind of you," I said.

"You're a sweetheart," Angie added.

"Yes, you are," Mara said.

Henry's cheeks bloomed pink in the rearview mirror. I couldn't hide my grin.

Abigail turned from the front passenger seat and gave us a look.

Henry laughed nervously. "It's no problem. I'm headed that way."

There was a bit of traffic ahead, but thanks to most people taking the shuttles, it only took about ten minutes.

We were just pulling up when a man went over the wall into the garden again.

Before I could say, "Did you see that?" Henry was out of the car and running for the wall. I unlocked the front door quickly, and we all ran out the back to see Henry chasing someone across the cemetery in my backyard, but it was impossible to see the person Henry was chasing. However, I did notice that the intruder was tall and lanky, just like the guy who had been following me.

"Who do you think it is?" Angie asked.

"No idea." I told them about being followed. "Last time it happened, it was a reporter who scared poor Tommy to death. Could be someone from the press, or the guy who hit Ewan over the head."

"Or the killer," Mara said.

We all shuddered.

"I'll be glad once this is over."

"I'm so glad we were here," Abigail said. "Do you think Henry is okay? Should we call Ewan?"

That wasn't a bad idea. I pulled my phone from my pocket.

"Doc?"

"Henry is in pursuit of a man who climbed over my wall just as we arrived," I said.

"Heading your way," he said. "Get inside and lock the door. Do not try to pursue." He hung up.

"Do you think he was trying to break in?" Mara asked.

"Probably wanted information on the deaths. Everything was still locked, so he didn't get inside."

"While it's been good for business, I'll be glad when we get back to normal," Mara sad.

"Me too. And here I thought I'd be bored having to take a month off."

They laughed, albeit a bit nervously.

A few minutes later, Henry came back, but there was no one with him. Ewan showed up at the back door around the same time. I let them into the kitchen where we'd been waiting. I checked to make sure the bodies and files were still locked away.

"Sorry, sir. Lost him," Henry said. He seemed quite sad about it. "Whoever it was knew the woods. I lost him in the trees about halfway up."

"Did you get a look at him?" Ewan asked.

"Hooded black jacket, about six two, but I didn't see a face."

Ewan glanced at me.

I nodded. "Yes, it does sound like the man who was following me."

"He was fast," Henry said. "Like he knew where he was going. I'd say it was a local."

"Right. We'll need to make certain the doc's place is covered. We need to find out what it is they want."

"Maybe it's someone from the media trying to get a look at the bodies," I said. "I mean, it's gruesome and awful, but it wouldn't be the first time."

He nodded. "Have you talked about the case with anyone?" He smirked. "Except for your little crew."

"I take offense to the *little* comment," Mara said.

"Me too," Angie said. "Just tonight, Abigail gave the doctor a clue."

"Please share." He stared pointedly at Abigail.

She explained about Hamish's dad.

"However, I can't see him doing something like this," Abigail said. "He's always been nice to me and Tommy, and he's taken care of his family."

"I'd forgotten about his father," Ewan said. He had a weird look on his face. "But he also has an alibi for the first death."

"They all did," I said. "Maybe we're looking at two killers."

Everyone stared at me.

"I mean, Davy could have helped Bram like Destinee said, but then one of the band members found out and took exception. It's also possible that they all did it and are protecting one another."

"It's plausible," he said. "But . . ."

"How do we prove it?" I asked.

"Any chance the DNA results have come back on Davy's clothing?" he asked.

"Not yet. Bethany said she'd get them to rush, but it's been a few days."

"I'll speak with her."

"That said, they were all together. It would be easy for a lawyer to say that the DNA transfer could have happened at any time."

"Have you all been watching *Vera* again."

"No," I said. "*Professor T* and *Annika*."

He smirked.

"But I'm right."

He sighed. "You are. We need the murder weapons."

"I don't think we're going to find them," I said. "One is probably out at sea, and the other . . ."

"What?"

"Did you guys go through the trash at the B and B? I mean, there might be a chance, right?"

He shrugged. "I'll get my team on it."

"Still, even if you find it, they may not have left fingerprints," I said.

"Yes, but if we find it there, then it was someone staying at or visiting the B and B. That will narrow down our search."

"True."

"In the meantime, someone will be on guard. Whatever our runner was after, we have to make sure they don't get it."

I nodded.

"Do you need me to stay the night?" Mara asked.

"Or me?" Angie asked.

"Abigail and Tommy are here," I said. "And like Ewan said, he'll have someone posted."

After everyone left, I was exhausted. Still, I checked twice to make sure all the doors and windows were locked up.

As I climbed the stairs to my bedroom, I wondered if this might be the first case we wouldn't be able to solve.

I really didn't like the idea of someone getting away with murder.

Chapter
Twenty-Five

On the day of the memorial service for Bram, I woke up early so that I could help Mara and Jasper set up for the small gathering after the event. The band had said I'd be on the list, but I wanted to make sure I was there. Helping my gang was a way of making that happen.

At first, the memorial was supposed to be a private affair but that had changed. The record company, who was now in charge of everything since Davy had been killed, had received backlash from fans. I, along with most of the people in town, had been surprised that they kept the event in Sea Isle.

The whole town swarmed with people. Yesterday, several crews had arrived to set up tents in the multi-acre meadow behind the cathedral where the memorial would take place. They'd also allowed cameras and media inside the church so that the whole thing could be presented to the world. There were monitors in the tents outside, where they predicted thousands of fans would show up just to be close to Bram and to say goodbye. The inside of the church was for invited guests only.

Our little town wasn't equipped for that many people, but Ewan and his team were doing their best, and everyone in town was chipping in to help. Luckily, because there weren't any available rooms for people to stay, most of the visitors would be gone soon after the memorial. That was a blessing. Unfortunately, it also meant our suspects would be gone as well, and we were still no closer to solving the case. I was beginning to doubt we ever would. Whoever had murdered Bram and Davy had been incredibly clever. I'd be watching them all closer today, especially Hamish.

For the safety of everyone visiting, and our townies, only shuttles and authorized vehicles were allowed to go up and down the mountain to the old part of town where the cathedral was. Cars were parked along the seawall as far as I could see. Some people had chosen to walk up the mountain, and there were droves of them already headed that way. Others were queued up in long lines for the shuttles. Luckily, I hitched a ride in Mara and Jasper's catering van. After helping them load up, we joined the slow crawl up to town.

"I can't believe how fast they put this together and how many people have shown up," I said.

"I wondered how it would work when they said it would be private," Mara said. "The band is huge in Scotland and all over Europe. We had fans from Italy and Germany in the pub this morning. There were even a couple of girls from Iceland who had flown over."

"As terrible as the situation might be, it's put Sea Isle on the map," Jasper added. "I was so busy yesterday that I had to close early so I could get ready for today. The shop was packed, and I had a line waiting outside the door. I'd been worried about surviving winter, but I've made three months' worth of income in the last week. And yes, I know how awful that sounds."

"It's the same at the pub. Thankfully, we have extra help since a lot of the university students we use in the summer are home for the holidays. Otherwise, we might have had to close as well. Granddad has made three trips for supplies in the last two days."

"I wouldn't feel guilty," I said. "Think of it as providing a service to all these people from out of town who might have been very hungry without you."

"There is that," Jasper agreed.

"Do either of you know what they have planned for the service?" I asked.

Mara handed me a file folder with a schedule.

"Wow, that's a lot of people speaking," I said. Some were government officials, and others were celebrities.

"They think it will be a minimum of two hours, but it will most likely go much longer," Mara said. "I can't believe all of this has happened. Like, I'm still trying to get my head around it. I knew them all when they were just starting out. I feel guilty that it happened here. If I hadn't invited them to play, then maybe Bram and Davy would still be alive."

I shook my head. "Mara, it isn't your fault. Bram, well, he didn't have much longer to live. Someone took advantage of the situation. It had nothing to do with you. I have a feeling it would have happened no matter where they were. Someone wanted them dead."

If I could only figure out why, maybe I'd know the who of the equation.

"Any news you can share?" Jasper asked. "We know it's still going on, but maybe we can keep an eye out today for you. That is, if we have some idea what to look for among your suspects."

I smiled. My group of friends had helped me many times, and while I couldn't tell them everything, there were some things I could share.

"We finally received all the DNA test results, which was why we were able to release the bodies."

"Did it help?" Mara asked.

"Unfortunately, no. As we suspected, there were several different samples on the clothing and skin. We saw Bram hug fans and the band members that night. The DNA could have transferred at any time. And there was no blood, which would have helped pinpoint the suspect who most likely killed them. My hope was that it would at least help us narrow down our suspect list, but it didn't. Same with Davy."

"Real life isn't like the television shows you all make me watch," Jasper said.

I smiled. "I wish we could wrap things up that easily. I don't feel so bad since Ewan and Bethany are experienced law enforcement officers, and they are just as stumped. I just was hoping . . ."

"You could provide the missing piece of the puzzle," Mara said.

"Yes. It sounds so egotistical."

"No, it doesn't," Mara said. "As the coroner, you want to find out exactly what happened and solve the crime. I'd feel the same way. I do feel the same way. I want you to have this win because once you figure it out, you'll be safe from the person who has been following you and trying to break into your house."

There was that.

"Do you have any idea who it might be?" Jasper asked.

I breathed in deeply. "Like I said before, my gut says it is one of the band members, mainly because of proximity and history. There was a lot going on behind the scenes with them. I'd hoped the DNA would give us something more specific, but the killer, or killers, were quite careful. I've got nothing."

"So, tell us what you need from us today," Jasper said.

"Listen for anything that might be going on between them. If you hear snippets of conversations that might be interesting for us to follow up on, or if you see them arguing, let me know. They do that a lot, but from what I understand, it isn't unusual for them.

"It is wishful thinking, but part of me hopes this memorial will make one of them break, and that he, or she, will confess."

"You never know," Mara said.

"We will keep an eye out for you," Jasper added. "I love this Scooby-Doo stuff."

I smiled. "Just be careful, and don't draw attention to yourself. I don't want anyone to get hurt. Unlike the cartoon, we have a real killer who has murdered twice."

"You might want to take your own advice," Mara said, and she shuddered.

She wasn't wrong.

When we arrived, there was still two hours until the service began. I helped them unload the van into the kitchen at the other end of the cathedral. I was helping them set up in the hall for the private event after the service when my phone buzzed in my pocket.

It was Ewan.

"Hi," I said.

"Doc, we got a call that they need you at the B and B for a medical emergency," he said. "I was wondering where you were."

"I'm at the cathedral helping Mara and Jasper."

"Good. I'm just outside."

"My kit is in Mara's van. I brought it just in case we needed it."

"Even better. I'll meet you at the van."

By the time I let Mara and Jasper know what was happening, Ewan already had my kit out of the van. We headed toward his SUV police cruiser. He turned on the lights on top, and the crowd parted to let us through.

"Any idea what's going on at the B and B?"

He shook his head. "Mrs. Beatty called the station and said they had a medical emergency. We are about to find out." He parked the car in front of the B and B. Then he carried my mobile kit inside for me.

In the lobby area, the screaming coming from the front parlor was earsplitting.

"If she starts throwing things, I want you to toss them all out," Mrs. Beatty said. "They've been arguing all morning, and I dinnae think my nerves can take much more. Never in my life have I had more dramatic clientele."

"Hopefully, we can help," I said over the noise.

She rolled her eyes and headed off toward the kitchen mumbling something about bread in the oven.

221

Ewan didn't bother knocking. He opened the pocket doors and walked inside.

"Thank God you're here," Destinee screeched. "One of them tried to kill me while I was sleeping. Like Davy, I'm going to die any minute. You have to do something, Doctor." She was wide-eyed and panicked like a wild animal in a trap.

I turned to Ewan. "Constable."

"Gentlemen," he said to the band, "we will give them some space." He ushered them out of the room.

I approached her slowly so as not to startle her any more than she already was. She was curled up in one of the wingback chairs with her arms around her knees. Her face was covered in mascara because she'd been crying, and her skin was blotchy with red spots.

"Why don't you tell me what happened," I said softly. I opened my kit.

"I was getting ready this morning, and I noticed this bruise on the inside of my arm. There's a red mark inside like a pin hole. I think one of them stuck me with a needle, and I probably don't have much longer to live. There's no telling what kind of drugs they shot me up with. Can you save me?"

"Let me examine your arm."

She held it out for me. I grabbed my lighted magnifying glasses out of my kit.

"Can you figure out what kind of drug it is in time?" She was shaking hard.

"Take a deep breath for me and hold it."

She did as I asked.

"Now let it out slowly."

While she did that, I examined her arm. There was a small scratch inside the bruise, but it wasn't a puncture. "You're going to be okay," I said. "No one stuck you with a needle. It's just a scratch. You must have brushed up against something."

She yanked her arm away and stared down at the bruise. "But there is a red bump."

"Right, but it's a scratch. Would you like to use my magnifying glasses?"

She waved a hand. "Are you certain? After Davy and Bram . . . I thought they tried to kill me."

"Who is they?"

"One of the band members. The same ones who killed Davy. I don't trust anyone anymore." Given what had happened, I couldn't blame her. I would have been suspicious as well. Unless she was trying to throw suspicion off herself.

I pursed my lips. I remembered that Mara had said she didn't think Destinee had the knowledge to kill her friends, but who knew at this point?

I wish I did.

Destinee took another deep breath. "I'm an idjit. I'm so wound up right now. I feel like a guitar string pulled too tight, and I might break at any moment."

"That is understandable," I said. "You've been through a great deal of trauma over the past week. You're also getting ready to say goodbye to a dear friend, and you've lost another one. Not to mention you were also in a car accident. My guess is that the bruise happened a while ago. It can sometimes take days for contusions to show up."

She sighed. "And I took too many pills that one night. I wish we weren't having this memorial service. I could use a pill right now, but I can't show up looking like a zombie. The press would have fun with that."

I had a feeling she was asking for something to help calm her down, but I had a better idea.

"Breathe with me. We're going to breathe in for four, hold for six, and exhale slowly for an eight count."

I took her through it a few times. By the last round, her shoulders dropped and the shaking subsided.

"Wow. Who knew?" She smiled. "I'm so embarrassed, though. What will I say to the guys?"

"I think they'll be happy to know you're fine."

"And crazy," she said.

"We don't use that term. And after everything that's happened, no one would blame you for being a bit . . ."

"Paranoid?" she said.

I shrugged. "Whenever you feel overwhelmed, try that breathing exercise or boxed breathing."

"What's that?"

"Same sort of thing, except four counts for everything and you hold the bottom of the breath once you let it out." I showed her.

"I can't believe how much calmer I feel."

I smiled.

"How is she?" Ewan asked from the doorway.

"Much better," I said. "She'll be fine."

"Where are the guys? I need to speak with them," she said.

The band rushed in, and I walked back to the lobby with Ewan.

"Everything okay?" he asked.

I nodded. "Just a bruise, but she thought it was a puncture." She thought it was drugs, though. Did that mean she didn't have a clue about the embolisms? Or, again, had she been trying to throw suspicion from herself?

Ugh. Circles. This case was nothing but circles with few clues.

He raised his eyebrows.

"If I were her, I'd be paranoid as well, but she's fine," I assured him.

I glanced at my phone. "It isn't long until the ceremony starts. We should probably go."

He nodded as he picked up my kit.

When we were back in the car, he hesitated for a moment.

"What?"

"Do you think it was a ruse to throw suspicion off herself?"

"I thought the same thing at first. But no, I don't think so, because she was pale and shaking so horribly. She was headed toward shock. I believe she was truly frightened."

He started the car. "I just wondered."

"If she was faking it, she's one heck of an actress. She'd deserve an Oscar for that performance."

"I wish they'd never come here," he said under his breath.

"Mara was saying the same thing earlier. But once they leave . . ."

"It's going to be nearly impossible to find the killer," he said.

He wasn't wrong.

Chapter Twenty-Six

The cathedral was packed and standing room only. I sat on the end of one of the rows in the balcony with Jasper and Mara. One dignitary after another talked about the contributions of Bram to Scotland and the world of music. But it was when Boscoe spoke for the band that I felt my eyes water.

"We may have come from different mothers and fathers, but he was our brother," Boscoe said, and then his voice caught. Hamish and the others stood with him. Destinee took his hand in hers and nodded.

"None of us would be who or where we are if it hadn't been for Bram. He was our North Star, and yes, we all know how corny that sounds, but it is true. We are lost without him." His voice caught again, and tears burned my eyes.

Mara, who was crying, handed me a tissue.

When he finished, people clapped, which seemed odd at a memorial. Then several musicians played pieces Bram had written. Many of the songs were quite moving for the occasion.

When it was over, more than half of the mourners left. The rest joined the band in a banquet room at the back of the cathedral. I'd offered to help Mara and Jasper, but they, along with their servers, had things handled.

Several pieces of memorabilia from Bram's estates had been placed around the room. There was everything from original pieces of music he'd written to art and photos. There were even some of his journals where he'd jotted down songs and notes of his adventures. Everything was in chronological order, and it was fascinating to see how his artistic endeavors had grown in depth over the years.

But there was something in the song journals that bugged me for some reason. I couldn't quite place what it was. I took my phone out of my pocket and snapped a few pictures. I wasn't sure why exactly, only that when things weren't so crazy, I wanted to sit down and analyze some of the pages. There was something strange I couldn't quite pinpoint, but maybe it would come to me later.

"I dinnae know you were such a fan," Boscoe said from beside me.

I jumped a bit and slapped my hand on my chest.

"Did I frighten ya?"

I smiled. "No, and yes. I'm a bit jumpy these days. I've become a fan of you all. I love your music. And you did a wonderful job during the service."

He grinned. "Thank you, Doctor. What do you think of all this?"

"The anthropological and scientist part of my brain is fascinated by how your band has grown in fandom over the years. I also admire how much depth and meaning your songs have. I get really caught up in his writing."

"Aye, he had a gift," Boscoe said.

"Do you think all of this will end up in a museum some day?"

"Before he died, Davy was working on it. They were looking at locations the last I heard. There had been some sort of endowment for the arts or something. So, I'm fairly certain it will happen."

"Maybe, since Sea Isle is his hometown, they'll set it up here."

He shrugged. "Perhaps. But my guess is they'll pick one of the bigger cities for tourist reasons."

"That makes sense."

"I actually had another reason for chatting you up," he said.

"What's that?"

"After this morning, I'm really worried about Destinee's mental state. We have all been under a lot of pressure the last few months, and then . . . She and Bram were, uh, closer, and his death . . ."

"Do you mean they were lovers?" This wasn't the first I'd heard about that. If it were true, I felt sorry for her. He had been a flirt, and that couldn't have been easy for her to watch.

He shrugged. "Off and on over the years. She's always loved him, and I think he loved her, but he was never much for anything long-term. He didn't believe in traditional relationships or marriage. It's been rough on her. She pretends she doesn't care, but his death was probably harder on her than any of us. I just want to make certain she is okay."

I pursed my lips. "Technically, she's a patient, and I can't discuss her medical condition. But I'm glad she has you looking out for her. I wouldn't leave her on her own for long. She needs time and some good friends to help her through this rough patch. Hanging out with her is the best thing you can do for her right now."

"Should we consider putting her in a facility?" He glanced around to see if she was close. She was talking to some executive-looking man in the corner.

"Again, that's not for me to say and that should be her decision. The most you can do for her right now is to just be there for her. Maybe keep her mind on other things. You've all been through a great deal. A distraction wouldn't hurt. Maybe think of something she likes beyond music."

"We will do our best." He turned to leave.

"Wait. I'd like to ask you something," I said.

"You still want to know if one of us killed them," he said. "I'd like to know the same thing. I've been with these guys since I was in college, and I can't imagine any of them hurting Bram and Davy. That's the truth. We are family. Yes, we had disagreements and awful fights sometimes, but we loved one another."

I nodded as he walked away. What I didn't mention was, more often than not, people were killed by family or friends every day. As difficult as the truth might be, it was more likely that Bram and Davy were killed by someone they knew.

I mean, from what Destinee said, Davy helped kill Bram. Now, we just had to find out who killed the manager.

I stayed awhile longer to make sure that Mara and Jasper didn't need any help. Before heading back down the mountain, I stopped by Angie's shop to pick up a few more gifts.

"How did it go?" she asked when I walked into the shop. It was crowded with people who were mostly likely doing some holiday shopping.

"About how you would expect," I said.

"We watched on the telly. I may have teared up a few times."

"You aren't the only one," I said. "There were times when it was quite moving. I had no idea the impact he had on Scottish culture or what an icon he was to the rest of the world."

When I made it closer to the counter, she leaned over. "Did you learn anything new?"

I shook my head. "No. I wish someone would have broken down and confessed in the middle of everything, but we weren't so lucky that way. I guess it will be up to the police now."

She scrunched up her face. "I'm sorry. I know how important it is to you to solve these cases."

"Even though it's not really my job, you're right, though I don't think I realized how much it matters until this one. I do feel like I have an answer to something, but I also feel like I'm missing the information I need to connect the dots. I don't really know how to explain it."

"When I get off work, why don't we grab something to eat? Then we can head to yours, and you can go over the whole thing with me. It might help to talk things out."

"Thank you," I said. "Are you sure?"

"Of course."

Someone came to the counter with a handful of items.

"You're busy. I was going to pick up a few more gifts."

"Take your time," she said as she went to help the customer.

While I shopped, I thought about everything I'd learned in the last week. Angie was right. I needed to sit down and go through each piece of evidence. Something would probably pop out that I'd missed.

When the customer left, I piled my gifts on the counter.

"How do you like your new coat?" Angie asked.

"I love it, and I don't feel like a marshmallow."

We laughed.

After making my purchases, I headed down the mountain in one of the shuttles. The crowd had thinned out, so the trip didn't take long.

In my office, I found a note from Abigail on my desk. They'd fixed the boiler at their home, so she and Tommy had left.

The place felt empty without them.

After making some coffee and putting cheese and crackers on a plate, I went around gathering files and my notebook on the case. I piled everything onto the kitchen table. I started with the medical files.

The two men had been killed with different instruments but in the same way. The killer had at least a bit of medical knowledge. However, after doing a search on the internet, I realized it wouldn't have been that difficult to learn what to do.

Then I went through my notes on the band members. I had exactly two suspects in mind: Destinee and Hamish. Still, I couldn't figure out why Hamish would kill his friend.

Destinee definitely had the strongest motive, especially now that I knew she and Bram had been lovers. But I had nothing more than hunches, and that wouldn't help the constable or Bethany arrest anyone. Also, she was short. I didn't see how she could have stuck that corkscrew into the base of Bram's skull.

"Ugh."

I turned to the notebook pages that I'd found at Hamish's house, and I printed out the ones from the photos on my phone. Then I set them side by side. It took me a few minutes, but then it hit me. The handwriting was very different. Even though Bram's mental capacity had been altered, his handwriting wouldn't have changed this much.

I checked each letter between what Bram had supposedly written in a strange scrawl and what Hamish had written. The letters were mostly the same. Why would Hamish say Bram had written the first bits? That didn't make sense. If Hamish wrote the songs outright, why wouldn't he just take credit?

I was about to call Ewan when there was a knock on the front door. Thinking it was Angie, I opened it.

Destinee and Hamish stood there, neither of them looking particularly happy.

Chapter
Twenty-Seven

Hamish shoved Destinee inside, and if I hadn't moved quickly, we would have tumbled over each other. I caught her before she fell to the floor, but I didn't miss the gun he carried.

This is bad. I'd never been a fan of guns—even less so when murderers carried them.

"Stop it," she growled. "Why are you doing this?"

"You know why," he said. "You know what happened." He shut the door behind him. Part of me wanted to run for the bat that was just behind the door in my office. But bullets went much faster than I could run, and I didn't want to risk him hurting Destinee.

"Maybe if you explain it to me, we could figure out something less violent," I said. Keeping him calm was the only way out of this. I put my hand in my pocket and found my phone. I hit 999. At least, I hoped those were the numbers I pushed. Then I muted it as I turned away.

"Why don't we sit down and talk this out." I motioned toward my office. "I'm afraid I'm at a loss right now. Did you have something to do with Bram's and Davy's deaths?"

"Why are you asking me questions?" He was angry. "I saw you taking the photos of the journals. You figured out what I did."

"I took pictures because I'm a new fan and I liked the lyrics." I wasn't much of a liar, but I had to try.

"I don't understand," Destinee said. "So what if she took pictures? It's not a crime."

"She knows about the songs," he said.

Destinee stared at me, wide-eyed and confused. I didn't blame her. I'd only put it together myself.

"Let's at least sit down, Hamish. Think of your mom and your little brother. They wouldn't want you to do something that might get you into trouble."

I walked toward my office, praying he didn't shoot me in the back.

"Just stop. Whatever you are trying to do, it won't work," he said. "I'm doing this for my family. They need me. No one can find out what I did. You are smart, Doc. As soon as I saw you taking photos of those journals, I knew you understood what I'd done."

But not really. "Right. About that. I haven't really pieced it together, except I know the handwriting that you told me was Bram's is actually yours. What I don't understand is why."

I'd made it to the doorway of my office. The bat wasn't far away, but there was no way for me to get it without raising his suspicions. I had no plan, except to keep him talking. I prayed whoever might be on the other end of my 999 call would figure out what was going on.

"I thought if I could tell everyone they were songs I helped Bram with, they'd take me more seriously. He told me about his condition and that he didn't think he had much longer. Someone was going to have to take over the writing if the band was to continue. They're great songs. I was copying them from his notebook and trying to make them look like I did it."

"But he found out what you were doing."

"He found the notebook the night we played here. I'm not sure how."

I took in his watery eyes, runny nose, and pupil constriction. "But it wasn't just about the notebook, was it?" How had I missed the symptoms? Well, because they mimicked signs of grief.

"What do you mean?" he asked nervously. Then he used the butt of the gun to scratch his arm.

"He found your stash," I said. My guess was MDMA, otherwise known as Molly, was the cause of his unease. I saw more than my share of cases when I worked in Seattle.

Destinee gasped, and Hamish's eyes went wide.

"Drugs?" she said. "You know how he felt about that. Hamish, no."

"You should talk. You take prescriptions like they are candy."

"To sleep or for depression, but that's it," she said. "Why, Hamish? You're so talented. How long have you been on drugs?"

"None of that matters," he said.

"It does to me," she said. "You matter to me."

He shook his head. "Not enough to walk away from Bram for good. You told me that you just needed time. But I saw him coming out of your room that afternoon after rehearsals in Amsterdam. You promised me it was over."

She frowned. "What?"

"He was buttoning his shirt, Destinee. You told me you'd never sleep with him again."

He was in love with her. Everything came into focus. This was about much more than drugs and songs lyrics.

"No. It wasn't what you thought," she said. "He had a spot on his shirt he wanted to wear that night. I used my special pen to get it out. That is all, Hamish. I meant what I said when we were in Amsterdam. I was finished with him. I couldn't take it anymore.

"But I was honest with you about needing time. I didn't want to jump from my screwed-up relationship with Bram into something with you. You know I love you. We have been friends for most of our lives. I did not want to ruin what we had between us by jumping in too fast. I explained that to you."

"But . . ." He sniffed. Tears streamed down his cheeks. He put the gun down on the desk. Then he sobbed.

Destinee handed me the gun and then wrapped her arms around him. "Hamish, luv. I'm sorry for all of it. Tell me what you've done, and I'll help. I promise."

He cried even harder.

I stuffed the gun in my sweater pocket. I'd probably get in trouble for handling it, but I wanted it out of sight in case Hamish changed his mind.

"Tell me, Hamish. Why did you kill Bram and Davy?" she asked.

"They were going to kick me out of the band. All that work for so long, and they couldnae give me one break. Bram called me that night and told me to meet him at the beach. Then he had the nerve to laugh at me for writing songs and thinking I was as good as him."

"Did you plan to kill him?" I asked.

He glanced at me as if he'd forgotten I was there. He shook his head. "Nay. He had the corkscrew and a bottle of wine. Said he wanted to have one last drink with me. He was so calm, and it made me barmy. I took the bottle and the corkscrew and tossed them in the trash." Hamish sighed. "I was walking away from him. Told him to stuff it.

"Then he said, 'Destinee will never want to be with a drug addict.' I lost it. I grabbed the corkscrew and shoved it into his head. I dinnae know what would happen. I promise you that, Destinee. I was just angry."

She sniffed. "I believe you. But what happened with Davy?"

"He figured it all out. Bram must have said something to him that night about the drugs. Davy had been acting weird toward me and kept eyeing me suspicious-like."

With good cause it turned out.

"After what I did to Bram, I did some research. I had to get rid of Davy."

"Wait. Destinee, you told us that Davy was the one who killed Bram. That he'd confessed."

She took in a deep, shaky breath. "Because I knew you suspected me," she said. "I was trying to throw you off me."

Ewan burst through the door, and we all jumped. Bethany was right behind him, as was Henry.

After they arrested Hamish, Destinee went with them.

Ewan stayed behind. I pulled an evidence envelope out of my office and put the gun into it.

"How does he have a gun in Scotland? I thought that was nearly impossible."

He shrugged. "His family lives on a farm. 'Tis probably licensed to them."

"His poor mom and brother. Did you hear the confession?"

"Aye. Brilliant of you, Doc, to do what you did. We were able to record everything, but we were worried about your safety."

I threw up my hands in surrender. "I didn't go after it this time, though I did make the mistake of opening the door without checking my video. That's the first time in a long time that I've done that. I thought it was Angie coming to hang out. Boy, was I wrong."

He chuckled. "You handled the situation like a professional."

"I'd say that was due to Destinee's quick thinking. There was so much more to that story than I ever expected."

"True, but now it all makes sense. I'm not sure we would have ever caught him."

"Oh, you would have. He was incredibly unstable. I'm mad at myself for not catching his symptoms earlier. I should have known. I've seen drug addiction far too often in my career."

He shrugged. "We all missed it. The good news is that you're okay." He said it softly as if he really cared.

I may have blushed.

"Do you think he was the one who hit you over the head with the cricket bat?"

"Seems likely, though why he'd been skulking around here, I don't know."

"I bet he was after the journal. He was worried that someone might be able to prove it was faked."

"I still don't understand that part of all of this."

I shrugged. "In his drug-addled brain, I think he perhaps felt like if he could write the songs, he could keep the band together. He wanted to take Bram's place, especially in Destinee's heart."

"Love does make people do strange things." He gave me a sweet look that I didn't understand at all.

We stared at each other for a moment.

Awkward.

He cleared his throat. "I should head to the station."

I nodded. I was about to say something, but there was a flurry of activity down the hall.

"Is she okay?" Mara was asking.

I laughed as she and Angie pushed past the guards Ewan had posted. They swarmed us, checking me over.

"Tell us everything," Mara said.

Angie waved the constable away. "Shoo. She will not say a word with you around."

He laughed and shook his head.

As for me, I was grateful to have friends who cared about me.

"You'll never guess what happened," I said.

Chapter
Twenty-Eight

O n Christmas Eve, the town buzzed with activity. Tonight was
the Christmas crawl. While I'd finished my shopping earlier
in the month, I still had a few presents to wrap, but I was interrupted several times by patients who brought small gifts to thank
me. The same had happened earlier in the month when it was
Hannukah. I'd received so many breads, jams, jellies, cakes, and
pies that I was glad I'd have guests later in the evening to help me
eat them.

As I placed the last of the presents under the tree in my den, my
breath caught as I admired the decorations, lights, and music. It was
the first time since I was a kid at my grandmother's house that I'd
celebrated the holidays. My eyes watered just a bit that this was also
the first time my house would be filled with loving friends who had
become the most important people in my world.

The buzzer on the front door rang. I was surprised to see who it
was. I rushed to open the door. It was Peggy, one of the archivists at
the town hall. "Afternoon, Doc," she said. "I hope you dinnae mind
me stopping by." She'd been helping me research my ancestors, but
we hadn't come up with much other than I had a great uncle, Theo-
dore, who used to be a vicar in Sea Isle.

She held out a file folder. "The info I requested from the national archives finally came in, and I made some printouts for you. We still have not found your clan, but we are closer. You are from the McRaes, though. As we suspected, the name was changed to McRoy when your ancestors went to America in the 1800s. Your great-great-grandfather is listed, and I thought it might be a starting point for your genealogy search."

I swallowed hard. There were times when I felt so alone in the world, at least until I'd come to Scotland, that I would have given anything for this connection. My new friends had helped so much with that. Still, I was desperate to know about my family.

"Thank you so much. You could have waited until after the holidays. I'm sorry to take you away from your family."

"Nay. I know how much it means to you. The information came in this morning, and you have been waiting months. I thought it might make a nice holiday gift for you, especially since you did such a wonderful job caring for my Dobb."

Her husband, Dobb, had come in with pneumonia a month ago.

"That's my job," I said. "It was no trouble."

"And this is part of mine," she said. "I hope these documents give you some comfort. Happy Christmas!"

I waved goodbye. Then, I went to the kitchen and sat down at the table. I opened the file folder and brushed my fingers over the manifest that had my grandfather's name on it. Finlay McRae had taken a ship in the 1800s to South Carolina. There wasn't any information about what he did once he arrived in America, but hopefully, I could figure that out on ancestory.com.

I was about to search for my laptop when my alarm went off on my phone. Darn, it was time to meet up at Mara's.

The pub had closed early, but the door was open. We'd be going to my place last. That's where we'd be opening our gifts and eating the main meal, provided by Abigail. But we had different types of foods at each house. First up, appetizers. Then we'd have soup at Jasper's.

By the time we were heading to my place, a soft snow had begun to fall. We'd also gained a few more friends along the way. Angie and Damien had decided to do the holidays with her grandparents here in Sea Isle. Even Ewan had shown up at Jasper's. Mara had invited him.

When we arrived at my house, it smelled amazing. Abigail had run ahead from Jasper's to get dinner started. She'd set Tommy up in a corner of the den with his gaming system, a small monitor, and, of course, his requisite noise-canceling headphones. He never minded hanging out with us but did sometimes complain we were loud.

He wasn't wrong.

By the time we'd eaten and drunk too much wine, it was time to open gifts. I'd never received so many thoughtful presents, not even when I was a kid. Most of them had to do with keeping me warm. I probably needed to stop complaining about the Scottish cold.

In the warm glow of the holiday lights, sitting around with my friends, I couldn't have been any happier.

Ewan joined me on the hearth of the fireplace, and handed me a small wrapped box. "This is for you, Em," he said. "And thank you for the tweed cap."

I glanced at him and smiled. "You're welcome, but you didn't have to get me anything."

"Open it," he said.

Inside was a beautiful gold necklace with circles forming the trinity knot. "It's gorgeous, but it's too much, Ewan."

He shrugged. "After everything you have been through, Em, you deserve something nice. I just want you to know how grateful I am that you are here. 'Tis a triquetra. It represents the past, present, and future. I hope the future will be here in Sea Isle with, um, us."

I blinked. "Thank you," I said. "Look at them." I pointed to our friends, who were laughing about something Damien had said. "I've no plans to go anywhere. This is my happy place."

He grinned. "Mine too, now that you are here." He jumped up to go join the fun.

What did he mean by that?

Acknowledgments

First, I want to thank the fans, book clubs, reviewers, and mystery groups. Your kind words and encouragement with this series have meant everything to me. I'm grateful to all of you.

Thank you to Tara Gavin and the team at Crooked Lane for making my publishing experience so wonderful. You are all amazing, and you make everything so easy.

Jill Marsal, thank you for putting up with my crazy and guiding my career. You are the best agent out there.

Lizzie Bailey, there are no words for how grateful I am to have you as my friend. You are a fantastic human being, and I'm so happy you are in my life.